BLACKOUT
M.J. Schiller

CHAPTER ONE

*F*aith

    He was there. I remember it all—the crowded street, Max holding the car door open, a bus passing by—and then he was just there, looking...as good as ever somehow, but not looking the same. I froze and everything faded away—the honking, Max's laughter, the tires on the road, the sounds of construction. As if God pressed His giant mute button. And Eli stood there, peering at me from across the street, and I couldn't breathe.

Instead of his khaki green flak jacket he wore a navy, cotton jacket, unzipped. The wind tugged on the ends of it as he glanced around. His hair was shorter, but it was definitely him, hands shoved into the pockets of tan Dockers, (Eli, in Dockers?). He leaned a little against a light post, his feet crossed in front of him. When his gaze landed on me, he straightened. A bicyclist passed in front of him, a bullet of color. My mouth froze in mid-smile and my throat suddenly ached.

And then, like some cosmic explosion, everything came speeding back into place.

"Babe?" Max turned and glanced across the street, but he didn't seem to see Eli. How, I don't know. "What's wrong?"

"N-nothing. Nothing," I finally spat out, looking up into his warm, brown eyes.

"Well, are you going to get in?" He gave me a teasing smile, his handsome face serene. Max's sandy, red-brown hair was not as long as Eli's had been, but long enough to show a hint of sexy curl. He wore his beard closely-cropped and carried himself with a confidence and style which was inherited from his successful parents.

"What?"

"In the car, you nut."

He bent and kissed me on the lips, a sweet, simple kiss, but I pulled away; suddenly it was all wrong. He didn't notice. He was too happy. Too happy I finally said yes. I gazed back across the street and, even though he wasn't near enough for me to see his eyes, I knew what they looked like. I knew by the way he turned and hurried away. And Eli's pain was mirrored in my own.

ELI

"Eli. Come check out this honey," Aarron called.

I turned from where I had my foot hiked up on a girder, bent over, joking around with Max. She wore some goofy pink waitress outfit and had a bulky, white cardigan sweater pulled over it, which was unbuttoned. She was clutching it to herself as a stiff breeze was channeled straight down the boulevard into her face. Right from the start, Faith was nothing short of incredible.

My stomach, which had been doing the rumba all morning, tightened when I caught sight of her. Her hair was blowing in the blustering wind, and she stole one of her hands from her sweater to push it back. It was long, and a kind of honey-brown color, with gentle curls at the end. Her face was clear and bright, a little rosy from the cold—or maybe from the over-warm diner, I don't know—but those eyes. Those eyes nearly knocked me over. I knew the other guys were watching her ass—and she possessed a killer one, no doubt—but she had these cat-like green eyes which pulled at my core.

"Hey, angel. How 'bout you serve *me* up a little something?" Aaron grabbed his crotch and all the others gave lusty chuckles. It was Faith's misfortune that: (A) we, the top crew of J. Drew Construction, were working on a corner across from her building, so she was forced to stop right in front of us, and (B) the light turned red.

Aaron sidled over to the chain link fence in front of the site and clutched the wires. He must have looked like a salivating dog in a kennel. Faith tried to ignore him, but she shifted her weight in the canvas shoes she wore with no socks and kept looking up for the WALK signal. Most of the pedestrians crossed to the other side of the street, instead of risking their luck under our covered walkways in the construction zone, so she was all alone on the corner.

"Come on, sweetheart. Why don't you let me help you out of that apron and we can—"

"Don't," I heard myself saying, my throat dry. Without even realizing it, I had moved closer to where Aaron stood at the fence, heckling her. She shook hair out of her eyes and chanced a quick, anxious backward glance over her shoulder to make sure Aaron stayed on his side of the fence.

"—get to know one another, and—"

"Don't!" I shouted, louder this time, tapping Aaron on the shoulder and giving him a warning look.

"What's wrong with you, Batronis?" He turned his shoulder to glower at me through bloodshot eyes. The meaty brute, a yellow hardhat perched precariously on his shaved head, had been up partying with me the night before; thus, my riotous stomach and his red-veined eyes.

I lowered my voice so only he could hear me, glancing in Faith's direction. "Can't you see you're making her nervous? Knock it off, would ya?" I stole another look and caught her eye. Her head was lowered, but she turned and looked at me gratefully, with just the corners of her lips turning up. In that split-second our gaze connected I swear those green eyes miraculously made me feel warm, even in the chilly weather. My own lips quivered in response, but I forced myself to turn my back to amble over to where Max was still sitting.

"What? You want a piece of that?"

I could have killed Aaron. Shoot, if the guy didn't have eighty pounds on me and wasn't as strong as a bull, and if I hadn't been feeling so green around the gills, I might have taken him on. But as it was, I spun around, my jaw tight, and told him again to knock it off.

By this time, the light turned green and Faith hurried across the street.

I saw her again a few days later. I was up about ten feet on some scaffolding. The late fall day had turned hot—Indian Summer, I guess—and I had abandoned my sweaty shirt near my Thermos on the ground. I was supporting a steel girder with my shoulder and my hands, while Max did some quick welding work down on one end, when she came into view. She wore the same outfit, minus the sweater of course, and her hair was whipped up into some kind of clip. The others hadn't caught sight of her yet, and I prayed with her the light would turn green and she could get across before they did.

"Hey. A little higher. Eli?" Max snapped back his visor and followed my gaze. "Well, hel-l-l-lo, beautiful," he murmured to himself.

I peered at him and he turned back, looking at me with a grin. Then he let his visor fall down over his face, muffling his voice as he called out, "Higher."

Max was all right. Maxwell Theobold III, actually. He was a student, making his way through med school by doing construction with J. Drew. We all called him, "Doc." He fit in with the other guys, mostly. He didn't holler at every girl who sauntered down the street, or wolf-whistle, but he could still appreciate a pretty woman. He maybe dressed a little nicer, drank a little less. He might study in his loft while we went out to kill the time at some bar. Some of the guys were a little intimidated by his formidable intelligence, but he and I got along just fine. We both possessed the same sort of goofy, somewhat sarcastic sense of humor, and when one of us would get on a roll, the other would feed him lines. Some people didn't get us, but we thought we were pretty damned funny.

While Max worked, I watched Faith hustle up her apartment steps. I'll admit, I was happy to get a glimpse of those long, luscious legs of hers when the uniform rode up as she climbed. When she disappeared inside the brick-fronted building, I imagined her clamoring aboard an elevator, somewhere in the belly of that place, and riding it up to her cozy little apartment, because I was sure her apartment would be cozy. Was it the one with the sad, little, droopy plant in the window? Or the one with the fire-engine red brassiere hanging from the curtain rod? Certainly not the one with the little boy who was watching me. I shifted my load so I could wave, and he waved back excitedly. Nice to know someone got a thrill out of me, even if it was a five-year-old.

I turned back to my work, but still thought about Faith. I longed to introduce myself to her, but I figured she would lump me in with the other nimrods I was working with and turn me down if I asked her out. However, I began to hope my little act of gallantry, when I called Aaron off her—"Down, boy!"— might have, unintentionally, scored me some brownie points with her. So, that afternoon, when the others headed off for beers at Harry's, I walked up to the diner.

MAX

When Faith waltzed into my life, I was sitting on a steel girder messing around with Eli. I turned, I'll admit, curious, when Aaron called out to Eli, "Hey, Eli. Come check out this honey."

Where Eli seemed to be emboldened by her presence, I was struck dumb. She was the prettiest little thing I ever laid eyes on, and that was saying something.

Back in my hometown of Albany, the Theobolds made quite a name for themselves. My Dad was a renowned plastic surgeon. My mom one of the best orthopedic surgeons in the country. Before I ticked Dad off and he decided to use "tough love" on me, and make me earn my way through med school, they used to inundate me with pretty, little, rich girls. Girls who could have been the models for the surgeries my dad performed, their features were so well-made. Some of them, I was pretty sure, had already had some plastic surgery, to enhance certain female attributes, even at their very young age. By the time I was twenty I had nearly dated all of the beauties in Albany, rarely giving them a repeat performance. But, when I left for New York, I had my fill of empty-headed, bejeweled little divas. I was ready for something different. And Faith was different.

She was as much of a breath of fresh air as the breeze blowing down the street that day, pushing against her stained apron. She possessed an amazing natural beauty, a soapy-clean kind of sexy that radiated out from behind the "Hello, my name is FAITH, I'll be your server today," name tag on her high, firm chest. Her long, silky hair drifted to me in my dreams. But it was her eyes that did me in. A flash of green behind the kind of curling lashes which didn't need to be batted to be shown off.

I think Eli was smitten by her on that first day, too, and so we began to search her out, both of us from our eagle-eye perches far above the street.

Only, it was Eli who had the good fortune to be with her during the blackout. How I wished it would have been different.

FAITH

The first time I laid eyes on him, I thought he was cute. The second time I laid eyes on him, I thought he was a god. Eli had his back to me as I approached, and I was glad of it. That way I could watch those beautiful muscles ripple without fear of his catching me at it. His shoulders were broad, his arms, taut, as he hefted his end of the steel beam while Max worked with a blowtorch on the opposite end. They always seemed to be working together, those two. I noticed that when I searched him out. A girl had to have something to fantasize about, and he provided ample material. At that moment he looked for all the world like Atlas, carrying the Earth on his huge, bronzed shoulders. Gracious, there was nothing like a man with a healthy, construction worker tan. From his strong back, my eyes worked their way down to his waist, circled by worn jeans. I could see the denim was darker where his sweat made it damp.

When I passed him, I longed to turn around and get a frontal view, but I could feel their eyes on me. His were green eyes, I'd noticed, the first time we'd "met" on the street. His voice was warm and deep, his hair a rich brown, thick and wavy, and, at the time, long. It was all so innocent then, an easy distraction on the way home I looked forward to.

He was a mystery man, so I could provide the details for myself. He was single, of course, or maybe a heart-worn widower. He worked construction to support his sick grandma. I dreamed of him silently following me to my apartment.

I never dreamed we'd meet for real.

MAX

I hollered at Eli, who was standing near his pickup. "Hey, E. We're going out for some beers. Wanna join us?"

"Uh, no. Thanks. I thought I'd just grab something to eat."

The only thing I'd ever seen Eli eat was pizza, fast food burgers, stale sandwiches in a beaten up, paint-scarred metal lunch box, which looked more like a tool box, and...cold pizza. Eli generally drank his dinner, so I was instantly on alert.

"Going to the diner?"

"Yep." He gazed up the street in that direction as he pulled a shirt out of his truck to slip on over his t-shirt, also something out of the norm.

"Gonna introduced yourself to that cute waitress?"

He laughed nervously. "That's the plan."

"Yeah. Well, good luck with that," I said starting to walk away, but I didn't mean it. "Are you sure you don't want to come out with the guys? I've decided to go for a change."

"No, man. Not this time. I'll catch you next time." He swung the door of his truck shut with a loud clang, as the door wasn't exactly square in the frame. At some point a while back, Eli had opened it into a light post while stumbling out, drunk, from its worn interior. The door hadn't been fixed, and I didn't think it ever would be, since the car was such a rusted out piece of junk. But it got Eli to work—most of the time—and that's what he needed. "See ya," he said with a tilt of his head and a smile, and then he turned to stride down the street toward the diner.

I watched him and the giant shadow he made duck into the black of the covered sidewalk, and he was gone. I vowed right there and then I would eat at the diner the next night and introduce myself to the girl, but the next day was the day of the blackout.

CHAPTER TWO

F*aith*
When he came into the diner I nearly passed out. He slid his long frame into a booth that wasn't in my station, but I bustled over anyway. First come, first to serve, I always say. Once I got to his table, though, I didn't know what to do. He had on a plain, navy t-shirt, snug over that glorious chest of his, and a soft-looking, faded, button-down shirt, left, mercifully, unbuttoned over it. It was white, with a sort of plaid pattern in baby blue; I noticed because I'd never seen him in anything but a t-shirt. When he looked up, I saw, for the first time, how incredibly, intensely green his eyes were.

He shifted in his seat. "Hi."

For a minute, I didn't realize he was talking to me, even though I was the only one standing in front of him at the time. "Oh, hi. My name is Faith, and I'll be your waitress tonight," I blurted out, going on automatic pilot mode. The heat rose to my cheeks.

"Faith. That's pretty. It suits you."

The warmth of my face turned into a full-force blush. His hands were long and slender as they rested on the table. Beautiful hands. Then again, everything about him was beautiful.

"Umm..." I mumbled, disconcerted, "can I get you something to drink?" Relief flowed through me. *That's it, Faith my girl. That's the question you're supposed to ask him.*

"Yeah. I'd love a tall, ice-cold Coke."

"Sure. I'll be right back." I didn't write anything down on my tiny, green pad of paper with the pen I was holding, not trusting my shaky hands, so I walked away thinking, *Coke, a Coke.* It was vital for me to remember.

ELI

She was so damned cute. I'll admit I'd entertained a fantasy or two where she walked over to me as I was sitting at a table in the diner and offered to serve me in various racy ways. She would wear the same uniform, only it would be cut much shorter and more of the buttons would be undone, letting me in on those sweet curves of hers. She would chew on her pencil, or do something equally provocative and cliché, and in these daydreams we generally wound up on the table, knocking the glass jar of straws so they shattered to the floor in our haste.

But when she walked up to me for real, my mind went blank. It was never that way in the daydreams, I always came up with some slick one-liner that would have her simultaneously laugh and lust after me. Yet there I was, without a word at my command.

"Hi," I spat out after a long beat. Okay, not an especially good start, but a decent one.

She seemed to be zoned out. "Oh, hi," she said brightly, if a little breathlessly. "My name is Faith, and I'll be your waitress."

Faith. Now I had a name to put with my fantasy girl. Faith. It suited her. And, to my amazement, I found myself telling her that. She was so damned cute when she blushed I wanted to scoop her up right then and take her home, but I figured that would make someone call the cops on me, so I ordered a Coke instead, or maybe it was ice tea, I can't remember.

I watched her amble away, and released a breath that was strangled inside of my lungs. "Idiot." I closed my eyes and ran a hand over my face. I promised myself I would do a much better job when she came back.

A few minutes after Faith left the table, another waitress approached. She was blond, and leggy, and *very* friendly. "Hi, there." She seemed to purposefully lean in to me to set a glass of water on the table next to the one Faith already gave me. As she pulled her hand back, she brushed it against mine, where it sat on the table. Her perfectly make-upped blue eyes stared boldly into mine. "What can I help you with?"

Well I've got to say, I'm not quite used to a woman coming on that strong, so I was taken a little off-guard. As my mouth tried to frame a reasonable response to her question, I glanced over her shoulder and noticed Faith draw near. When she saw the blonde at my table, she came to an abrupt halt, spilling some of my soda onto her hand.

"Hey." Blondie rested her long painted fingernails on my cheek, and turned my face to hers squarely, taking my eyes from Faith's for a moment. "Listen, handsome." She rubbed my hand again, sensually. "Why don't you let me take your order, and when you're finished, we can go," she gestured vaguely, "somewhere...together?"

I gulped. Her strong sell really started to make me nervous. Faith slammed my Coke down onto the table, splashing some of it on us.

Her voice shook. "Here's your Coke, sir." Her green eyes blazed like emeralds set on fire.

The blonde shook soda off her hand. "Geez, Faith. Watch it." Her switch from seductress to prissy bitch was head-spinningly fast. The mean edge to her voice when she talked to Faith made her ugly, her pleasing features became sharp, hard, and dark. "I've got him already. Take another table."

"Sure, Glo. He's all yours." The fire had left her eyes and left behind a sad sort of resignation. She marched away without looking back.

I spent the next forty minutes defending advances from the blonde, Gloria, and watching Faith work her tail off. The place was packed and I'm guessing from the amount of time Gloria spent with me, Faith picked up her slack, too. She whizzed like a ballet dancer between tables, dropped off plates of burgers and heaping fries, filled water glasses, and cleared dirty dishes. She didn't look my way again, but I watched her, watched her as beads of sweat began to form on her forehead, watched her smile at men other than me, and women and children, too. She seemed to have some regular customers who were glad to see her, and whom she seemed glad to see. It was impressive, the amount of food she brought out, and the grace with which she did it all.

Until Gloria got pissed, that is. I'm guessing she was ticked off because I was looking at Faith instead of her, but I'm pretty sure she stuck her foot out. Faith walked past my table with a half-dozen plates extended up and down her arms, seeming bent on avoiding eye contact with me. She headed toward a large, round booth occupied by a bunch of male yuppies. The next thing I knew, she was sprawled on the floor with food and broken dishware everywhere. The crash was tremendous and was accompanied by the sound of the air which left Faith's lungs in a rush.

In the next few seconds, several things happened at once. Faith let out a moan of probably both pain and embarrassment. Two of the yuppies from the nearby booth jumped up to help her to her feet, and several of her regulars scrambled to pick up pieces of the plates that skidded everywhere. But above the flurry of activity came the bark of the diner's owner.

"Faith!" He scuttled around the counter, a big guy, about Aaron's size, but in his mid-fifties or so. He wore a white t-shirt and jeans and had a full head of salt-and-pepper colored hair. He started picking up pieces, shooting Faith a dark look as she stood—with the help of the two men—and looked a bit dazed. "This'll be coming out of your check at the end of the week." His voice stung. "Why don't you get out of here? Sissy is here now and you've already been here over your shift by an hour. Go home."

An elderly man stumbled to his feet. "B-but *she*—" He pointed at Gloria, his frail hand shaking. "–tripped her." His face was red and contorted in anger.

Faith went over and put her arm around him. "It's okay, Mr. Stanislaski. I'm sure Gloria didn't mean to." The glare she gave the blonde contradicted her words. "I'm fine. I was just rushing too much." She escorted the man back to his table, where he sat with his tiny wife. "I should have been more careful. I'll go home and have a nice rest and be as right as rain tomorrow." He started to speak but she interrupted him, giving his arm a squeeze. "Don't you worry. And Sissy is here now." She gave him a nod. "I'll see you Monday." She turned to the little old lady across the table from him. "Good night, Mrs. Stanislaski. Take good care of him for me."

"I will, dear. You take care of yourself, now. You're likely to be sore after a fall like that."

"I'll take a bath when I get home. I'll be fine." She patted the woman's arm, too, and then turned and blew past me without a word. The table of yuppies stared at the owner accusatorily. The guy looked a little remorseful, but I got the sense it was more for yelling at Faith in front of customers than for yelling at Faith period.

I had jumped to my feet when Faith fell, too, and now Gloria stepped up to me, playing with a button on my shirt. "Now. Where were we?" Over her shoulder, I saw Faith leave the diner.

"Why did you do that?" I growled.

"Do what?"

I just stared.

She shrugged. "Faith is clumsy."

Before I could comment, the owner yelled, "Gloria! Order's up."

"Coming. Coming," she snapped. She looked at me. "I'll be right back."

But as soon as she left I pulled out my wallet and laid a ten on my table for my Coke and burger, hurrying to follow Faith. When I got to the street, she was nowhere to be seen.

FAITH

Instead of heading home, I took off up the street, my anger and humiliation driving my feet against the cold concrete sidewalk. The breeze stung my cheeks, hot from embarrassment, and drove the tears I'd kept in out upon my cheeks. I brushed them off as rapidly as they fell, furious with that dumb Gloria for tripping me. In the twilight hours, I seldom walked farther than across the street to my apartment house, but tonight I traipsed a good five city blocks before turning back. By that time, I had cooled down some. My feet and legs ached from being on them all day and I was exhausted. As I neared my apartment, I began to look forward, in earnest, to the bath I talked about. That's when I looked up and saw him.

He sat casually on the short brick post at the end of the concrete banister/wall that hemmed in my staircase. When he saw me, he slid to his feet and jammed his hands in his pockets. Had he sat there the entire twenty minutes it took me to calm down?

"Hey," he said as an opener.

"Hey." I looked anywhere but in those eyes, my jaw clenched as I thought about Gloria stroking his hand.

He cleared his throat. "I wanted to check on you. I've seen you come home this way before. Not that I was like...stalking you...or anything..."

It was hard to stay mad at him when he so obviously struggled to be nice to me. "I'm okay, thank you." I sighed, dropping my gaze as I exhaled the last of my irritation over the situation.

He moved forward and grabbed my arm. I took an instinctive step back, my gaze flew to his face to judge his intent, but he didn't notice. He looked at my arm. "You're hurt."

"Hmm?" I mumbled, a little dazed by his closeness. I was thinking about his voice. It was better than I imagined it would be, a sort of dreamy blend of high and low tones that softened when he was concerned, but always contained a sort of sexy rumble underneath. I knew it would send me over the edge if I was ever in his arms. I looked at my forearm lamely. A piece of glass had sliced about a four-inch cut, but it wasn't deep. "Oh. That's mostly spaghetti sauce." I wiped at it with my other hand.

"Oh." He laughed, the image perhaps struck him as funny. But I realized the mess I must be, covered in blood, spaghetti sauce, and brown gravy, some of it already made stiff in my hair.

A new wave of embarrassment heated my cheeks. I tried to barrel past him. "Goodbye, then."

He stepped into my path, blocking the way to the door. "Wait."

"What? So you can continue to have a good laugh about..." My exhaustion and emotional turmoil choked me.

"Hey," he said tenderly, again placing his hands on my arms and bending to try to look into my eyes. "I'm not laughing at you. I...okay, I was *kind* of laughing at you. It's just...spaghetti sauce can be...I don't know...funny."

It was an odd thing to say, but somehow right. I chuckled quietly and he laughed some more, deep and pleasing. "It's not funny you're hurt, though." He drew a thumb in a line beneath the cut, as he examined it. His calloused hands surprised me with their softness.

An unreasonable urge to kiss him stole over me. His lips were full and inviting, and he smelled wonderfully, dizzyingly masculine. He looked up and caught me examining his face. I wet my lips, my throat going dry in an instant. "I-I'm okay." I breathed. Stepping back, I rubbed my arm without thinking. "Thanks for coming to check on me, but I'm fine." I attempted to sound dignified and maybe a touch mad still, but I knew if I said anything more, I would come out looking stupid. I hastened up the steps, my heartbeat pounding in my head in rhythm to my feet as they slapped at the concrete. When I turned he watched me through the glass entry doors as I got on the elevator, his brows furrowed. Then the doors closed between us. I leaned back against the handrails, exhaling loudly and cursing myself for not coming up with something cute or clever to say. When I got to my room and rushed to look out of my window, he was gone.

CHAPTER THREE

E*li*   The next day began like any other, with my tiny, personal jackhammers wreaking havoc with my head before I'd even made the site. Aaron grimaced with each loud noise, too, and I concluded the shot war we were involved in the night before had claimed a few brain cell casualties in his head, too. It was a Saturday, but we had nearly a full crew as we were behind schedule. My gaze kept straying to the brick-fronted apartment building across the way, and I was rewarded after a time by a sighting of my pretty, little waitress.

But this time, she wasn't dressed in a uniform. She had on a navy, nylon jogging suit, mittens, and a wool headband. Her hair was pulled into a high ponytail, floating above the headband keeping her ears warm. The weather had turned colder overnight. I had a flannel shirt on top of my usual t-shirt, and I could see her breath coming out in a cloud of white. I watched her move sinuously down the street, and caught her again when she returned, forty minutes later, but didn't see her for the rest of the morning. I wondered what she could be doing in that apartment of hers.

We broke for lunch around one. The sun had come out, warming things up a little, and it turned out to be a beautiful day. As I sat with Max and Aaron, chewing on a stale sub sandwich I got out of a cooler at a convenience store, high heels could be heard stamping down the sidewalk, a sound that automatically got our attention. A tall blonde swung into the yard. She was dressed in a pink business suit and looked as cool and crisp as the fall day began, but she gave us a disarming smile. She appeared to be in her mid-forties with big hair and a...well-proportioned body.

"Good afternoon. Would you two gentlemen know where the boss is?"

I watched, amused, as Max and Aaron exchanged a look and chewed their food as rapidly as possible so they could be the one to answer her question. Max came out on top, while poor Aaron started coughing and had to take a sip of his soda to clear his throat. Max stood gallantly. "Why don't I show you the way?" He held out his arm, and she slipped hers through his with a light laugh. The pair ambled over to the boss's trailer, amid a shower of whistles and envious looks, and disappeared inside.

Fifteen minutes later, as I was about to get back to work, they sauntered out again, arm-in-arm. They walked up to me, each smiling as if at some personal joke. "Eli Batronis, I'd like you to meet Amber Dulle. Amber, this is Eli." She held out her hand, and, after wiping mine on my jeans, she shook it.

"Eli," she said coyly, "how'd you like to earn a little extra cash?"

The way she eyed me up and down, like a meal prepared by the personal chef I felt almost sure she had, I had to wonder what I would have to do for this money. Before I could answer, Max spoke up. "Ms. Dulle is having some renovations done to her penthouse across the street. She has a crew over there, but she could use a couple of extra hands. The boss said it was okay, or at least he did after Amber gave him a grand a piece to have loan of us today. So what do you say?" Max grinned like the proverbial cat with yellow feathers hanging out of its mouth.

I shrugged. A change of pace would be welcome. "I'm in."

"Good, good." She latched on to my elbow so she had one of us on each side. "Let's go then." We waltzed through the yard to a second chorus of cheers and soon we were in the Faith's building, riding the elevator up to her penthouse. Once the doors closed, Amber began to examine both of us like a slave trader in the marketplace. "Wow. You certainly are muscular," she praised as she ran her hands up our biceps. "It will be a pleasure to watch you work." Max grinned at her, but I was beginning to feel a little uncomfortable.

When the door opened up on her penthouse though, I had to admire her style. The place was huge, with tall ceilings, terraces, and expansive picture windows. It was decorated all in white, except for the splashes of color gracing several large canvases hanging here and there. One was a nude, done in yellows and blues, of a woman who seemed to be contorted into an impossible position. Amber caught me looking at it. "Do you like it?" Her voice was low and sensual. She walked her long, painted fingers up my chest and slid her hands to link behind my neck.

"It's...uh, nice." I had trouble swallowing the second come-on I'd gotten in the past twenty-four hours. Max winked at me over her shoulder.

"Can I get you gentlemen a drink?"

"I'd love one." Max followed her over to a drink cart.

I glanced around, trying to shrug off an uncomfortable feeling. "Uhh...where is your other crew?"

Max and Amber's heads lifted. They glanced at each other and he shrugged.

"They're...out to lunch."

Max frowned and walked over to me. He put his hand on my shoulder and led me off a couple of steps while Amber looked on with a raised eyebrow, clinking ice into etched crystal tumblers. "Uhh, Eli...there isn't really a job, per se, but Amber here is really lonely and would love for us to spend the day with her, which I, myself, am up for." While we were talking, Amber had made her way back over to us and now slid her arms around Max's waist, clasping them across his midsection.

I laughed. "I couldn't do that with you around, man."

Max chuckled. "What? Afraid of a little healthy competition?"

"That's okay." Amber sighed. "I can take you one at a time. I'll start with Max, here, since he seems to be...in the mood. Here, Eli." She handed me a hundred dollar bill, but didn't really look at me. "Go and get us something to eat at that cute little diner across the street. I'm sure I'll be famished." She focused her attention on Max who took his cue and swept her off her feet.

"Yes, Eli. Run along." Max smiled and Amber squealed as he carried her off.

I chuckled and shook my head, but turned to leave with no hard feelings. "Take your time," Amber yelled over Max's shoulder. The last thing I heard was her high-pitched giggling as I closed the door behind me.

I snickered again on the way down in the elevator, wondering over the hundred-dollar bill she gave me; it would buy a *lot* of burgers and fries. Then I thought about how nice it was to have an excuse to go over to the diner—Dino's, I found out yesterday, was its name. Maybe I would run into Faith and things would go a little smoother than the first time. I hoped Gloria wouldn't be there to cause trouble for me today.

But when I got there, neither Faith, nor Gloria was around. I got my food from the burly boss-man from the day before, Dino, I supposed, and toted it back across the street, taking my time as instructed. I took my package back to the penthouse and found a note on the door.

Leave the food on the table. Thanks, man. -Max

The door was cracked open so I entered and set one of the bags down and left before I could see or hear anything that made me any more uncomfortable than I already was. Max was something else. He had regaled all of the guys on the site before with tales of his exploits with women, and I'd always thought the good doctor "doctored" his stories up a bit. But maybe he hadn't. Maybe all those wild things he told us were really true. After today, I would have to give him more credence.

My experience was far less...well...just far less. Not that I hadn't had my fair share of offers, but I always found sharing myself in such a way to be so intimate. It wasn't something I wanted to do with just anyone. I was a bitter disappointment to all of my co-workers when I didn't have any stories to tell them the morning after we'd been out together and someone hit on me, but it's just how it was.

I left and boarded the elevator feeling a little alone, like I was an alien among another species. I tried to decide where to eat my burger and fries and still shook my head and laughed over Max's behavior, when the elevator came to a stop on the tenth floor with a friendly *ding*. As the doors parted Faith waited on the other side. She had on her uniform again, with her hair swept up in some sort of fancy knot behind her. Her eyes went wide when she saw me.

I smiled. "Hi."

"Hi." She stepped in quickly and turned her back to me to stab at the button for the ground floor, even though I had already pushed it. It was as if she couldn't wait for the elevator to take her there.

"Faith..." I started, but I didn't get a chance to finish as she whirled around.

"Listen. I'm sorry for the way I acted yesterday. I was kind of rude. I guess I was still upset—"

Before she could complete her thought, we heard a funny *whirring* noise like something winding down and then the elevator came to an abrupt, jerky stop, knocking us both off our feet. We landed together in a pile of arms and legs in complete blackness. Her weight on me was pleasant and I was engulfed by a sweet fragrance that was uniquely her. It was as much a feeling as a fragrance. It felt like I closed my eyes and turned my face to the warm sun. If that peaceful, sunshiny contentment had a scent, it would smell just like Faith. She scrambled around to try to disengage herself from me in the dark.

"Are you okay?" It was a pretty jarring stop.

"Yes. What happened?" As she spoke, an emergency lantern in the corner came on, bathing us in a strange, yellow-brown glow. I could see her face now, and she looked...terrified.

"I think it might be some sort of power outage."

"What do you mean?" Her voice was pitched high. "We're stuck in here?"

I tried to look around and assess the situation as best as I could. "Yeah. For the time being. I—"

"No." All the blood drained from her face and her eyes darted back and forth. "We can't be!" she wailed. "We can't be," she repeated. Her choked voice came out with a note of quiet desperation.

"It's okay, Faith. It—"

"No!" she screamed, then took a step back and gulped in air. "No, it's not. We've got to get out." She banged her fists against the door. "Help! Help! We're stuck in the elevator." She shouted for several minutes, but to no avail. No one answered her call. "Please," she sobbed, laying her cheek against the stainless steel door, her eyes squeezed shut. "Won't somebody help me?"

"Faith." She didn't turn. "Faith." I laid my hand on her shoulder. "It's okay. They'll come for us in a bit."

She jerked away and stumbled sideways a few feet. "You don't understand," she cried out. Her eyes shone like an animal caught in a trap. I looked on in utter confusion until it finally dawned on me—she was claustrophobic.

FAITH

How can this be happening? my mind screamed. Not here. Not now. Not with him. The humiliation of it all rose inside of me and tried to choke me.

It wasn't enough I made a complete fool out of myself the day before, now I was going to totally fall apart on him.

I thought I was over it. I abandoned the stairs years ago and forced myself into the elevator to overcome my gut-wrenching, all-consuming fear. And I'd gotten good at it. My palms didn't even sweat anymore. Despite often refusing to get on when more than three people were in there, I did manage to ride down most of the time acting like a normal human being. I was used to the doors closing in, shutting out that gap of space and freedom on the other side, knowing I would be at the bottom and out in a short time. I thought I was better. But I had been kidding myself.

I was still as terrified as ever. The stifling darkness, no one hearing my cries, the air, strangled in my lungs…I had to get out. But no one heard me…

And now, he was here. He looked at me with such confusion, not aware of the horror show replaying in my mind. My breath came in ragged, frayed gasps just short of filling my lungs. My head swam, and for a minute I thought I would pass out.

He held my arms and I let him, their strength reassuring. "Are you claustrophobic?" His voice was kind.

I stared at him, dumbfounded. He'd guessed my secret. The one I tried so hard to hide away from everyone. *Well, I guess it's not that hard, Faith. You're practically hyperventilating on him.* I nodded my head, aghast over the tears which now poured down my face.

"Okay." He slipped his arm around my shoulders. "Tell me what I can do to make it better."

"I don't know," I moaned.

"Well, how about we sit here, and I'll talk to you. I'll just keep talking and take your mind off things until they come." He helped me to the floor.

I closed my eyes to clutch at the pieces of me that were shattered and spread all over. "Yes." A tiny bit of air leaked into my lungs. "Yes. Talk to me."

"Okay. But I don't know how exciting it will be. I'm not exactly Scheherezade." He referred to the heroine of *The Arabian Nights* who had to tell stories for a thousand and one nights to keep a mad sheik from slaying her.

I smiled at that. "Well, it's okay, 'cause I'm not going to kill you when this is over." I was surprised by how easy it was to joke with him in my current condition. He sat with his legs stretched out in front of him, his arm still protective around my shoulder. I curled my knees up under me and leaned into him with no sense of pride, just a need for the shelter of his strong arms. I closed my eyes and breathed in more good air. "But first, you have to tell me your name."

"Oh. I forgot I never told you. I'm Eli."

"Eli." I didn't move or open my eyes. "It's good to know the name of the man whose arms you are in," I added, joking, then realized how forward it sounded. "I mean...I mean..."

"I know what you mean." His hand rubbed my arm in a soothing, mesmerizing way, and I realized I wasn't scared anymore.

ELI

She sat next to me, so trusting as she leaned against me. A smile played over her lips. Her eyes were closed, which gave me ample opportunity to look at her face. She laid herself so open to me, closed her eyes, not watching over me, but giving herself freely, something that both exhilarated and frightened me. I was barely able to take care of myself. She was wrong to trust me.

I stroked the bare skin of her arm without thinking, and she relaxed muscle by muscle. She was so warm and soft. Her breathing was more regular now; that was good. "Let's see..." I settled into my role of storyteller. "I was born in Beacon, New York, a little town about an hour north of here—"

She opened her eyes and straightened a little, obviously more at ease. "You're kidding. I'm from New Windsor."

"Really?" We had almost been neighbors, then, when we were growing up. I smiled down into her face. She was just like a little kid when she was excited. "What brought you to New York?"

Her face fell, and she shrugged. "I needed to get out." She didn't explain, but dropped her gaze to mess with a seam in her uniform. There was a story there, I was sure of it, but I didn't press. She turned to face me. "I want to tell you...to explain...why... Why I am like I am. Why I'm scared...in here." She glanced around the small confines as if she waited for a monster to tear through the steel sides of the elevator and claw us to death.

"You can explain if you want. But you don't have to. My mom was a little claustrophobic, so I know what it's like to a degree."

"Well, I'm more than a little claustrophobic." She shifted her weight around so she sat across from me, but our bodies still touched. I missed her warmth by my side, but I could look into her pretty face this way, so I was satisfied. She ran a finger up the seam of my jeans while she talked, I think, unaware she was even doing it. But I was hyperaware. It sent waves of desire through me I squelched as I listened to her. "When I was six...my brother and I were playing hide-and-seek." Her eyebrows scrunched up and her upper lip quivered for a moment. "I climbed inside this foot locker he had. I don't know where my parents got it for him. It was about a foot wide, and as long as his bed. Nathan painted it white and stuck a bunch of stickers from *Mad* magazine all over it. You remember *Mad* magazine?"

I nodded. "Spy vs. Spy?" It was a cartoon in every issue.

She laughed. "Yes. Anyway...I climbed inside of it to hide. It was stupid. I knew better. But it was such a good hiding spot. Big enough for me, but small enough he wouldn't think to search for me there. It..." She struggled now to get the words out. "It became locked...somehow." Tears ran down her face. "I screamed and screamed, but nobody came. When they found me, four or five hours later—no one was sure when I went missing—I had passed out, a mass of sweat, my throat sore from crying out. They took me to the hospital, and I was okay, physically. But ever since then, I've had a hard time..."

My face must have shown the shock I felt. "That's awful." I reached up to rub the tears from her cheek. "I'm sorry that happened to you." My eyes searched hers and I drowned in their swirling green depths. She seemed to try to read me. Her lips trembled again.

"That's not true," she burst out. "That's not what happened." A half-sob escaped. "I've never told anyone this—not even my parents—but..."

I could tell it was important for her to tell somebody whatever deep, dark secret from her childhood lay hidden behind her fear. I took her hand. "What happened?"

"He—Nathan, my brother—he wasn't right. He had problems. He was eleven at the time—" She scrambled to her feet. "I can't believe I'm telling you this. I-I shouldn't—man. It's not like this is some therapist's couch. You didn't get on board this elevator to have some hysterical girl unload her whole twisted childhood on you." She turned her back on me and bent her head to cry into her hand, her other hand wrapped around her middle as if to hold herself together.

I stood and gripped her shoulders gently, then pulled her against me.

"I'm sorry. I'm sorry." She turned her head toward me.

"No, it's okay. You can tell me, if you want."

She twisted around and gazed up at me. Tears still fell over her lower lashes. "No." She laughed. "You're a captive audience. You must feel very uncomfortable having some strange girl fall apart on you. If we were out there—" she gestured to indicate some world beyond our elevator "—you could make some polite excuse and ditch me."

"First of all, you're not all that strange," I said, making her chuckle again. "And I wouldn't want to make any excuse to you." I moved some of the hair that fell loose from her pins out of her face. "I want to hear what you want to tell me."

"Why?" She laughed, then she looked up and her eyes searched mine.

"I don't know," I said honestly.

She seemed to make a decision. "Nathan had some problems before, but nothing serious." She swallowed. "The locker shut with a padlock. He locked me in there and he told me I could yell all I wanted to, that Mom and Dad would never find me. His voice was so strange, so different than normal... It was eerie. A voice without a heart. You know what I mean? He left. He just left me there. I loved him so much." She fell apart in earnest now and I took her into my arms. She beat her fists against my chest. "Why'd he do that? Why?"

"I don't know," I murmured into her hair. I held her while her hot tears dampened my shirt, held her until the tears would come no more and she was limp and exhausted. "Do you want to sit?" She nodded and I sat, but she ended up laying her head on my knee. I think she was ashamed to look at me. I stroked her hair, thinking about all of my deep dark secrets and how good it would feel to be unburdened of them. She was only six, a year younger than I had been...

"I'm going to owe you a bundle, Dr. Eli." She sat with a rueful smile. "Your 'Elevator Therapy' is quite revolutionary." She became more serious. "I'm sorry."

"I'm not. I'm glad you told me." I ran my hand down the side of her face. I couldn't quite seem to stop touching her. Her stomach growled and she put a hand over it, laughing.

"What else embarrassing is going to happen? I was going to get something to eat at work but—"

I reached for the sack that fell into the corner of the elevator. "Well, here," I offered.

"No. I can't take your food."

"Come on. We'll share it. There's no telling how long we'll be in here." I split the burger and gave her half. She chewed on it, but looked up at the emergency light.

"How long do you think it will last?" She gestured with her head to the light.

"Oh. I think they're supposed to last quite a while."

She nodded, seeming a little relieved. I couldn't imagine how horrible it had been for her as a little girl, locked in a trunk in the blackness, not knowing if anyone would come for you, a kind of live burial of sorts. She finished her half of the burger and brushed her hands off.

"Not some of Bruno's best work," she commented. The burger oozed grease.

"How do you know Bruno cooked it?"

She smiled. "Because he always puts too much mustard on it."

"Speaking of which, you have some in the corner of your mouth." She started to lick her lips to search for the wayward mustard. The move was so innocent, but so provocative at the same time. I was completely turned on.

"Uhh—" I mumbled, my voice husky in my own ears, "—it's here." I reached out and wiped the mustard away with my finger. We sat for a moment, frozen. My heart beat harder and wilder than the rhythm of any jackhammer I had ever used. I wanted to kiss her, but I knew if I did, I'd have to have all of her. Where the thought of Amber was slightly titillating, but wrong, the thought of being with Faith swam through my veins and made me dizzy, and I knew, without a doubt, it would be perfect and right. "Faith..." My hand drifted to the back of her neck and my thumb rubbed experimentally across her bottom lip. My gaze moved from her lips to her eyes as I poured my heart into them. "Can I kiss you?"

Instead of answering, she leaned in closer to brush her lips across mine, her breath warm and enticing. I drowned in her, like a shot of tequila, drank her in more deeply, more greedily with each kiss. She responded, her lips as hungry, which sent a shudder through me. When I thought I would lose it altogether, I found an unusual ounce of self-restraint, and pushed gently on her shoulders to separate us. "I'm sorry. Talk about a captive audience. I should never have started something in a place where you might feel like you were being forced to—"

"Eli." She put a finger over my lips. "I was the one who kissed you first." She removed her finger and looked down. "And truth be told, I've wanted to do it for awhile."

I couldn't help but grin. "You have?"

A voice echoed down the elevator shaft, interrupting us. "Hel-l-l-o-o-o-o-o. Anyone in there?"

Faith sprang from my arms to the door. "Yes! Yes! We're in here."

"Faith? Is that you?"

"Yes, Mr. Girardi." She smiled. "It's me."

"Are you okay, hon? In there alone?"

"I'm fine. And I'm in here with Eli."

"Eli? Eli, who? Do you feel safe? If you don't, I can get someone to help me get down there?"

Faith eyed me teasingly. "Am I safe, Eli?"

My Lord, the girl was hot. I grabbed her by the hips. "I don't know. Depends on what you mean by 'safe'?"

She laughed. "I'm fine, Mr. Girardi." She looked at me with a wicked smile. "I'm actually in good hands."

"Who is this Eli fella?" the older man insisted.

"He works across the street."

"What's he doing here, then?" he rumbled, sounding testy.

"I don't know. What *are* you doing here?"

"I was doing a job in the penthouse."

Faith's spine straightened. "You were upstairs with Amber."

"Yes. You know her?" I deflected. I sensed a change in her mood.

"O-o-oh, yes. I know her. And I know just what kind of job she'd want you to do for her, too." She squirmed out of my grip.

"No. No." Obviously Amber had a reputation. "Let me explain."

"No need." She ripped at her uniform and undid the top more, like I fantasized about. "Man. It's hot in here." A bead of sweat rolled down her cleavage; she was scared again. "You don't owe me an explanation. I'm just some girl you got stuck on the elevator with and you thought you could find a pleasing way for us to spend the time." She strode around the small elevator like a caged panther.

"Wait a minute." My own temperature increased.

"No, Eli. It's okay. Obviously you were up there being *entertained*, worked yourself up an appetite and went to the diner. Then you—"

"Faith," I gripped her shoulders, making her stop her dizzying laps. "*Max* is up there with her right now. I didn't want anything to do with that so they sent me out, as their little errand boy, for food."

The elevator chose this moment to jerk to life, and we were forced to grab on to the railings to right ourselves. A shout of elation went up throughout the building. Faith's face was a mixture of confusion, hurt, and anger as she stared back at me, and then the elevator doors opened. A round, balding man in a thin, white undershirt, who I assumed was Mr. Girardi, stood outside. Faith broke from my grip and rushed out of the elevator past him. The older man glared at me for a beat, then took off after her.

"Faith. Faith. Are you okay? Did that kid hurt you?"

I couldn't hear her answer as she stormed out of sight.

CHAPTER FOUR

F*aith*
　　What was it about Eli that brought out the idiot in me? In my few moments with him I managed to trip and go sprawling amidst a myriad of food items, act like a loon in an elevator because I was scared, go all jealous-girlfriend on him after one kiss, and apparently for no reason. I'd scored an Embarrassment Trifecta. If I was him I'd've run as fast as those gorgeous long legs could take me.

After our release, I showed up at the diner and got yelled at by Dino for being late, even though I'd had no choice in the matter. I sulked through my shift and trudged home at eight. But my face lit up as I neared my apartment on the tenth floor. Sitting in front of the door was a tiny vase with daisies and alstroemeria, which spilled over its rim. A small card was propped up in front of it with my name on it. Maybe it was from Mr. Girardi. He had seen how upset I was. What a sweet gesture. I opened the card and read-

I offered the elevator repairman fifty bucks to make sure it stops again for a few minutes the next time we're on it. What do you say, Faith? Up for a ride? -Eli

My smile broadened and my heart warmed inside my chest, then skipped a beat when his honeyed voice came from behind me. "So, what *do* you say, Faith?"

I turned and he walked toward me wearing a black t-shirt with a black, button-down shirt over it and a nice pair of jeans. He looked incredibly sexy. He gazed at me in a way that would have any woman responding positively. I tilted my head to one side with a smile.

"You must be a glutton for punishment." He put one hand over my head on the door and leaned in, his smile wide, his lips tantalizingly close. "What do you have in mind?" I asked breathlessly.

"I don't know. Maybe a little dinner. Or did you eat at the diner?"

"No," I answered, as if appalled. "I don't eat that junk."

He laughed.

"I'd have to take a quick shower and change?"

"Fine by me."

I opened the door to my apartment, and brought the flowers in with us. I walked over to set them on a window ledge by my bed. "Thank you for the flowers. They're the first flowers I've ever received."

"You're kidding?"

I turned and caught him looking around my apartment, what there was to look at.

"The rent here is more than I can afford, really. But it saved me from needing a car to drive to work, and gas money...so I moved in. I don't have a lot of money for extras. Or even necessities." I laughed.

The room was bare except for the queen-sized mattress on the floor near the windows and a phone, hooked up and lying in the middle of the empty room. In one corner, though, sat my laptop on its empty box, my only splurge.

"I like it. You've got the whole bare minimum thing down to an art."

I laughed and swatted at him.

ELI

"Make yourself at home. You can sit...on my bed, I guess."

She left the bathroom door open a crack while she talked. "I don't have many guests up here." She raised her voice over the sound of the shower she started.

I picked up a book from a small stack next to the bed to page through it. Before I cracked the cover, I glanced up, and through the crack in the door I could see her reflection in a floor-length mirror. She was shimmying out of her waitress uniform and I gaped at the sight of her long legs stepping out of the ring of pink fabric, the black lacy underwear she had on barely covered her behind. She brought her hands up between her breasts to undo the clasp of her matching black bra. I had to force myself to look away, knowing she had no idea I was watching her. When I yielded to the temptation to look back a second later, the steam had fogged up the mirror and stolen away my view. I flopped back on the mattress with a groan. The book clattered out of my hand onto the hardwood floor. Being a gentleman with Faith, as I had vowed to do, was going to require willpower, something which I was notorious for lacking. The sound of the water running, as I imagined it sliding over that smooth skin of hers, was ratcheting up my nerves, so I got up to pace the apartment.

The room itself was large. Large and empty. The hardwood floors were a light, honey oak that made your footsteps echo in the vacant space. Three of the walls were white, bare, with light wood trim. The fourth, the one facing the streets, was brick, with several long, arched windows reaching nearly to the floor. The room itself was broken up with white, boxed support posts, or perhaps plumbing or wiring ran through them. I ran my hand over the wood covering the posts as I walked around them, admiring the crown molding at the top.

I looked over as she came out of the bathroom. Either she put on more perfume, or the water released some of its former scent, or she used some kind of fragrant shampoo or lotion. In any case, when she walked out, wearing snug jeans and a green, thin, ribbed turtleneck that set off those riveting eyes all the more, I stopped in my tracks, inhaling her, letting her pulse through my veins with each heartbeat.

She stopped, smiling at me but studying my expression. I must have looked stunned, because that's how I felt. No woman had ever had the staggering effect on me she did. Being with her was like downing a shot; it sent a warm shiver of excitement through me and made me slightly off-kilter, with the same promise of feeling sorry in the morning. Should I even be here with her? She was beautiful, and wholesome, and pure. And I? I was not.

She sauntered over to me; I didn't move a muscle. "What are you thinking, Eli?" she asked softly, coming to stand in front of me. My hand slid up the pole and I gazed down into her face, totally struck by her.

"I was thinking..." I said slowly, my voice gruff, playing with her hair, "maybe I shouldn't be here."

"Don't say that," she whispered. Her gaze danced across my face.

I bent my head as if by force and kissed her, long and deep. Her body molded to mine. The tightness I carried around with me unwound itself. It had become a constant presence I wasn't even aware of until I surrendered it to her. The cartoon angel on my shoulder said, *Don't do this to her. She deserves better. You'll hurt her eventually.* The devil responded, *You need her. You deserve some happiness, too. She can make it all go away. She's the key.*

I brought my hands to her waist, just under the taut fabric of her sweater where the jeans met the flesh above her hips. I thought of taking her there, I admit, of seeking and pillaging dark pleasures with her there on her mattress on the floor. I wanted it hard and fast and mindless. This is why I avoided women. They made everything so damned complex.

I pulled away and stared into her face as she slowly opened her eyes, dimmed by her passion. I cleared my throat and messed with her hair again. It was so silky soft. "We should probably go."

"Okay." She smiled enthusiastically and bopped away. "I have to quick dry my hair."

I laughed a little, releasing the sexual tension built up in the last couple of moments, light again. "You may want to grab a coat. It's gotten colder out there."

When she came back she snatched a black down vest with a faux-fur collar from the doorknob of her closet and we set out.

It had, indeed, gotten colder, the temperatures plummeting in an effort to set records. We walked, her arm through mine, my hands jammed defensively in my pockets, not speaking much, but smiling brightly. "Where to?"

"Wherever you want."

We were walking past Harry's and someone pounded on the front glass. Inside sat Max and Aaron and the guys, knee-deep in suds. Max had no doubt described his afternoon with Amber in lurid detail.

"Aren't those your friends?"

"Yeah. But they can be jerks."

"Oh, no. They look like they're having fun. Do you want to join them?"

I hesitated. Would I love to show her off? Sure. Was there potential for an embarrassing moment or two with the guys? Definitely. "We don't have to..."

"No. I'd love to meet your friends. Come on." She pulled me into the pub, undaunted by the boisterousness beyond the pane of glass.

Loud cheers went up as we approached the table.

"Hey, hey. Look who's here?"

"Hey, darlin'. Aren't you the waitress from the diner?"

I received a couple of rib jabs and *Way to go, Eli* s, but she melded into the group seamlessly. Her hands were stuck into the pockets of her vest as she chatted. Her cheeks glowed from the nip of the night air, eyes shone with excitement, and I couldn't take my eyes off her.

A few beers later, Finger Eleven's "Paralyzer" came on and she screamed, "I love this song. Do you want to dance?"

"Eli doesn't dance," the others hooted as I shook my head.

"I'll dance with you, doll," Aaron offered. She was already bopping and belting out the lyrics. She looked at me.

I laughed. "Go ahead."

Aaron reached for her hand over the table and lifted it over the other guys' heads to lead her out onto the dance floor. He jerked around like a bird about to take flight, a bird with broken wings, maybe, and Faith enjoyed herself all the same. I watched her dance, and occasionally she looked up and smiled at me. She had a cute style of dancing, confident, but not in-your-face; sexy, but not slutty. She just looked like she was having fun. She danced with all of the guys, except Max. He was being strangely quiet tonight.

She came back to the table, laughing. She was on her third beer and headed toward tipsy. I was on my third pitcher. A slow dance came on and she put her arms around my neck and swayed. I put my hands on her hips and followed suit, my forehead resting on hers.

"Are you having fun?"

She nodded, her smile alcohol-loose. We rocked back and forth by the table while conversation went on around us.

"Look. Eli's dancing," Aaron hollered out as the song ended. Everyone clapped sarcastically.

I bent down to whisper in Faith's ear. "You want to show them what real dancing is?"

"I'm all yours, Studly."

I took her out onto the dance floor while my friends uttered various expressions of surprise. When I hit the little square of multi-colored space, I looked pointedly back at our table and dramatically held my hand out to Faith. She laughed and placed her little hand in mine, and I yanked her in, like a puppet on a string. She whirled gracefully into my arms, a testimony to her coordination and style, not mine, and laughed as I grinned and nodded back at the table. The guys stared back enviously, but hollered out their praise as I held my arm up and she twirled beneath it like a figurine inside a music box. We danced and laughed and one time, when she was close, I pressed my lips to hers, meaning to stop, but getting caught up in the kiss. The boys caught sight of us.

"Whooo!"

"They're so immature," I said against her lips, starting to work my hands, again, under her sweater.

She put her hands back to quickly stop mine and pulled away. "Somebody's had too much to drink."

"Who?" I looked around in an alarmed way.

She smiled. "You."

"Oh. Sorry." I guess the shot Aaron bought me, tequila and kahlua, which was surprisingly good, had taken hold of me.

"No. That's okay. But maybe you should take me home."

"Umm...most definitely. Let's not even say goodbye. Let's just walk out together."

"Okay."

We swung by the table so she could pluck her vest off a stool wordlessly, and then turned to leave. She trailed after me as I held her hand.

When Aaron noticed, he jerked his head in our direction, alerting the others. "Hey, check out Batronis." Several shouts and whistles followed us out the door.

We strolled silently for a while, though still chuckling over the guys' reaction. I turned my head toward her. "They can be a little obnoxious."

"I thought they were fun."

We walked farther. "I can be a little obnoxious, too. Sorry I got carried away on the dance floor." The chilly night air had sobered me some. A tingle of alarm shot through me. "Are you mad?"

She looked at me out of the corners of her eyes. "Not at all. I just wanted to get you all to myself."

I exhaled and stopped. "And what, may I ask, are your intentions?"

"Umm..." She put a finger to the side of her mouth and tilted her head, then smiled and slipped her hands around my neck. "I intend to take you up to my apartment, and..." She hesitated, long enough to drive me crazy. "And see how things unfold."

"Mmm," I purred as I brushed my lips over hers. "See how things unfold. I like that."

"Um-hum." She nipped at my chin, then turned and hurried on down the sidewalk, dragging me happily after her.

We took the stairs down, but she pushed the elevator button for the trip up. We stood aside while a couple got out, and I recognized Mr. Girardi, from earlier in the day. Mrs. Girardi gave me a friendly smile, but her husband didn't look nearly as friendly. In fact, he practically glowered at me.

"Hello, Faith," the woman said, her voice musical. "I heard you got stuck in the elevator earlier. Is this the young man you were stuck with?"

"Yes, Mrs. Girardi. This is Eli."

"Hello, young man." She took my hand in both of her frail, papery ones, giving it a warm squeeze. "You take care of our Faith, now." She winked at Faith and whispered loudly, "He's cute."

"I think so, too," Faith whispered just as loudly, giving me a dazzling smile. We climbed on board and waved goodbye to the pair as the doors closed. Then, all of a sudden, she was on me. She untucked my shirt and slid her hands, delightfully cold, over my back, her mouth pressed to mine with a blinding wildness. But, as fast as it began, it was over. A *ding* sounded and the doors opened behind us. She spun, guiltily, and stood in front of me, her hands on the side of my legs. A guy stood outside. He looked at us with a hint of confusion on his face, probably having caught the flurry of activity as the doors opened.

"Going down?"

"No," I responded, moving my hands to Faith's shoulders. "Definitely going up."

"Oh," he mumbled, still looking bewildered as the doors closed on him.

Faith doubled over in laughter. I chuckled along with her. "I don't think your neighbors are getting a very good impression of me."

"Are you kidding?" She giggled. "Mr. Girardi loves you." I shook my head and she tried to sober up. "He's just a little overprotective of me. He told me once I looked like his Estelle, his first wife, when they were married." She became more serious and didn't touch me for the rest of the ride up.

I followed her out of the elevator to her apartment door. She turned as if to say something then whirled back, focusing on her key in the lock. I waited outside when she went in.

"Aren't you coming in?"

"Are you sure you want me to?"

She came back and pulled me inside, then closed the door behind me. "I'm a little nervous," she admitted. "When I said earlier I hadn't had many guests up here...well...what I should have said was...I haven't had *any* guests up here in the entire five years I've lived here. Only the super, the Girardis, a couple of other neighbors, Glo, once..."

"I could come back another time."

"No." She took my hands. "I want you here with me."

I shifted, feeling slightly uneasy. "Okay."

She hung up her vest, but still moved in slow motion. I studied her. She turned back, her mouth opened as if to speak, then she lowered her head. Her voice was almost a whisper. "I mean, this is what people do, isn't it? They go out for a couple of drinks, and come back... It's done every day. Just not by me," she added under her breath.

The bed felt like a living, breathing thing in the room with us, a dragon lying in wait. She led me over to it, and sat awkwardly, the bed being so close to the ground. Her comforter was a lemony yellow color that brightened the room.

"Faith," I said, stroking her cheek. "Let's talk for awhile. We don't have to do anything you're not ready for. Heck, I don't even know if I'm ready for it. You only learned my name a few hours ago." I smiled to relieve the tension and leaned back on the bed, twisting on my side to rest on one elbow.

She flopped straight back with a groan. "I'm doing this all wrong."

I moved a few hairs from her face as I tried to reassure her. "You are doing nothing wrong. Nothing has to be done a certain way. Nothing has to be done at all. We're two friends talking, right? We're friends?"

"Yeah." She reached up and ran her finger across my lips and I tightened.

Taking a breath, I forced myself to relax and played with her hair. "You've been here five years then, and—"

Just as the words escaped my mouth, the lights went out again. A collective groan went up from the building, and a loud, male voice yelled, "Shit! Not again."

Faith giggled beside me. "Hold on. I'll get some candles." The outside lights provided a small amount of vision in the dark. She stumbled into the kitchen and came back to set three, thick pillar candles, which I suspected had been used for the same purpose before, on the window ledge near the flowers. The sulfur smell of the match filled my nostrils when she lit them, and then came back beside me. The candlelight made her all the more beautiful and hard to resist. She resumed her position so I looked down on her while her hair fanned out on the comforter, a pillow now pressed under my armpit to rest on.

When she went to the kitchen, I was trying to do the math. She'd already been here five years? How old was she? The candles guttered in the not-well-insulated windows. As if reading my thoughts, she spoke.

"I was only seventeen when I moved here. I lied when I signed my lease. It would only be legal if I was eighteen, so-o eighteen I was."

"You came alone? Not knowing anyone?" She nodded. "Boy. Things must have been bad at home."

She rolled over onto her stomach to pull on a loose thread in the comforter and then run it through her fingers as she talked, leaning on her elbows. "They were. Once, when I was thirteen and Nathan was...eighteen, I guess, I came home from school, and he was there. I'd made straight A's for the first time, and I was excited. He could tell I was happy, and that ticked him off. He ripped the report card out of my hand and read it, and next thing I know, he slammed me up against the door and had a knife to my throat. He said he was going to kill me and cut my brain out and eat it and then maybe he'd be smart. And he wasn't just talking. I could see it in his eyes. He would have done it." She shivered. "Luckily my parents got home, and he must have decided it wasn't worth the effort."

She stopped talking. I was stunned.

"He wasn't that way all the time, though. Sometimes he was really sweet. He would take me to the mall, or to the park, or whatever...That's what made it hard." Her words choked off and again she was silent.

"You're very brave," I said at last, my voice raw.

"No, I'm not. I graduated early, and then, as soon as I could, I ran away. A brave person wouldn't run away. I couldn't take it anymore. My parents understood, but they couldn't help me financially. Nathan's doctors cost too much." She rolled back over, and then changed her mind and snuggled into my arms, her back to me. I kissed her neck, glad she couldn't see how overwhelmed I was by her. "I came to New York because I wanted to write, but I needed to know more of the world first. Funny, because I still don't know anything. I'm stuck on this block for the most part, going from work, to home, and back. My world's less than a block wide." She sounded sad. I rubbed her arm, wishing I could take the hurt away. She shifted and placed a hand on my cheek as she looked up into my face. "What is it about you that makes me reveal my innermost secrets to you? Are you some kind of sorcerer Eli...what's your last name?"

"Batronis."

"Are you some kind of sorcerer, Eli Batronis? I have never told anybody the things I've told you. I didn't think they'd understand. There's a certain amount of shame..." She stared off into space thoughtfully.

I took her chin and gently turned her to me. "You have nothing to be ashamed of," I insisted. "You are not your brother—" *And I am not my father.* "—and, from what you say, he was just troubled anyway."

She drew me to her and kissed me, then, pulled back.

"You are wonderful. I mean it. And it's not just because I'm madly in lust with you," she said with a wicked smile. "You are a fantastic listener, and are so non-judgmental."

"I'm not like that. I'm not the man you think I am," I blurted out.

Her brow knit as she peered into my face and pushed the hair back on my forehead. "Maybe you're not the man *you* think you are." She pulled me in again and kissed me, and it was as if I could feel her letting go of her fears.

She opened herself to me, pure, and gentle, and unbelievably good. Her need for me was imbedded in each kiss but I was not nearly as brave as she was. And I was not as strong either. I could not say no to her, not even close.

She moved to kneel in front of me and slowly pulled the turtleneck off over her head. Silently, I straightened and knelt in front of her, too, my hands going to her hips. She was built like a swimsuit model, and I wondered how she was able to hide this gorgeous body under a polyester waitress uniform. The way the black lace of her bra traversed the curves, enticing, alluring.

I let my gaze fall from her face, and traced the lines. She sucked in her breath. I slid my hands up the lines of her slender neck. Her pulse underneath my fingertips fluttered and I felt alive, so alert. The electricity surged through my bloodstream like quicksilver. She bent her head back so her hair swung loosely behind her, until my fingers reached her chin, when she brought it forward. Her eyes burned in the darkness and my breathing stopped. I wanted to lose myself to her, to relinquish my burden, but I was frozen.

She stretched up and ran her fingernails under the back of my hair to pull my head down gently until our lips touched. I drank her in, drank deeply and long. She moved her hands to my shoulders then yanked at my buttons until she finally pulled my shirt off, throwing it across the room with a twinkling smile. I smiled now, too, and wrapped her in my arms, squeezing her to me with a laugh. I pushed her back and we fell together onto the mattress. I held myself above her, my arms extended. She reached behind me for the tail of my t-shirt and tried to pull it over my head, but it was awkward. I helped her the last little bit, and then swung it around my head and threw it somewhere like a male stripper. We fell together in a heap, laughing, kissing, rolling over and over, until we almost rolled off the bed, except for my hand coming down on the hardwood to brace us.

I tugged at her jeans and she lifted her hips so I could slide them off. I stood by the bed and undid my belt buckle while she watched, rolling on her stomach. Her chin rested on her clasped hands, her elbows bent. A huge grin slid across her face, and she raised her eyebrows at me, kicking her feet behind her while she lay there in that lacy bra and panty set driving me crazy. When my pants hit the floor with a loud clang, she scrambled under the covers and held them up for me. I dove in next to her and then it was all smooth flesh, heat, and need. When I drove into her it was heaven. I wanted to take it slow, but my body raced on without me. When she moaned out my name it almost pushed me over the edge, but I held on while we swayed together in the candlelight, until she cried out and melted into the sheets. Unable to stop myself, I too released with a soul-shattering shudder, blinded with pleasure and contentment. We lay together, panting, spent and liquid; blissful. For the first time in a long time I could say I was happy, lying naked next to her, underneath the thick, down comforter, warm and at peace.

Somewhere during the night I woke, the candles an inch or two shorter, the light still flickered madly about the room. I carefully rose on one elbow to look at Faith. I jostled her a little and her head fell to one side, an arm bent, fingers curled, lying on the pillow beside her. Her face was so peaceful, a smile still played around her lips, and my heart swelled with love for her. She accepted me into her world, into her private thoughts and most intimate needs, into her.

And then a chill spread over me, rising from the middle of my back and creeping over my shoulders. But she didn't know the real me, it indicated, and when she did, she would be gone. I bent as far as I could and blew out the candles. I slid back beneath the covers, next to her warm body. The rhythm of her open heart soothed me and I pushed the chilling thoughts away. What we had together was good. I could change. It was enough for now. It would have to be enough.

CHAPTER FIVE

M*ax*   Well, Lady Amber was a winner. She knew her way around the bedroom so well she could offer tours. She may have kissed without putting an ounce of heart into it, but the end result was the same, or so I told myself. We didn't even know when the lights went out because what we were doing was best done in the dark anyway. Later, when the lights came back on, we sat in her bed; she wore my shirt, and I had just put my jeans back on. We scarfed down the burgers Eli was such a dear to bring up. Slurping her soda through the straw, she reached over and grabbed my hand.

"Ooh, Mark." I had quit correcting her by this time and simply decided to be Mark for the day. "You've really got to clean your nails. I know you are a construction worker and all, but that's a real turn-off. To think, those hands were...well, you know where they were," she added with a laugh.

"Yes, I do." I grabbed her hand and brought it up to kiss. I looked at my nails myself. "Hmm...I don't think that's from work. It's clay, from my sculpting."

She raised a manicured eyebrow. "You sculpt?"

I shrugged. "It's a hobby."

"Then you must do me," she squealed.

I took her hand and kissed her knuckles. "Madam, I believe I did. Several times."

She slapped my shoulder. "No, silly. Do a sculpture of me. I'll pose for you, nude."

"You mean the portrait isn't enough?" I gestured to the mammoth painting of her in the buff—straddling a Queen Anne's chair, no less—that hung on the wall behind her bed.

"Well, it's nice and all, but a sculpture...now that would be something. Your hands, molding clay into the shape of my body. Ooh. I'm all atingle."

I came to the conclusion Lady Amber was a sex addict, and it showed in every aspect of her life. She kicked me out soon after that, taking my number so we could set up a time for me to sculpt her, and, no doubt, screw her at the same time. I left her apartment feeling pretty proud of myself.

Until Eli walked into Harry's with Faith. She was bright and cheery and delicious in that green sweater of hers, and she was on Eli's arm. It took the wind right out of my sails. I watched them all evening, listened to the melody of her laughter, dazzling and tinkling, and the low rumble of Eli's words to her that provoked it. I watched him as he watched her, out on the dance floor with all the guys. He couldn't take his eyes off her, and it was obvious she felt the same about him. And when they danced together, it was both sexy and fun and patently magical. No one noticed when they got set to leave, except me. I saw the weighted looks exchanged, felt the energy from them as they anticipated being alone together...and I ordered a double. My tumble with Lady Amber seemed like nothing more than a cheap sex now, which was exactly what it was. Cheap, and empty, and suddenly not at all satisfying.

FAITH

When I woke up in the morning the sun was streaming in the windows, and the lights were on. For a minute I was confused, then I remembered the blackout and I remembered Eli. I turned to see him asleep beside me and listened to his soft, even breathing. It was the first time I'd woken up with a man, and it was...nice. Very nice. I wanted things to stay like that forever, just Eli and me, wrapped up in each other's arms, buried under the warmth of my comforter. But reality rushed in and a wave of panic swallowed me. I looked for my alarm clock. It blinked at me benignly, 12:00, the power outage took care of that. Eli had a watch on the hand that was flung over his head. I lifted it and squinted at the numbers. Eight o'clock.

"Eli!" I hissed, poking him in the ribs. "Eli, get up!"

"Huh? What? What's wrong?"

"It's eight o'clock. You've got to get out of here." I hopped out of bed and shivered as the room was so long without heat in the blackout it was freezing. I covered my breasts with one arm and retrieved Eli's pants from the ground, flinging them at him. "Here."

"What's the hurry, babe? Why don't you come back over here?" He lifted the covers with a playful grin.

I took his t-shirt, which I found hanging off my ficus tree, my one and only plant, and balled it up to throw it at him. "You're going to be late."

"Nah, I've got plenty of time. I'm right across the street."

"You mean you're not going home to change?"

"No. I figured I'd wear what I wore yesterday."

"But they saw you in it. They'll know you spent the night here."

"So?"

"They'll know we...you know." Heat rose in my cheeks.

"Slept together?" he said with an irritating grin.

I stuck a hand on my hip and exhaled in exasperation. "You're really enjoying this, aren't you?"

"A tiny bit."

"Ugh." I threw up my hands. "*I* have to get to work." I marched into the bathroom. When I stepped into the shower, the warm water felt fantastic and my irritation lightened as if it washed down the drain with the water. I thought about the night before, dancing with Eli, talking with him, then feeling the way his strong hands stole over my body in the darkness of my room, making each nerve dance in succession as they swam over my flesh, and finally about the dizzying plunge into molten lava when I achieved that sweet release with him. I was so wrapped up in my own personal peep-show I didn't hear him until he was there. His arms came around me to lean against the wall, the water falling between us.

He gave me a shit-eating grin. "I decided to take a shower after all."

I thought about protesting. I did. But he looked so good, with the water running down his muscular chest, and I loved him. Even then, I loved him. I gave in, saying, "Oh, what the hell," and threw my arms around his neck. That was the first time we made love in the shower. He took me to strange, new places of pleasure and desire, and I was glad to find my way there with him, each act we did new and exciting. I can still remember the joy of that first time in the shower—the way the water made our bodies slide together, kissing his chest and feeling the doubled sensation as the water rushed over my lips, warm and refreshing, the way the steam rose around us, as if to hide us from prying eyes. He was my first, and I thought he would be my only.

In those first couple of months, we became each other's worlds, though Eli was determined to broaden my world beyond my block, as I intended to do when I first moved to New York. So though we were constantly together, we were also constantly on the run. We visited all the sightseeing places together—the Statue of Liberty, the Kennedy Center, and Radio City Music Hall. We even ventured to The Guggenheim, though, perhaps, a little out of our league there. He surprised me with picnics in Central Park later, and wowed me with the awe-inspiring beauty of Grand Central Station. I remember walking in and standing in the middle, spinning in slow circles, mesmerized by the way the light streamed in from above. I watched the shadows of the pigeons as they cooed on the windows' ledges, their wings often beating against the glass.

I started to believe I was living an enchanted life meant for someone else. Eli was so free and easy, and I was so unbelievably happy. We made love every night, and basked in the knowledge that we did the next morning, and that we would do it again the next evening. Our love hung over us during the daytime hours like a secret, shimmering umbrella, and whispered seductively to us at night as our bodies merged and became one.

But sometimes lingering doubts overtook me. Why was I allowed to have what I had with Eli, when others would never be allowed to even feel for another person a tenth of what we did for each other? Why was my life in those days so perfect, so idyllic, when others suffered from heartbreak, or loneliness? Or was it all an illusion, make-believe, could it really be this good?

One day he took me ice-skating at Rockefeller Center. It was one of those perfect winter days. Huge snowflakes fell slowly to the ground as if enjoying the trip down. It was like we were living inside a snow globe. Eli had on his green flak jacket, and I had on a thick, multi-colored sweater with a matching knit cap, and my down vest. He held my hand as I skated, patiently instructing me, or holding both hands and skating backward in front of me and pulling me along. He would let go every once in a while and take off, crouched like a speed-skater. He whizzed around the ice at terrifying speeds, weaved in and out of surprised skaters and passed me with a rush of air that practically knocked me over, although, to be honest, that didn't take much.

By the end of the afternoon, though, I was a fairly competent skater, with a fairly bruised backside and aching ankles. I thought he was the most beautiful thing in the world as his long legs sliced gracefully over the ice and the wind blew back his hair.

We sat at a table afterward sipping hot chocolate and I became moody.

"You're quiet all of a sudden."

I was thinking about this waitress that had been overly familiar with him the night before at Harry's. "Have you taken any other girls here?" I asked suddenly.

He laughed, which irritated the hell out of me. Seeing my scowl he took both of my mittened hands in his. "No. No one. You're the only one I've ever wanted to take anywhere."

I knew he'd been with other women before. Aaron had done me the great favor of informing me Eli "hadn't slept around much" before he met me. But try as I might, I couldn't put his imagined previous lovers out of my thoughts. To think someone else had kissed his lips, and moreover, he'd kissed someone else's lips, made me sick to my stomach. Had he thought he loved them? Were they better in bed than I was? Prettier? I knew it was unreasonable to be angry over women who came before me, but, I still was. I hated them. Hated them for having touched him, for having pleased him.

This baffled Eli. He insisted no other woman ever meant anything to him, not like what he felt for me. And I wanted to believe him.

At Christmas time, he bought a tree and snuck it into my apartment to surprise me. My heart did a little flip when I saw it. It was so sweet and so perfect, and it made the place more ours. We didn't really have any money for decorations, so I bought some cheap, lacy ribbon for garland, a box of candy canes, and a few strands of white lights. We'd make love and then lay awake holding hands and watching the lights twinkle in the dark, bouncing off the windows behind the tree. It was the most wonderful Christmas ever.

MAX

As the days passed and this thing between Eli and Faith blossomed, I threw myself into my studies. I tried to convince myself I was happy for them. Eli was a great guy, he really was. And Faith? Faith was fantastic. With each passing day I grew to like her more. Okay, to love her more. I'd never met anyone with a more generous spirit. She gave herself to her customers, to her neighbors, to me. She was even good with the guys at work, knew all their names and their wives' and kids' names, and asked after them on a regular basis. She remembered whose daughter had a big test coming up and whose wife was waiting on a doctor's test results. She went out of her way to help others—cooking meals for the elderly couple in her apartment building when the woman fell and broke her hip, watching someone's kid while they took night courses, even taking that bitch, Glo, to the hospital when she cut herself at work. She was funny, cute, sexy, all rolled into one. Her wit was sharp enough to serve me up with a fast comeback; but her heart was good enough to make sure I knew she didn't mean it later. And I couldn't get her out of my mind.

Even as I sat, night after night, hunched over some anatomy book under the beacon-like light of my study lamp, I found myself thinking of her. About the way she tilted her head back and laughed loud and full at something I said when Eli and I had come to lunch that day. Or about the way her eyes would sometimes melt when she was looking into Eli's while they were slow dancing at Harry's, as I watched on pathetically, brooding over my beer. At home in my loft at night I would lift my head from some thick book or other, and see her ghost-like reflection in the glare cast by my lamp on the window. And in my dreams, her willowy form undid me, calling to me on the edge of ecstasy and then disappearing with the morning light.

It was New Year's. Amber invited me to her party to celebrate my completion of her sculpture that I finished in time for the holidays. I just took my first sip of champagne when Faith walked into the room on Eli's arm. He had purchased a dress for her for Christmas, in anticipation of the party, and man, could that girl set a room on fire. The dress was short and slinky and jade green, and my heart performed like some kind of trick contortionist as it twisted in my chest. Her hair was mostly pulled up high behind her, but she let several curling strands flow out from where it was gathered, making her neck look even longer. She wore a small diamond cross, as always, on such a thin silver strand it looked like it was suspended on her chest. I put my hand out to stop a waiter who was walking by with a tray of champagne flutes and downed the rest of mine in a single drink, put it on the tray and snatched another.

"Good man," I said to the waiter, not taking my eyes off Faith. She looked up and saw me and she smiled wider. Amber greeted them, but now took Eli's arm and led him away. He looked back and mouthed an apology to Faith. She stood for a few minutes by herself, looking around, fiddling with the strap on her little purse, and then found me again and smiled, taking a step toward me. But as she did, one of her neighbors rushed up to hug her.

Later, I sat out on Amber's terrace feeling sorry for myself and got good and ripped. At one point Faith rushed through the French doors to my right. I sat in a wrought iron chair in the corner by the door, leaning back against the wall. I had loosened my tie and unbuttoned my shirt about halfway down. Now, I sipped my champagne and watched her. She bent over the railing, breathing deeply, clearly upset.

"What's wrong?"

She jumped a mile and put a hand over her heart. "Oh, Max! You scared me." She smiled at me, taking a moment to catch her breath. "It's just... I don't like Amber. She keeps looking at Eli like he's a piece of meat, and she's decided to give up being a vegetarian."

"Don't worry," I replied blandly. "Eli only has eyes for you." Something in my tone struck her, I think, and she looked at me more closely.

"What about you Max? What are you doing out here?"

I hesitated, still eying her speculatively. "I like the city at night," I said finally. It wasn't a lie. "It's peaceful, stretched out like a sleek black cat at my feet." I drank again.

She smiled. "That's very poetic," she returned, with a hint of teasing.

"I pull it off every now and again." Inside people shouted out the final countdown.

"Oh. I didn't realize it was so late." Noisemakers went off, accompanied by champagne corks popping. Faith moved to go back inside, but as she passed me, she bent down to kiss me tenderly. With her hand still on my face, she said quietly, "Happy New Year, Max," and then disappeared inside.

I closed my eyes and breathed her name. "Shoot, Faith. Why'd you have to go and do a crazy thing like that?"

Sometimes, when Faith worked late and Eli and I got to spend some time together one-on-one, it would be like the old days. The old days when I didn't seethe inside for what my best friend had, and I would remember why we became friends in the first place. Still, for some reason I kept torturing myself, joining Eli at lunch at the diner so I could see Faith.

One day, I was walking back from the diner with Eli and Faith. It was one of the first days in early March with a touch of warmth that promised spring wasn't too far away. Although it only got up to fifty-five, everyone was walking around without jackets, the warmth being relative after a chilling winter. It's funny, because I knew the same people in short-sleeves today would be in sweatshirts in fifty-five degree weather in the fall, when we were in the warm summer mode. Faith's shift was over, and Eli and I were heading back to work. We both had an arm around her and were teasing her about something; I don't remember what. She was so cute when she was embarrassed, trying to shrink into her shoulders and squirming, telling us to cut it out. When we got to the site, Aaron and the guys stood around talking, all of them gazing up.

Eli breathed, "Holy shit!" and I looked up, too, finally seeing what they were all looking at. Four floors up, a guy balanced on a girder. He looked like a young Drew Carey, complete with black suit, white shirt, and tie. He was heavyset with a round face and thick, black glasses. He was running his hand through his short, spiky, blond hair with one hand, while holding on to a corner support with the other. Strangely, he had kicked off his work shoes. Better to be safe when you're trying to commit suicide, I guess.

Before I knew what was happening, Eli took off running toward the building. Faith shouted after him, "Eli? What are you doing? Eli!" I tightened my grip on her, unsure of what he was up to, but wanting to make sure she was safe.

Eli started shouting up to the guy. "Hey! Hey up there. What's your name?"

"Name's Chuck. What's it to you?" I could tell the kid was scared. Scared, but desperate. That's a bad combination.

"Did someone call the cops?" I asked Aaron.

"Ten minutes ago," he answered sourly, never taking his eye off the potential jumper.

"Chuck, I want to talk to you." Eli pulled off his work boots and socks. Some guys felt they got a better grip with their bare feet. I'd never seen Eli do it though. I'm not sure if he was trying to make the guy feel more comfortable or what.

"Nah, man. I'm done talkin'."

"No, listen, Chuck...you did a good job getting up there. You think I could do that? If I did that, would you let me talk to you then?"

The man on the ledge jeered. "Yeah, sure man, whatever."

I heard Faith exhale, "Oh, my God."

I turned to look at her and her face was deathly white. I squeezed her shoulder. "It's okay. He knows what he's doing." Although I had no idea whether he did or not. The crew held its collective breath as he scaled the building, starting at the corner farthest from the man, which is what, I suppose, the suicidal maniac did, and angling toward him. He shinnied up like a monkey, quickly, never once faltering. It all happened so fast, we hardly had time to be scared for him. He talked with the kid for about...I don't know...five minutes or so, and then they shook hands, Eli in the open, not holding onto anything else, and the kid, still clinging to a corner support. Then, slowly, Eli began to lead him back in the direction from which they'd come.

He'd only gotten about a third of the way across when the man lost his footing. He slipped off one side, but was able to somehow grab the thin bottom edge of the girder he was just standing on. Everyone gasped as he hung there in midair and then Aaron said what we all were thinking. "Sweet Jesus."

Eli turned back carefully, like a gymnast on the beam, and crouched down. Only this beam was four floors up. He was on the middle of a girder, the nearest support bar a yard away. Faith whispered, "Oh, Eli, no." Her voice sounded strained. It was the strangest feeling, watching from below, knowing we might be about to witness someone's death, and realizing there was nothing you could do about it. I thought about what that would do to Faith, and my stomach dropped out.

Eli grasped the girder. The guy was screaming. "Help! Help me! Don't let me die."

Nice, jerk. Now your instinct for self-preservation kicks in. Now that Eli is four stories up.

I watched as Eli moved his hands out carefully until he was lying flat on his stomach. He hooked his bare feet around the girder and wrapped one hand around it on the side opposite from where the man was clinging. He reached down with the other hand to grab the guy's forearm. Eli was strong, but I knew he had no chance of pulling old Chuck up; it was physically impossible. But as I watched, the guy started flailing his legs.

"What is he doing?" Faith asked desperately.

I watched a few seconds more and determined he was trying to hike his leg up on the girder, unsuccessfully. After a pause in the action, the guy made one last attempt. Eli released his grip on the girder to grab Chuck's pants leg and yanked him up onto the girder, with the guy's help. A cheer went up, but, simultaneously, Eli slipped. His momentum from swinging the guy up took him over the other side, and with one hand on the business man's forearm, and one on his pant leg, he had nothing to even grasp with.

He fell, and fell, and fell. It seemed to take forever for him to come down. Beside me, Faith screamed. I'll never forget the sound of that scream; it still haunts me in my nightmares, echoing her frantic terror. Finally, he hit with a dead thud. For a second or two, no one moved. We couldn't believe it. Then I was running, running toward him without thought. When I got to him, he was a mess, blood everywhere, lying on his back, his leg crumpled up under him. "Oh, man." My hands were sweaty, my heart started beating like crazy, and a wave of nausea hit me. Aaron and Faith reached us.

"Eli," she cried out weakly, tears already streaming down her face. "No. No." She shook her head. Her hands trembled as she brought them up to cover her mouth, her eyes wide with disbelief. Looking at her galvanized me.

"Faith," I said harshly. "Go back to the diner and get some towels." She moved her eyes from Eli's face to mine but the words couldn't reach her where she was in the midst of her horror. "Faith. Now." Without a sound, she turned and took off running. "Where the fuck is the ambulance?" I wiped my face. "Aaron, get me something to brace his leg with."

"Like what?"

"I don't know," I snapped. "Maybe a couple of two-by-fours, short ones." He left and I took my t-shirt off and began ripping it into shreds.

"Is he okay?" the jerk above me asked. I didn't bother to answer him. "He's gonna be okay, isn't he?"

Aaron and Faith arrived back at the same time. "Faith, press a towel to that cut on Eli's head and apply even pressure." She did what she was told. As I took his vitals, I got a glimpse of Faith, and her hands weren't shaking anymore, though her lips moved in silent prayer. I worked quickly to stabilize him, after a few minutes glancing again at her. She had stopped praying and cried as the blood started to saturate the thick towel she pressed to Eli's head and it squeezed out through her fingers. "That's good, Faith." She looked over at me searchingly and for a second I could imagine her, pigtailed and freckled, crying over a scraped knee. I swallowed and looked back at Eli. He was looking awfully gray. I could hear sirens approaching.

By the time the EMTs made it to us, I had rigged up a makeshift brace, tying the boards together with strips of my t-shirt. The EMTs decided to leave my brace as is, to reduce the amount of time in the field, but as they were putting him on a backboard, Eli moaned.

I closed my eyes. "Thank God." I wiped the sweat from my brow, knowing his waking and feeling pain was a good sign.

I looked at my hands, covered with Eli's blood, and then over at Faith as she stood shakily, blood streaked all over her cotton-candy pink waitress uniform, a dazed look on her face.

After that, I remember shouting, firemen and policemen arriving, people running around, and ladders being put into position. I remember Chuck saying, "Hey, I'm sorry man," as he was led off between two policemen, and Aaron saying, "You did good, Doc," in his simplistic way. I remember the ambulance doors closing on Eli on his stretcher, and bystanders talking to cops with notebooks, but not understanding their words. I don't remember Aaron hustling Faith into his truck to take her to the hospital, but I was told later that happened. I don't remember anything the EMTs said. I remember being alone, standing at the feet of an imprint of Eli's body in the loose dirt, misshapen by pools of blood in parts, perfect in other spots, lying inches from the concrete slabs that made up the building's base that would have definitely killed him. I stood there a long while, as my shadow stretched over the Eli-hole. Then I walked to the back of the site and threw up.

CHAPTER SIX

E*li* I don't know why I did it. I only know I could not sit back again and watch another man take his life.

When I woke up in the hospital, Faith was with me. I had a doozy of a concussion, but no bleeding on the brain. My wrist was broken, the one thing that hit the concrete, and my leg was badly sprained from being twisted under me. Stitches closed the gash on my head, and glue the one on my arm; don't ask me why they chose to do it that way but that was how things ended up. They kept me in the hospital for two days while I recovered from my blood loss, and on the third day Faith came to take me home to her place, where she intended to nurse me until I lost my mind.

She was so sweet, spending every minute with me that she wasn't at work. The nursing staff let her sleep in the recliner the first night, and she snuck back in after visiting hours the second night. They didn't have the heart to kick her out. They told me Doc probably saved my life. He told me the cadavers were more fun to work on than me.

Aaron and Max helped Faith to get me up to the apartment, but when the door closed behind them, she turned on me. She was quiet all morning; I should have known she was working herself up into some kind of state.

She was looking out of the window when she first spoke. "Eli," she said evenly. She spun around slowly, her eyes zeroed in on mine. "Why did you do it?"

I was clueless. "Do what?"

"Why did you climb up after that man? Why?" Her hands fisted at her sides and her face grew redder by the second. I'd never seen her like this. Ever.

"I had to, Faith. He was going to jump."

She crossed the room to stand in front of me. "So, you get to plunge four stories instead?"

I didn't answer. What could I say?

"Do you know what it was like for me to watch you f-fall?" The tears started. "Do you?" She poked me in the chest with her finger and it hurt. Hurt like hell.

"Oww! I'm still kind of sore."

"Tough," she shrieked, hitting an all-time record decibel level and poking me harder, tears spurting out of her eyes and flying everywhere. "Do you know what it's like to have to sit there and watch the man you love's body falling through mid-air...and then to see you like that, broken, and bleeding." Sobs ripped from her and she became incoherent until I touched her. Then her head flew up. "Don't touch me. Don't you touch me, Eli Batronis! I'm pissed at you."

"I'm getting that."

"Why? Why would you do something so incredibly asinine? The police were on the way, and firemen, people who are trained to handle situations like that." She put her hand on her forehead, pushing her hair back and holding it on top of her head. "Why in the world would you risk your life," her voice cracked, "when it wasn't necessary? Why didn't you just let them do *their damned jobs*!" With each word she jabbed me, almost knocking me off my crutches.

"Damn it. That hurts."

"I don't care. You know what? I don't care if it hurts. You shouldn't have gone and got yourself hurt like that."

"Do you understand how crazy you sound? You're going to go on hurting me because you're mad I hurt myself."

"Don't use logic on me. There's no place for logic in this conversation. I'm upset."

"You've made that perfectly clear. Now," I could see she was running out of steam. "Why don't we go over, and you can help me into the chair you bought."

She'd purchased a secondhand recliner for me and a small TV set. When she got me into the chair and set the crutches down, which I was glad to see she didn't intend to use as a weapon, she knelt beside the chair and sobbed.

"Oh, come on, honey. Don't do that." I rubbed the back of her head. "Sugar, come on... You're getting my cast all wet and it's not the waterproof kind."

This got a small laugh out of her between catches in her breath. Slowly her breathing came back to normal. She rose on her knees and stretched over me. "God, Eli. I'm so pissed at you."

She kissed me, her wet face brushing against my stubbly one. And then she kissed me again, passionately. And before long I was glad I injured my knee and not my hip because we initiated that chair into our place in a fine way. It had been too long for both of us, and broken wrist or no, I ripped off her clothes and by the time we were finished, she was completely naked in my lap, her hair whipping everywhere, and sweat rolling down between her breasts, and I had only unzipped my jeans.

As she lay over me afterward, gulping in air, I managed to say, "Damn, woman. Maybe I should piss you off more often."

She slapped my chest lightly and I swatted her backside not-so-lightly and she kissed me again. "Don't *ever* do that to me again. Don't ever get yourself hurt like that."

"I won't, baby. I won't." I kissed her.

She stole over and got the comforter off the bed and curled up on my lap, lay her head on my shoulder, and then fell asleep. I stayed awake for a long time, thinking about what I had done and why I'd done it. It made no sense, even to me.

FAITH

I worried I had hurt the big jerk. Jumping him when he'd only been home from the hospital for fifteen minutes.

When I woke up, it was dark in the room. He was stroking my arm. I didn't move my head from his shoulder. "Eli?"

"Hmm?"

"Why did you do it?"

He sighed. "I've been sitting here trying to figure that out."

I didn't say anything.

"I guess it has to do with my dad," he said finally.

"Your dad?"

He brought the chair back to a more upright position and I shifted so I was facing him, although I couldn't really see his face in the darkness. I could tell by the tension in his voice this wasn't easy for him. "Get me a drink, and I'll tell you the story."

I obediently got up, wrapping the blanket around me as I tripped to the kitchen and poured him a scotch on the rocks. I came back and sat. He rolled the scotch around in his mouth then swallowed it and exhaled sharply from the sting of the liquor.

"Mmm. I'd forgotten how much I missed that."

I waited patiently for him to begin.

Seeming emboldened by the alcohol, he said, "When I was seven...on my seventh birthday," he articulated the last carefully, "my dad took me by the hand and walked me out to the woods and shot his brains out."

I sucked my breath in so fast it cut into my throat. "What?"

"He shot his brains out."

My stomach dropped. "But...how could he? You were so young."

"He was miserable. Sick. Dying from cancer. They'd discovered a brain tumor and done everything they could, but it was a matter of time. He must have realized that. And I think the tumor put pressure on his brain. He wasn't in his right mind those last few months."

"Oh, baby." I curled my arms around his head, pulling it into my chest.

"Actually," his voice cracked, "it was worse than that. I've never told anyone this, not even my mother." He took a shuddering breath. "He asked me to do it. Asked me to hold the gun. But I refused. I begged him not to do it, and he got angry with me. 'Why won't you help me, son? Don't you want me to be happy?'" Eli sobbed, and it pierced right through me. "But I couldn't do it. I loved him. I loved him too much. Or maybe not enough, I don't know..."

"Eli. My God, you were only seven years old. He should have never put that kind of pressure on you."

"I know. I know," he moaned. "It was horrible. He explained it all to me. 'I'll put this end into my mouth, and you'll pull the trigger,' but I cried and shook my head telling him, no, Daddy, I don't want to shoot you." He broke down then and cried until he was exhausted.

I held him, crying for that little boy inside of him.

I almost thought he'd drifted off to sleep when he spoke, startling me, his voice dead. "He got a stick and—" Someone opened their door across the hall, spilling more light into the hallway and under my door and I could see his face. He wasn't there with me. He was back in those woods, his voice now small and disbelieving. It was the first time he told anyone about the dark secret his father shared with him. "—and the gun went off." He put his hands over his ears and they were shaking. "It was so loud. Right by my ear." He sounded like he was in shock. "When I got back to the house, I was covered in his blood and his brains, and maybe even some of that god-awful tumor. And my mom knew. And I knew, though she never told me, he asked her, too."

I could see this was the final betrayal. His mother had not protected him. She had let it happen.

"We never spoke of it. Still never have. And things were *never* the same with us again." His bitterness hung in the air like the stench of mold. He reached down and picked his glass up off the floor and finished his drink in silence.

I was sitting on the arm of the chair and I cradled his head, laying my cheek on the top of his head while my hot, silent tears fell. Now I understood. No, he couldn't sit there and watch *another* man take his life.

ELI

And so I told her. And then it was there between us. I don't think she noticed, but I knew. I'd sullied what was good between us with my dark past, and nothing would ever be the same.

I tried to tell her the next day, tried to explain to her the man who my dad was. She nodded her head and tried to understand, but I could see it in her eyes. She hated him for what he did to me. And part of me did, too. And that's what made it so hard.

I didn't want to hate him; I loved him. I loved everything about him. Yet I became all he wasn't. Where I worked with my hands, with my brawn, he was a banker. A tall, slender man with jet black hair and a wooly mustache.

He wore glasses that perpetually slid down to the tip of his nose. He loved to play games with me, all kinds of games, from tic–tac-toe, to Parcheesi, from hangman, to hide-and-go-seek. And he would always act like he couldn't find me, even though I hid in plain sight, under a table with no tablecloth, giggling.

And he loved me. Oh, how he loved me. He would take me to work with him and sit me behind his big desk and have his secretary come in and take dictation from me. And the sweet woman would write down every bit of nonsense that came out of my mouth.

I wanted to forget it all—the dark woods, the hide-and-go-seek, the mahogany desk in his office—but, at the same time, I was terrified I would. No one would be left to remember him. And as terrible as the thing was that he did, he did not deserve that. Drinking helped to numb the memories. They were still there, but without the sharp, stinging edges. His laugh, the way crinkles would appear beside his eyes when he smiled, the way he swaggered when he was especially proud of something he did at work—those could not disappear. But they must be muted. Must be muted because of the thing that happened in the woods. Now I had told her, that made it breathe again. I began to drink more to dull the keen, ever-present pain.

MAX

Eli had told me about his father once when he was very drunk and I was slightly less so. But the story sobered me up in an instant. I knew he told Faith, too, after his fall, because I could see the sadness in her eyes in the days after he returned from the hospital. I knew, too, because of that darkness, he would eventually hurt her. And that energetic little tumor would claim another victim. What I didn't know, what I failed to fathom, was Faith's infinite capacity for forgiveness.

FAITH

Something was wrong with Eli. *Could a head injury have changed his temperament?"* I'd heard that happens sometimes.

Whatever it was, our little excursions to the city stopped after his fall. We were still together every night—sometimes at my place, sometimes at his place, when I worked the late shift—but something changed.

He shared a dingy little apartment with Aaron about ten blocks away from the diner. They had more furniture than I did, but the white painted walls had turned gray and chipped, the florescent lighting was dim and dismal, and it forever smelled of stale beer. More often than not in those days, when I would get off work at eight and change before meeting Eli at Harry's, he would be well on his way to becoming plowed. I'd take him home, and most of the time he'd pass out before I even got under the covers. I'd turn over on my side, cold and lonely, and think about the way things used to be between us.

And the next night it would be the same. It began to eat at me, drag me down, making me unbearably sad.

One night in particular, I walked into Harry's and located his group immediately by their boisterous behavior. When I walked up to the table, he grabbed me and dipped me, kissing me so ardently I could hardly catch my breath. He tasted like beer.

"Hey, Faithy," he said with a sloppy grin. "Where've ya been?"

Embarrassed, I wiped my mouth with the back of my hand. "Working."

"Oh, yeah. Well come here so I can kiss you again." He grabbed me roughly and pulled me onto his lap. "Let's go home so I can do you. Do you know, guys, she makes the cutest little noise right after she's finished?"

Everyone at the table sat with their mouths hanging open, except for Aaron, who began giggling with him. Mortified, I snatched my purse off the table and turned to leave, but Eli grabbed my wrist.

"Where are you going?" he slurred.

"Home."

"Oh, goodie."

"Without you!" I shook my hand free. "And, for your information, you won't be hearing that cute little noise again for awhile."

I stormed out, but over my shoulder I heard him say, "As long as you do me, and I get to make my cute little noise."

He and Aaron fell together in a riot of laughter, knocking a stool over in the process, but by that time I was almost out the door.

"Faith. Wait."

I didn't turn. "Doc, I'm not in the mood."

"Come on. Let me walk you home. You shouldn't be walking home alone at night."

"I'm fine. I'm—" But I couldn't keep it in any longer. I started to run for home with him on my heels. I stopped finally, a stitch in my side, and began to cry in earnest. Max took me into his arms in the middle of the sidewalk while people passed us, giving us wide berth.

"Faith. Faith," he said quietly. "Come on, honey. He didn't mean it. He—"

I lifted my head from his chest. "Don't you defend him, Doc."

"I won't. I can't. What he did was not worthy of defense. I just—" He reached up and brushed the hair away from my face. "I don't like to see you like this. And I know he loves you."

I slid my arm around his waist, calmer now, and started walking with him toward my apartment. "I love him, too. But...how am I supposed to look at those people again? He made a fool of me. Of our most intimate—" I stopped, embarrassed all the more.

He turned toward me. "Faith, honey, none of those people are going to remember jack-shit tomorrow."

I laughed. Max always had a way of making me feel better. I lifted my head to give him a smile, but he was looking at me strangely. The next thing I knew, his warm lips covered mine. For a second, I let him kiss me. I was shocked, I guess, and...it felt so good. It had been awhile since I'd gotten more than a drunken, sloppy kiss from Eli. I lost my head. And when I pushed him off, it was with a struggle on my part. But as soon as we parted, the wrongness of it was clear as a cloudless day. Nausea rose to choke me. I tried to speak, but I couldn't. So I turned and walked quickly away.

CHAPTER SEVEN

M^{ax}   I don't know why I did it. I lost my head. It was the last thing I wanted to do to Faith, add to her grief. I watched her walk away with a sinking heart, then spun on my heel, disgusted with myself, and stormed back into Harry's. I strode right over to Eli, who was still laughing raucously with Aaron, grabbed a hold of his t-shirt and yanked him off his stool.

"What the hell?" Eli grumbled.

"Come on."

"What the hell are you doing, Doc?" he repeated belligerently.

Aaron stood to get in my face. "What's your deal, Doc?"

"Listen, Aaron, as big as a badass as you are," I spat at him through clenched teeth, "I swear to God, if you interfere with what I'm doing right now I'll rip you another asshole." And, unbelievably, I was so pissed, I think I actually saw a flash of fear in his eyes.

He shrugged and sat down to his beer. "Whatever."

I dragged Eli out of the place. The bouncer stood like he was going to step in and help him, but seeing the fire in my eyes, I guess, he sat down. I slammed Eli into the passenger seat of my BMW, a leftover from my days in Albany. When I got in on the other side, he started up again.

"What the fuck, Doc?"

"Shut up, Eli." I squealed away from the curb, testing the beautiful high-performance engine as I rarely did.

"You got some kind of problem with me?"

"No, Eli, you're the one with problems. But you will have a problem with me if you ever do anything to hurt Faith like that again."

"Faith?" he said, incredulous. "What's this got to do with Faith? I'd never hurt her."

I slammed my brakes and pulled over so quickly I was lucky to not cause a multi-car pileup. I turned to him. "I know you're not this stupid, Eli. You can't really believe she'd be okay with your talking about the most intimate details of your love life." For a minute, even in my blind rage, I thought about what her face would look like, what her voice would sound like when she climaxed. I shook the thought away.

Eli hung his head and was silent for a few seconds. "Geez, Doc. Don't you think I know what a jerk I was? That I have been?" He put his head in his hands. "I love her, man, I do. More than I ever thought I could love somebody. But I can't seem to stop hurting her." I could feel his frustration radiating out from him as surely as the stench of beer emanated from his pores.

I sighed, putting a hand to my forehead, awash in guilt. "All right...this is what we're going to do. I'm going to take you back to my loft, and you're going to take a cold shower and sober up. Then, you're going to go back to Faith's and get down on your fucking hands and knees and apologize to her, got it?"

He nodded morosely and I pulled slowly back out into traffic, exhausted by the whole affair.

ELI

I let myself into Faith's apartment with my key. The lights were on, but she was nowhere to be seen. I stuck my head into the long, narrow kitchenette on the far wall, but she wasn't there either. Alarmed, I was about to run back out the door and start searching for her, but a light came out from underneath the bathroom door. I walked over and tried the handle but it was locked.

"Faith? Faith?" I waited for a response but none came. I laid my head on the door, wiped out by all that happened. "Come on, babe, open up. Please."

To my surprise, the lock clicked back and the handle turned underneath my fingers. I stepped back and she walked out, straight past me, without even looking at me. She still had her vest on. Had she been sitting, locked in there, all this time? All the time I was at Max's place sobering up? She trudged over and flung herself on her mattress, stomach first. I lumbered over, too, taking my flak jacket off and depositing it on the floor, and laying beside her, on my back. We turned our faces toward each other. Her face was worn and tear-streaked. Had I done that to her? She was absolutely still.

"I'm sorry."

She squeezed her eyes shut as if my statement caused her pain. I reached out and ran the back of my hand gently across her cheek. Her eyes opened, and I could see her heartache swimming in them. And then she did the one thing I dreaded most. She started to cry, silently, still not moving, big, hot tears rolling out of her eyes and down her face as she stared into mine.

"I can't do this anymore." Her voice was barely a whisper.

Fear stole over my heart like a fog seeping from the ground. "No. Don't say that."

"I love you, Eli. So much. But I can't live like this. I can't stand to see what you're doing to yourself. What you're doing to us."

"Faith, I was just a little drunk tonight." My terror made me sound angry. "So, I have a big mouth—" Rage sparked in her eyes. "Not that I'm trying to minimize it, 'cause I know I screwed up."

She flew up. "It's not just tonight. It's all the nights. All the nights I have lain here beside you when you passed out, wanting you." She swallowed a sob. "Do you even remember the last time we made love? Because I don't."

I reached for her. "Well, if that's what you want..."

She slapped my hand. "That's *not* what I want. I want you. All of you. I want to laugh again, share my thoughts with you again, I..." Words seemed to desert her. She got up and moved over to the windows with her back to me, her arms crossed, staring blindly out into the darkness. "I'm tired, Eli." And she sounded like it. "Tired of trying to keep alive something that—for some reason that I can't understand—has died between us. I can't make you happy anymore. I've tried, but I can't." Her shoulders began to shake.

I scrambled out of the bed and went to her, putting my arms around her and squeezing her against me tightly so I could speak into her ear, hoping then the words I would say would find a straight path to her heart. "You are the *only* thing that makes me happy. The only thing that has *ever* made me happy. Please don't take that from me. I need you. I know I haven't been showing you that lately, but I can change. I can." I saw our reflection in the windows and suddenly it sickened me, what I had done to us. "I'll stop drinking." I started to kiss her ears, a move I knew she was particularly susceptible to.

"Mmm. Don't do that," she moaned, and she tried to move away but I tightened my grip.

"I'll stop drinking. I swear. And I'll make it all up to you somehow." I started kissing her neck and making promises in her ear, and she melted. The despair that had rocked me earlier was replaced with hope. *I haven't lost her altogether yet.*

I won her over eventually and made love to her until the pink rays of the sun began to glow in the east. I fell asleep determined to do a better job.

And I did. For two months I stayed sober, coming to the diner when the day was over to hang with Faith until she was done, and then going back to her place and renting a movie or something; we'd finally popped for a cheap VCR. When her days off coincided with my days off, I'd take her places, like I had done when we were first going out. To a Mets game or the Empire State Building. And to my relief, we recaptured it, those easy, happy days from the beginning of our relationship. And pretty soon, it was as if there'd never been a rift at all.

FAITH

"Heya, handsome." I leaned over the counter to give him a kiss. I was blissfully happy to have my Eli back. He wasn't drinking anymore and we were as happy as when we first fell in love. "How was work?"

"Good."

"Then what's with the glum face?"

"Well, I've got some bad news."

My pulse quickened. "What?"

"Tommy has the whole crew going to Albany to do a job for his brother-in-law. I'll be gone for two whole weeks," he said, disgruntled. "He's paying for the hotel and everything for us, so he thinks that makes it all better."

"Oh. Well, that stinks."

"And that means I'll be gone during our anniversary. We were going to go to that play."

"Oh." I was trying to mask my disappointment. "Well, that's okay. We can go when you get back. It's only a day on the calendar."

He grabbed my hand, looking into my eyes. "Not to me. We've been through a lot lately, and I really wanted to make that night special for you."

He had a way of making my heart beat like no one else. I leaned over and whispered to him, "You make *every* day special, babe." I kissed him. "I love you. And as long as you're extra careful while you're away and come back to me in one piece, I'll be fine."

But it was harder than I'd imagined. This was the most time we'd ever spent away from each other since the day we'd met. I hardly knew what to do with myself. When I got home, the apartment was empty, and I wasn't even able to look forward to going out with him later in the evening. I began to wonder what I ever did with myself before Eli, and it had only been six months. We limited ourselves to every other night phone calls while he was away, and the first night I paced the floor waiting impatiently for the phone to ring.

"Hey."

His voice infused me with warmth. "Oh, gosh. It feels so good to hear your voice. I already miss you so much."

"Me, too, babe. Aaron refuses to snuggle with me. Ouch." He was laughing.

"Well, I would hope so."

I could hear Aaron in the background saying, "I'm out of here."

"Dork threw a pillow at me. So...now that we're alone together..." He made his voice low and seductive. "...how are you really?"

"Hopelessly lost without you," I answered with a dramatic sigh that wasn't too far off the mark, to be honest.

"You sound tired."

"Ugh. I am. My feet are *killing* me. We got in a bus of band kids. Filled every seat in the joint. And, let me tell you, band kids are not great tippers."

"Oh, poor baby." I could hear the smile in his voice and it made my lonely heart feel light. "Did Glo help you out?"

"What do you think?" I flopped down on the bed, still in my waitress uniform.

"Why don't you ever rat her out?"

"Because ratting out the boss's daughter doesn't get you too far in life, and my goal is to someday take over Dino's, and then, the world."

He chuckled then sighed. "I'm pretty tired, too. We've been making a lot of progress already, though. Maybe we'll be able to knock a couple of days off and come home early."

"Don't tease me, Eli. I'm a weak woman."

"I'll do my best, Faith. You know I will... How have you been sleeping?"

"Horribly. I guess I need your snoring to put me to sleep."

"If you think my snoring is bad, you should hear Aaron's. It's one thing having to sleep a room away from him at home. Being in the same room is absolutely impossible. I'm worried if the fire alarms go off I won't be able to hear them."

I laughed, and then exhaled loudly. "You sound *so* good."

"What are you wearing?"

"Ooh. Are we going to get into some kinky phone sex now?"

"No. I'm not that imaginative," he quipped, then, demanded, "answer the question."

"I'm still in my uniform. I didn't want to be in the middle of changing when you called."

"All right. I'm going to give you fifteen minutes to get ready for bed, and then I'm going to call you back, okay?"

"Okay." I wondered what he was up to.

"Faith, wait."

"I'm still here."

"Don't get changed yet. Just brush your teeth and wash your face and do whatever else it is that you do before going to bed."

"Okay." I giggled and hung up. I rushed through my nighttime routine, hoping the phone would ring quicker, but it only gave me more time to wait.

When I answered the phone, he didn't bother with hello, just asked, "Are you ready for bed?"

"Yes." My smile hurt.

"All right. Turn out the lights."

I sauntered to the door, sashaying my hips, my smile even bigger, if that was possible. I flipped the switch. Now only the little, cheapy lamp by my bed was on. I moseyed over and turned it out, too.

"Are they off?" His voice sounded so sexy.

"Yes, they're off."

"Okay. Now...unbutton your uniform."

I did what I was told, feeling a little foolish, and having a strange urge to look around, as if someone were watching me.

"What are you wearing underneath?"

"Umm...the black and pink bra and panty set, hose, and my shoes."

"Okay, well those shoes have to go. Lie down on the bed and take them off."

I let my uniform drop to the floor, then lay down and pushed one shoe off with the toe of my other shoe, and used my foot to knock the one off on the other side. They clunked to the floor in the empty apartment. "Okay, the shoes are off."

"Peel off the stockings."

I peeled them off slowly, thinking about him as I did so. "May I ask what you're wearing?"

"You may. While you were getting ready for bed, I was too. And I'm now under the covers with only my underwear on."

"And Aaron is gone?"

"No, Aaron is here, getting off on our phone conversation. Of course Aaron is gone."

"Just checking."

"No more questions for you. Slide under your blankets."

"Okay."

"Turn on your side to face the windows. ...Now, close your eyes." I listened to his voice, my heart pumping in my chest. "I'm turning out my light...and turning on my side, too. Imagine I'm behind you." His voice became soft, and I could feel his lonesomeness through the phone wires. "Do you feel me, Faith?"

"Yes," I breathed, and my eyes were filled with tears.

"Okay, now my arms are coming slowly around you to undo the clasp of your bra. It closes in the front, doesn't it?"

I smiled. "Good memory."

"Only for the important stuff. Now...now that we've got that pesky bra out of the way, why don't we get rid of those darn panties?"

"I thought we weren't having phone sex?" I asked, reaching for coy.

"We're not. I just wanted to feel your skin against mine. Now you need to mold your body to mine like you do... Oh, I wish I could smell you. Have I ever told you how wonderful you smell?"

"From time to time." We both knew that he did it almost daily.

A deep, peaceful quiet settled over us. "Are your eyes still closed?"

"Yes," I lied. I'd opened them to look at the security lights from his construction zone across the street. But I guess he could read my voice.

"Liar. Close them."

"Boy. I never knew you were so into this whole control thing," I teased.

"Like you're not getting off on it?"

"Oh, no, baby," I answered, trying my best to sound seductive. "I'm not saying that."

"Then pipe down."

"I love you."

There was a pause. "I love you, too."

"Thank you for doing this." He didn't speak again for a moment. With my eyes closed the exhaustion took over. I stirred myself. "What if I fall asleep and I have an eight hour phone call on my next bill?"

"I'll take care of that. I'll make sure I hang up. You go to sleep." His voice was soft and soothing. He sounded sleepy, too. "I can't wait to do this for real. To be together again. To touch you, to feel your heartbeat next to mine."

"Me, too." I sighed then started to drift off again. My own body heat mimicked his soothing presence.

When I woke up later, the line was dead. As I lay awake, staring at the pie-shaped light on the ceiling from the construction site, I thought about our phone conversation and smiled and came up with a brilliant idea. Instead of spending our money on tickets to some play, I'd use it for gas money and a hotel room and go to visit Eli on our anniversary. I'd already arranged to be off anyway, and I needed to be with him. I only needed to wait until Friday. Three more days. When he called on Wednesday I hummed with excitement, wanting so badly to tell him, but savoring my secret at the same time.

Friday dawned bright and beautiful. After my shift I changed into jeans and a black, V-neck sweater I knew he liked. I got into his beat up old pickup. He had driven down in Max's Beemer with Aaron, Max, and another guy named Rocco, so I had only to cross the street to find my chariot. With the windows cracked to let in some of the wonderful fresh air, I hit the road to Albany. I turned his radio up loud and sang along—although I was getting my fair share of static—excited about seeing him again.

I pulled into the Motel 7 where they were bunking, checking the slip of paper with his room number on it one more time. While I drove, dark descended as thick as oil over the landscape, but the balcony was well-lit as I pulled up in front of his room number. I climbed the outside stairs quietly. It was silly because there was no way he could have heard me, but I was so anxious to surprise him by this time I was practically pulsating out of my skin. Room 207. As I crept down the hall/balcony I could see the door to his room was cracked a little, a piece of the drapes keeping it from closing completely, and I thought, all the better.

I pushed the door open, a giggle on my lips. The light by the bed shone on Eli's bare back as he sat in bed, half under the covers, and hands with painted fingernails were laced around his neck. My eyes grew wide and then I took in the trail of women's clothes leading to the bed. A black leather miniskirt, heels, a push-up bra... A strangled noise escaped my lips, and he turned.

I spun and ran without any sense of direction. Strangely I felt like I was intruding, peeping in on some couple in their most intimate moments, and then, I realized, I was.

CHAPTER EIGHT

E*li*   "Come on, E. You've stayed in every night since we got here. Faith wouldn't want you hanging around some hotel room by yourself. Come out and have one drink with me. It's my fucking birthday, dude."

I laughed. "All right. All right. As long as you promise to hook up with some girl and snore at her place tonight."

He raised his eyebrows comically. "That *is* the plan. Come on. We don't have time for you to doll up."

"Let me at least put on a fresh t-shirt. I've been working all day in this. The smell alone will keep the ladies away from our table."

"Like you care. You've got the hottest babe on the planet pining for your fucking return. Jackass. You've got five minutes."

"That's all I need."

We left and headed down to Duke's, some seedy dive on the north side of Albany where the jukebox played Aaron's country as opposed to my rock. Within half an hour I had a headache, and my ears were bleeding from the incessant twang invading the air, but the beer was going down good, although going surprisingly fast to my head. I guess laying off the booze for awhile decreased my tolerance. Aaron returned from the dance floor with the redhead he'd honed in on since we arrived, and a shorter brunette.

"This here is Sarah, Tawny's friend. Sarah, this is Rocco and Max and Eli is the one with the goofy grin."

"Howdy," I said, a little more loudly than I intended, and the others chimed in, too.

Sarah walked around to sit on the stool between Max and me. "Hey, boys. Aaron says you all work together?"

"That's right," Max spoke up. "We're all rock stars."

"Is that so?" She winked at me. "Maybe Eli here, but you impress me more as a...camp counselor."

"Ooh. She's got you pegged, Doc."

As the night wore on, Sarah became increasingly...friendly. She ran her high-heeled foot up and down my leg and bounced around on her stool, shaking her boobs to the music. Her black leather mini-skirt seemed to ride higher and higher up her thigh the later it got, or else it was some trick of the alcohol. Max did his best to come on to the girl, but she would have none of it. She seemed quite taken with me. Max mentioned Faith's name about a half-dozen times. "That's what Faith, Eli's steady girlfriend, said. Oh, Faith saw that movie, didn't she? Faith is Eli's girlfriend. She's so sweet." But it seemed the harder Max turned it on, the more the brunette kept coming on to me, until she ran her hand up my thigh and I decided it was time to go to the bathroom, planning to move my stool a little farther away when I got back.

But when I left the bathroom, she was waiting for me in the hall. "How 'bout you take me back to your hotel room—" Before I could react, she'd pulled my head down and pressed her warm, soft lips to mine. "—and I'll screw the hell out of you." My head was spinning. Could beer really affect you this way? She drew me in again, pressing me against the wall with her shapely little body. This time her tongue darted into my mouth, and, I've got to admit, certain parts of my body came to attention. Someone was coming down the hallway and I pushed her gently off. I looked up to see Doc passing us to go into the bathroom, glaring at me.

"Hey, listen, Sarah. You seem like a nice girl and all, but I *seriously* have a girlfriend and we've had some hard times lately, and I don't want to mess things up with her. So—while I'm flattered—I'm going to have to take a pass. And since I'm feeling a little drunk, I'm going to have to leave now. Good-night." I gave her hands a squeeze, as much in an effort to disengage myself as to soften the blow, and walked out.

I went by the table and wished Aaron happy birthday one more time and headed back to my room. Within minutes I was in bed with the lights out thinking about Faith. Within minutes more, I was asleep.

At some point later someone grabbed me...in a *very* familiar way. I opened my eyes and realized someone was in bed with me. For a second, I thought, *Faith. Faith came to see me.* But just as quickly I understood an un-known, overbearing fragrance was filling my nostrils and I sensed something was not right. I sat and turned the light on illuminating Sarah, in the buff. For a second, only a second, my drunken eyes blurred her face and it merged with Faith's. I reached up to touch her face; then I shook myself, hard.

"H-how did you get in here?"

She smiled. "Aaron gave me a key."

I owe that bastard for this one. I found it hard to mask my irritation. "Sarah, I thought I'd made it clear that—" And that's when I heard someone behind me. I turned around, and my beautiful Faith stood there, staring at us with such utter shock and disbelief that I froze.

MAX

I couldn't believe it when I caught Eli lip-locked with that little barfly in the hall. With Faith at home, thinking about him and missing him, he hooks up with some trashy brunette. I wanted to pound him right there, but I de-cided to observe his body language while I passed. His hands were on her hips in a neutral position, not pulling her in, but not pushing her away either. His face was bent toward her, as if to receive the kiss, but she had her hands on the back of his head, so I couldn't tell for sure if he'd initiated things or if she had. Regardless, I gave him the eye as I went to the john. I guess I could give him the benefit of the doubt for a minute, while I went. *But I better not see anything when I come out.*

And I didn't. Eli was gone. That was good. The whole kiss thing kind of made me sick though, so I decided to leave and go get some pizza.

When I drove back into the parking lot, I was surprised to see Eli's old pick-up there. My lights illuminated the interior when I pulled in next to it and someone was slumped over the wheel. Curious, I got out of the car. That's when I realized it was a woman, and as I came around the front of my car, I realized it was Faith. I knocked on the window and she jumped and lift-ed her head to look at me. Her face was the picture of misery, tears running down her cheeks and her eyes wild. Reflexively my hand went to the door handle and I opened the door.

"Faith."

"No, Doc. I've got to go." She tried to pull the door shut but I wouldn't let her.

"You're not going anywhere like this."

"You don't understand. I have to go." She almost sounded frightened.

"Look, you're right. I don't understand yet what happened to upset you. But I do understand you are upset and in no shape to drive." I took a hold of her elbow firmly and pulled her out of the car.

"I *have* to go home. I can't stay here."

"Okay, okay. I'll take you home." I opened my car door and helped her in, shutting it and coming around the front.

"Faith!"

I looked up. Eli leaned over the balcony in his jeans, and then the girl from the bar rushed out of his room behind him, zipping up her mini-skirt.

"Damn you." I stared at him as I walked around to the driver's side.

"Wait, Doc." He was running down the stairs. "You've got to let me explain this to her."

"She doesn't need your excuses." I got behind the wheel, started the engine, and threw it in gear. I backed out of my space, but as I was about to put it in drive Eli came out of the darkness and put his hands on the hood of my car, as if to keep me there like the Incredible Hulk or something.

"Okay," I said through gritted teeth. I threw it into park and opened my door.

"Doc, no!" I heard her voice somewhere on the periphery of the rage boiling in my mind. I slammed the car door shut and stormed over to Eli.

"You son-of-a-bitch. How could you do this to her?"

"Oh, come on, Doc." He didn't back down an inch. "Like you wouldn't be glad if I messed up. Like you wouldn't be waiting on the sidelines to rush in and save the fucking day. You think I don't see the way you look at her? You don't think I notice the pain and envy on your face when you're watching us together?"

I shoved him, hard, in the chest. "Shut up. You're drunk."

"Max. Stop! *Please!*"

We both turned to look at her. She had gotten out of the car and stood behind the open door screaming at us. Then all of a sudden, she ran toward the building and bent over and retched on the scrawny patch of grass between the lot and the sidewalk.

"Geez," I cried, rushing to her side before Eli could even move. "I'm sorry. Let's get you back in the car."

She self-consciously wiped her mouth with the back of her hand. "Oh, God," she said weakly. "I'm sorry."

"No." I looked up again to glower at Eli, who was white as a sheet, looking at Faith with wide eyes. "*You* have nothing to be sorry for." I helped her back into her seat. "Hold on. I have some water." I walked around to my side of the car and got in, closing my door and making a pretense of reaching for a water bottle, then closed Faith's door and again put the BMW into drive, squealing rubber as we left Eli behind, staring after our taillights. After I'd gotten far enough to know he wasn't following me, I looked over at Faith. Her eyes were closed and her head was settled on the headrest, hair stuck to her wet face. She looked ghostly white. "Here. Here's some water." I handed her my bottle and she gulped it down. She closed her eyes again and I wondered if she were reliving whatever it was she saw back in that hotel room. After a while she nodded off.

I drove on and on into the night, putting mile after mile between us and Eli and his little slut. I couldn't believe he would jeopardize all he had going with Faith for a quick blowjob—or whatever they were up to in that hotel room—from some tramp. The more I thought about it, the more I seethed, and every time I looked down at the speedometer, I realized my anger had pushed me to 90-plus, and I would slow it down. As we neared the outskirts of New York City I glanced over at Faith. She was still white, and the hair still clung stubbornly to her face, which I thought was strange. She moaned in her sleep and that's when I noticed the beads of sweat on her forehead. I reached over to feel her face, but before I even touched her, I knew she was feverish. Heat radiated off her like a campfire. "Shit." I pushed the pedal down.

I finally pulled up in front of her place. Luckily, my hand came forward to catch her as she flopped forward. "Faith?" She didn't wake. "Oh, geez." I rushed around to her side of the car. "Faith? Can you walk?"

"Hmm?"

"Can you walk, honey?"

"I think so," she mumbled.

I helped her up to her room and onto the bed. I struggled her jeans off and slid her under the covers.

"Doc?"

"Yes, babe?"

"I don't feel good."

"Are you going to throw up again?"

She moaned. "I don't think so. It's just...I'm so cold."

I tucked the blankets around her tightly and got a damp washcloth for her head. I wiped her face and she sighed, seeming to settle down. Even with her hair bedraggled with fever and damp washcloths, she looked spectacular. She tossed and turned for hours, whether from the effects of the fever, or from replayed images of what she saw in Albany, which, I couldn't be sure. I stood watch over her, glancing from the window to the bed, and occasionally bringing a fresh washcloth. After some time she seemed to fall into a more peaceful sleep.

"Faith?" I called quietly. She didn't stir. I bent and swept my lips over hers then looked into her lovely face as I brushed her hair back. I closed my eyes with my head still bent over her trying to reel in my emotions. I snapped the little lamp off by her bed and stood gazing out the window for several minutes.

I walked back and watched her sleep for a little while, then glanced around her sad, little apartment; this was the first time I'd ever really been in her place. I thought about how much it differed from my own.

My loft had a huge semi-circular window taking up most of one long wall with panes separated by strips of honeyed wood in a ray-like pattern. My mahogany, claw-footed desk sat in front of it, with its green-shaded, brass, lawyer's lamp casting an appreciative glow. Glass-fronted book shelves were filled to capacity with all manners of books and a skeleton, a quirky, but useful home accessory for a doctor, stood in a corner. A huge, platform bed with black, silk sheets and a dark-chocolate brown comforter dominated the rest of the room. I had a coffee maker, bean grinder, and French press. I liked to cook, so I owned kitchen accessories that would make Martha Stewart weep with envy. In short, it was the anti-Faith's-apartment. What hers said in minimalism, mine said in extravagance, remnants of my youth in Albany and from parents whose "tough love" wouldn't allow them to pay the bills, but who still liked to dote on their only child.

I took another look around. Faith deserved so much more than this, my heart cried out. And certainly, she didn't deserve to be cheated on by Eli. The thought made me fume.

I took my anger over to the threadbare recliner and stretched out with my coat as a blanket. I don't know when I fell asleep, but sometime around two a.m. I heard a key in the door. I jumped to my feet, knocking my leather coat to the ground, and stood, legs spread wide, arms at my side, fists clenched, waiting for whatever, or whoever, walked through that door. The light fanned in as the door swung open, and I recognized Eli's silhouette.

"What the hell are you doing here?" he stormed.

I tried to push him out into the hall and close the door, hissing. "Dammit. She's finally asleep. If you wake her up, I swear I'll knock your head off your shoulders. She's sick, for God's sake."

"Sick?" he parroted, trying to look over my shoulder.

"Yeah, sick."

"Did she throw up some more?"

I sighed. Rubbing a hand along the bridge of my nose. "No. I think that was more about being upset. She has a high fever now."

"Is that bad? Should we do something?"

"*I* already took care of her," I snapped, but seeing the worried look on his face, I relented. "She'll be fine. It's only a bug." I glanced over my shoulder at her shadowed, sleeping form, and my ire began to rise once more. "Why did you come here? Don't you think you've done enough to her?"

"Doc, I didn't—"

"Save your stupid excuses, Eli. I'm sure you've had plenty of time to come up with some good ones."

"I took my time so I could sober up before driving up here. And that girl forced herself on me."

I laughed in his face. "Boy, that takes the cake. That's not even imaginative. Maybe I would have believed you if I hadn't seen you making out with her at the restaurant."

Fire flashed in his eyes. "I wasn't...you know what? It doesn't really matter what you fucking believe, does it, Doc? It's what she believes that's important."

"So you're gonna hand her that line of horseshit and hope she believes it?"

He straightened. "I'm going to tell her the truth," he said, calmly now. "Thank you for helping her. I appreciate it, I really do. But it's time for you to leave. Shouldn't you be getting back to Albany anyway?"

"Oh, so you're gonna throw me out now?"

He dangled his key ring in front of me. "I'm the one with the key, Doc. *Me*, not you."

I wanted, so badly, to ram that key right down his fucking throat. But, for Faith's sake, I didn't. I turned around and scooped my jacket off the floor where I had dropped it, and swung it over my shoulder. "I'll leave, Eli." I acted like I was going to pass him, but got into his face. "But you *better* treat her right, or you'll have me to deal with." He eyeballed me all the way to the elevator before stepping inside Faith's apartment.

I rode down in the elevator feeling like the interloping third wheel he wanted me to feel like. *Well, at least I kept her safe tonight. She didn't drive while she was upset, or sick...and whatever she has to deal with tomorrow, she'll have to deal with herself, I guess.*

But as I left the apartment building and stepped into the now frigid, pre-dawn air, I wished *I* was the one with the damn key.

I made the mistake of looking up at her window when I got to the street. Eli was looking down at me.

CHAPTER NINE

E*li* I was sorry I'd jumped Doc. After all, he made sure Faith got home safe. I owed him, at least, for that. I walked over and bent by the bed. Faith's face was pale in the light from outside and Max had put a washcloth across her forehead. I pressed it myself and was surprised by the heat radiating through it.

"Ah, babe," I murmured. I got up and ran the washcloth under cold water again and brought it back to her.

She stirred. "Doc?" she called out faintly.

It was like a knife to my heart. I should have been the one taking care of her, not trying to sober up in some cheap hotel room. Her breath was shallow, but easy. *Let her think I'm Doc. She'll find out the truth soon enough.* I tried to sleep in the recliner, but I kept stretching my neck to look at her, and it was uncomfortable. I got up after an hour or so and looked out the window. The girl's face from Albany swam in front of me and I was touching it. What if Faith hadn't walked in? Would I, in a drunken stupor, been unfaithful to her? The thought haunted me. The one thing I knew for certain was I didn't want to lose Faith. She breathed life back into me, resurrected me from my non-existence, or maybe my zombied existence, and I would not let that go.

I turned away from the window and went back to the bed. Tears filled my eyes as I peered down at her. I had to fix this somehow. I lay on top of the covers, turned toward her, and watched her sleep. I synched my breathing to hers and let my gaze absorb her face. As pale as she was, she reminded me of a fairy princess, caught in some sleeping spell, and I wondered if I would be the one to wake her from it. I kissed her, but she didn't stir. I watched her, afraid to close my eyes, afraid she would disappear if I did.

I could tell when the sun came up by the way the light changed on her face, bathing her in its pink glow. Somewhere close to eight she took a deep breath and snuggled deeper into the covers. I almost laughed. She looked so cute, like some kid hoping for a snow day. Then she opened her eyes slowly.

"Hey," I said softly.

For several seconds she simply stared at me, emotions changing her face like some strange magic show. A brief moment of joy was followed by confusion, sadness, and finally anger. Yes, she settled on anger.

She flew up into a sitting position screaming at me. "What are you doing here? Why did you come back? Get out. Get out! I don't want to see you anymore."

She grabbed her head; I think the sudden movement left her dizzy.

I reached for her. "Are you all right?"

She slapped my hand away. "Don't you touch me. Don't you ever touch me again!" Her voice pitched as she shouted.

For some reason, her display of anger struck me as funny. But I learned a valuable lesson. Never laugh at an angry woman.

"Oh. You think this is funny, do you?"

In no way did I think the tears in her eyes were funny. "Let me explain. I—"

"Ya know, I don't need for you to draw me a picture, Eli. Everything was pretty damn clear last night when I caught you—" Her voice wavered for a second, but she charged on. "—in bed with another woman." She threw the covers off and got out on the other side of the bed. She looked unsteady on her feet and stumbled over to hold on to the back of the recliner.

"Faith," I scrambled to follow her. "You need to settle down. You're sick."

"Don't tell me I'm sick. I know I'm sick." She looked down at her bare legs. "Did you take my jeans off?" She scowled.

So did I. "No, I didn't. Doc must have."

Her face, if possible, flushed even redder than with the fever. She started really crying then. "Just go. Leave me alone." She sobbed, turning her face from me.

"Honey, you don't need to get this upset."

"I d-don't need to—don't need to—" she sputtered.

"It was all a joke. A sick, twisted joke of Aaron's." She spun around, her mouth open in disbelief, but a lightening in her eyes gave me hope. "He gave the girl his room key. I was sound asleep when she came in." I reached over and ran the back of my hand down her cheek. "Dreaming about you." My voice cracked. "I didn't sleep with that girl. I would never do that to you. *Never.* Not in a million years." I hoped and prayed it was true even as I said it.

She hesitated one horrible second, and then sobbed and fell into my arms. I sighed, closed my eyes and pulled her close. "Shh, honey. It's okay now. Don't cry anymore."

After several minutes of weeping she raised her head from my chest where her tears dampened my t-shirt. "I feel like such an idiot."

"There's no reason to feel that way. It had to look pretty bad."

"It...it was awful. Wait...shouldn't you be in Albany?"

I laughed. "I told Aaron he better come up with one hell of an excuse for me or his ass was grass. He felt pretty bad about the whole thing last night, so he said he'd come up with a whopper."

She didn't comment.

"Are you okay now?"

She nodded her head.

"Are we okay?"

She managed a small smile. "Yes."

"How are you feeling?"

"Like hell."

I felt her forehead. "Well, you're not hot anymore. That's good. Why don't you climb back in bed and—"

"Oh, my gosh! I've got to get to work." She started looking for her uniform.

I took her hands and dragged her back to the bed. "You're not working today. I'll go over and explain things to Dino. Gloria can manage to pull her weight for once today. And I'll get some breakfast for us, too." When she got under the covers, I pulled them up to her chin, and bent to kiss her. She grabbed me and kissed me dizzy.

Then she made a little cry and said, "Oh, no. I'm going to make you sick."

I grinned stupidly. "It would be worth it."

She smiled and brought my face down to hers again, kissing me with less passion but more feeling. When she pulled back, she kept both hands on the sides of my face, looking deep into my eyes. "I love you, Eli."

"And I love you. Don't ever forget that."

When I walked into the diner, Max sat warming his hands around a cup of joe at the counter just inside the door. All I could think was, *he took her pants off.* I tried to rationalize he was going to be a doctor and she was sick, and he was helping her, and doctors were trained to look at the human body scientifically...but I knew that was not the way he would have been looking at Faith's body. While I stood there studying him, Glo walked up to the counter.

"Hey, Handsome." She looked out the window to the sidewalk. "Where's Faith?"

Max turned in his chair a little bit to look at me over the rim of his cup of coffee. "She's sick, Glo. She won't be able to make it in today. Fever...she threw up. I think she needs a little time to recover."

"Ooh, yeah. Keep her out of here. I don't need to catch that. I've got a big weekend coming up," she said with very little sympathy for Faith. She leaned over the counter a little, flirtatiously. "What about you? Got plans for the weekend?"

Max watched the exchange with interest.

"Yeah. Our six-month anniversary was yesterday, so I thought we might do something to celebrate," I answered smugly, loud enough to be sure Max heard me. And then I realized he had come to the diner in hopes of seeing Faith.

"Oh, how sweet." Glo straightened, giving up on me with an ease I found insulting. I ordered two breakfast specials to go, and Glo walked away. I leaned on the counter, next to Max. His jaw was clenched and he was staring straight ahead.

"So, aren't you going to ask?"

"Ask what?" He took a sip from his cup and continued to look straight ahead.

"How Faith's doing?"

He seemed to deliberate answering me, but finally said, "Yes. How is Faith?"

"She's fantastic. Her fever is gone, but she's still feeling a little under the weather." I paused. "Oh, and I explained the situation in Albany, and we've got that all straightened out."

He turned to look at me incredulously, his jaw dropping open, forgetting his pretense of acting disinterested. "She forgave you?"

"Really, there was nothing to forgive, as I tried to explain to you. Aaron gave that girl a room key, and she snuck in while I was asleep. I was in the process of kicking her out when Faith arrived."

He sat there dumbfounded for a minute, but countered with, "Did you tell Faith you kissed that little piece of bar trash earlier in the evening, or did you leave that little tidbit out?"

I shifted my weight, glancing around, hoping Gloria would return. "You know, I'd love to sit chit-chatting with you all day, Max, but I want to get back to Faith." He was starting to tick me off, so I added meanly, "I guess we'll lie around in bed all day today."

He eyed me steadily. "You didn't tell her. You didn't tell her, and you'll go right back with her without blinking an eye."

I turned on him. "*I* didn't kiss that girl, *she* kissed *me*."

Max got up and flipped through some bills from a wad of cash in his pocket, throwing some money down on the counter. He turned on me, teeth clenched. "You know, you can tell me that, and tell Faith that, and even tell yourself that, but we both know you were drunk last night, and if Faith hadn't shown up when she did, you may have been waking up with a different woman." He stared at me, a vein pulsing in his neck and then he left, slamming the door so hard the glass shook.

I went back to Faith's, but, somehow, Max's words got stuck in my craw, so much so that, eventually it was driving me crazy and I had to tell Faith about it, to clear my conscious. It haunted me the entire rest of my time in Albany, and even more so when I returned to Faith in New York. Her trusting face and bright smile were like guilt-vises on my heart.

It was our anniversary, and I took Faith out for a nice dinner in the city. She was wearing the dress I bought her for Christmas, the green one that looked so amazing on her that whenever she wore it I found it difficult to speak to her using coherent sentences. It was dusk, and we were walking through Central Park. An half hour later and this wouldn't have been such a hot idea. But, as it was, we stuck to the well-lit areas and had no problems. I held her hand. It was a magical evening, and now I felt compelled to ruin all that by laying bare my soul.

"Faith...there's something that has been bothering me."

"Yes?" she prompted when I hesitated. She stuck her hair behind her ear as she turned to listen to me.

"It's about...what happened in Albany...with that girl."

She halted abruptly and a look of fear crossed her face. "Okay." She withdrew her hand from mine and I could see her bracing herself for my answer.

"It's just...Doc didn't think I was being totally truthful with you, and...I guess I haven't been. But it's only because it didn't seem to matter...but now, I think maybe it does."

"I'm not sure I understand," she said slowly.

"That girl, she was at the bar earlier that evening, and she kissed me," I blurted out. "I didn't invite the kiss, I swear. She followed me to the bathroom and when I came out she...just laid one on me. I was surprised, and I told her in no uncertain terms that I had a girlfriend and I was *not* interested."

She stood stone-still for what seemed like an eternity, and then stuck her arm through mine, and continued to walk in the same direction we had been, in total silence as she digested what I said. I could tell it upset her, and I felt heavy with guilt.

After we walked for several yards, she stopped again.

"What else?"

"Huh?"

"What else happened that makes you feel bad about this. I want you to tell me."

Her eyes peered into mine unrelentingly and I knew she would have an answer to her question or she would be dissatisfied.

"The fact of the matter is, I was drunk. Way too drunk, and I'm scared that... I would never want to hurt you, Faith, but...what if I had?"

"But you didn't?" she asked quickly.

"No. I didn't. But what if had?"

"I don't want to think about that, and I don't think you do, either."

We turned and walked on silently for a while.

"I want to get help. For my drinking."

She stared at me, her mouth hanging open a little. "You do?"

"Yes. I think I have a problem. And if it has the potential of wrecking anything we have, I want to take care of it. Get professional help."

"Okay," she returned enthusiastically. "Then that's what we'll do." She squeezed my hand and a huge burden lifted from my heart.

The next day I began AA meetings in a church basement a few blocks from her place.

CHAPTER TEN

F*aith*
  I never got a chance to thank Doc for his help, because after that night in Albany, he disappeared. He called and quit his job with J. Drew Construction and no one knew where he went from there.

Things with Eli kept getting better and better. He took me to plays in the city and a concert or two, and nights were spent either at my place, or over at his and Aaron's. He attended his AA meetings without fail, and, one day, he told me he wanted to find his mother.

"At AA they tell us to seek forgiveness from those we have harmed, and forgive those who have harmed us. I've always had a hard time forgiving my mom for...not protecting me more from what happened with my dad. It's time to put that behind me now, and to do that, I need to see her and forgive her."

It didn't take long to find her. Old friends from Beacon had her address and her new last name; she had remarried. Ironically, she didn't live far from us, and if we lived in anywhere but New York City, we may have run into her before. She was very receptive to seeing Eli when he called, and he was excited to see her, and a little nervous.

She lived in a small, one-bedroom house in a neighborhood where all of the houses looked the same, bunched together as if in protection against downtown's vast skyscrapers. When we got there, she was waiting on the front steps. Eli's hand was sweaty in mine and his smile tight, but when he got close, he dropped my hand and ran the last several feet to embrace her. My heart caught in my throat as I stood on the sidewalk, feeling like an intruder in their very personal reunion.

"Momma," Eli said, finally releasing her and holding out one hand to me. "This is Faith."

"Nice to meet you, Mrs. Archuletti." She gave my hand a squeeze and shot me a quick smile, but her eyes returned to her son's face, as if to memorize every detail.

"Well, come in. Come in, you two," a voice bellowed from behind her. A robust man in his mid-fifties stood in the doorway with a round face, little hair, and a friendly smile. We were escorted into their living room, which was furnished meagerly, but was neat as a pin. White doilies lay over the arms of overstuffed chairs which were a dingy white with large blue and green flowers. A low coffee table in front of a matching couch was polished until the bowl of fruit on its surface showed a mirror image. I was glad I decided to wear a skirt and blouse, as that's also what his mother chose. Eli wore his usual jeans and t-shirt under a button-down shirt, but he looked so happy that it didn't matter.

His mother's eyes were likewise glowing. She was a slight woman, about five-three, I think, with dark, curly hair and green eyes like Eli's. Her face was sharp and angular, and she gave the impression of having worked hard for everything she had over her fifty-some-odd years. We sat on the couch, and the older couple took their places in the two chairs at either end of the coffee table. As soon as he sat, Eli's mother's husband stood back up and offered Eli his hand. "Al Archuletti," he said with a smile. He looked as pleased as punch himself, obviously gratified his wife's son finally chose to return to her. "Faith," he said, as he squeezed my hand warmly. "Such a pretty name."

"Thank you."

"So, Eli...you said on the phone that you are in the construction business?"

I looked over and Eli was holding his mother's hand. "Yes, sir. I work for J. Drew's Construction."

"Oh," he said, satisfied. "They're a big company. I've seen their billboards."

"Yes. I've been with them ever since I moved to New York City."

"And what about you, young lady? Do you work?"

"I'm a waitress at a diner near where Eli is working right now."

"I see." His eyes twinkled. "Is that where you two met?"

We smiled at each other. "Sort of," Eli responded for me. "We really met during a blackout, when we got stuck on an elevator together for awhile."

"Ahh." Al gave us a knowing smile, his broad hands on either knee. He stood. "Well, would you two like a piece of pie? Your momma makes a mean apple pie, if you remember, Eli."

"Yes, sir, I do." Eli gave his mom's hand another squeeze.

"Let me help you," I offered, rising to follow him.

Their kitchen, which was at the back of the house, was not much bigger than the one in my apartment. We had to walk through a less formal living room/dining room to get there, and once there, we kept bumping into each other as we reached down plates and sought out a pie server.

"I want to thank you, Faith."

"For what, Mr. Archuletti?"

"It's Al, now, angel. For bringing Eli back to his momma. She doesn't talk about it much, but I know losing Eli is her biggest regret."

"Well, I'd like to take credit for that, but it was all Eli's idea."

He laid his big hand over mine as I brought the knife down through the cinnamon-sugared crust of an enormous apple pie. "You may have not directly influenced his decision, but, let me tell you, he wouldn't be here if it weren't for you. We men can be awfully stubborn, and it's usually only the influence of a good woman that makes us sit up and take notice. And make changes in our lives." He patted my hand and then turned back to get glasses down; I found it difficult to see where I was slicing with the tears in my eyes. Such a sweet man.

When we walked through the door to the formal living room, Eli and his mom were standing in a tight embrace. Both Al and I stopped, and prepared to back out of the room.

"No. No," Eli's mom cried, letting go of him with one arm, while keeping the other around his waist. "Come in and let's have some pie to celebrate."

While we were eating, Eli reached over and took my hand. His face looked more serene and happy than I ever saw it before, and I couldn't help but think that this was a new beginning for him, and it was. When we left for the evening, amid a shower of hugs, Al and Betty asked us back for dinner the next Sunday.

Sunday dinner was great. Conversation flowed naturally and we played cards and Trivial Pursuit afterward. We asked Betty and Al over for the following Sunday.

We decided it would be better to have them over to my place than Eli's, even though mine was not much to look at either. The Girardi's let us borrow their small kitchen table and chairs and once we had things all arranged, it actually looked pretty nice. Eli insisted on cooking dinner, which almost turned out to be a complete catastrophe, until I stepped in to help.

His "lasagna" was cooking, and it smelled a little...funny. I went to investigate.

"Eli, did you use this cheese for your lasagna?"

"Yes. Why?"

"This is Swiss cheese. You needed mozzarella."

"Is there a difference? They're both white. They're both cheeses."

"Yes," I said slowly, "but that's like saying that cinnamon and chili pepper are interchangeable because they are both spices, but you still wouldn't want to have chili pepper and sugar on top of your toast in the morning."

He paled, holding the package of crescent rolls he was about to bang on the edge of the counter aloft. "What are we going to do?"

"Don't separate the crescent rolls," I ordered, checking the fridge. "I'll make a sausage roll. It's more of a breakfast item, but it will taste better than Swiss lasagna, no offense." I paused for effect. "The Swiss are not known for their lasagna."

He smiled, relieved I'd come up with a solution, but not willing to admit it. "Smartass." He swatted me on the behind as I pulled out the sausage and egg.

"Watch it, mister, or I'll leave you to finish this on your own."

"No way. I've learned my lesson. I bow to your superior cooking skills."

"Yeah, right. Just get a skillet out."

The sausage roll finished up as our guests arrived and was accompanied by some fresh fruit I cut up. It was a little unconventional, but we all enjoyed it. When Al and Betty left, after Eli and I trounced them in Spades, Eli lifted me up and swung me around.

"Not only are you the most beautiful girl in the world, you're the smartest." He kissed me happily. I was on cloud nine. It was the first time we entertained together, and it was a success. Eli and his mom patched things up, and things couldn't have been going any smoother.

And so, of course, a bump was necessary.

The following Sunday we were headed to Al and Betty's again. We decided we would take turns hosting Sunday night dinner. Eli was excited about spending some more time with his mom, and about the tickets he won from a radio station to a Mets game. We were talking about it as he drove—and then it happened. I glanced up and the light turned red, but Eli didn't slow down.

"Eli—" I turned to look at him as I warned him and out of the window behind him a city bus approached. "Eli!" I screamed in horror, one hand going automatically to the dash to brace myself, one to his shoulder. He turned slowly and saw the bus and yanked the steering wheel to the right to avoid it, not realizing he steered us into the path of a car on our right. It hit my door, and we were driven into a hot dog vendor's cart and then into the corner of a department store window.

I woke up once, in the car. My head was turned toward the driver's seat when my eyes opened, but it was strangely empty. The pain came blindingly into focus then, screaming through my head like a banshee keening. The firemen yelled at me to be still, they didn't want to hurt me while trying to cut away the pieces of the car pinning me to my seat. A chrome piece of the hot dog cart had already been removed from my face, where it was imbedded in my right cheek and they were working at freeing my mid-section, which was compressed by the dashboard which had been pushed back by the force of the impact into my abdomen and chest. *Why are they yelling at me? I didn't do anything wrong.* I wondered why they didn't shut up that woman who was screaming, until I realized it was me.

The next time I woke up, I was under some bright lights in the emergency room. The pain was still intense; it felt like an elephant was sitting on my chest and that cold air was seeping from my pores. I understood later that this sensation was due to the blood loss. A half dozen people stood around me, and they all seemed to be talking at once. I looked from one to another, trying to figure out what they were saying, but none of it made any sense, it was all garbled. I turned my head slowly, feeling like it was ratcheting with each inch like I was some jerky robot. My right cheek came to rest on the cool table. A nurse moved out of my line of sight for a second, and I could see through a plastic window in a door connecting my room to the one next to it. Eli lay with his eyes closed, spattered with blood, on a bed. Where my room was full of people, his was not. Was he dead? Had they given up on him?

I tried to call out to him, but something was over my mouth. I tried to lift my hand to take it off, but my arm felt like it was held down with lead weights. I had a fleeting image of Gulliver being tied down by the Lilliputians. Wires and tubes ran up and down my arm and I looked at them curiously for a second, and then noticed the nurse was talking to me. She pulled the oxygen mask off my face a few inches.

"What is it, honey?"

"Eli. Eli," I breathed, though the effort sent new sparks of pain shooting through me. "You...h-have to help him."

"What? Him?" She gestured toward Eli with one hand.

I nodded slightly, the small gesture forcing me to squeeze my eyes shut in agony.

"Oh, don't worry about him. *He's* fine. Not a scratch on him, like usual. He's sleeping it off."

She placed the mask back over my face with a smile, but I looked at her questioningly, tears forming, unbidden. Was she saying that he was drunk? But he couldn't be. He didn't drink anymore. I wanted to ask her more, but they were wheeling me away. I didn't want to leave Eli. I screamed, but no one heard me. I fought against the weight holding me down and the terrible lethargy, but even as I shook my head at the nurse, my vision turned to black.

When I woke up, I was alone in a white room. The contrast from the burning white light, and blackness beyond, in the E.R. and the chaos and noise and movement that surrounded it, to this stark, white nothingness, was disorienting. It was quiet as a tomb, and, for a second, I wondered if I *was* in a tomb. All I could hear was the steady, slow, rhythmic beeping of one machine, and a kind of intermittent hissing noise. Then someone bustled in with an I.V. bag. She took one look at me, and then turned right back around and left. The pain was gone, or maybe lost, somewhere inside me. I was floating, peacefully, like in the inner tubes at the lazy river at the water park. Only deep down, I knew something was wrong. I couldn't put my finger on it.

My hand, clumsily, came to my face, and I discovered a bandage, and then, beyond that, more tape and a tube.

"Uh-uh-uh. Don't touch that." A man in a white lab coat and horned-rim glasses bustled into the room with the nurse behind him. Seeing him reminded me of Eli for some reason. Where was Eli?

I remembered the bus, and the crash, and waking up in the car, and finding Eli gone, and then I remembered his bloodied body in the next room.

"Hey, now. Calm down. Calm down," the man repeated. "We put a tube down your throat to help you to breathe, but we're going to remove it now. We need you to cough when I say three. One, two..."

I coughed and it was like they were taking out my insides through my throat, like a long, hard snake was pulling on my insides, and digging claws into me to stop its momentum as they tried to pull it out. Finally, it was out, and I gasped air deep into my lungs, which seemed to be sticking together somehow, the air cold and raw.

"Eli," I rasped out, my voice sounding strangely old, or like I'd been chain-smoking for years.

"Does she have any family?" the doctor asked the nurse.

She nodded. "There's someone out there. I'll go get them." She left and he was talking again.

"You're very lucky, Ms. Robeson." He adjusted my machines and checked my chart. "We almost lost you twice on the operating table, but you're going to be fine and make a complete recovery."

The nurse came back in, and Betty Archuletti rushed from behind her. "Oh, Faith," she cried, and a huge smile lit her face.

But I was oblivious as tears poured down my face. "Oh, my God. He's not...he's not..."

"What? Oh, honey. You mean, Eli? Oh, no, honey." She grabbed my hand. "He's fine, sweetheart, just fine. Well, he's in a little hot water right now with the law, but Mr. Drew is taking care of that. Going to bail him out."

"Why? What happened?"

Betty looked up at the doctor, her eyes wide. "Doesn't she know? Can't she remember?"

The doctor looked at me with a frown. "Ms. Robeson...what do you remember about the accident?"

"We were going...to Al and Betty's..." I looked at Betty for confirmation and she nodded her head. "Eli...ran a red light, I think, and we were hit by a car, and...that's all I remember really, except for seeing Eli here. Is he hurt badly?"

The doctor shook his head his brow furrowing more deeply. "He walked away from the accident, or stumbled away, I should say. His blood/alcohol level was nearly three times the legal limit."

"But Eli doesn't drink. He's a recovering alcoholic."

The doctor hung my chart back on the end of the bed. "Well, I'd say he had one hell of a backslide, then."

"B-but, he seemed fine."

"Most of them get where they can hide it pretty good."

"But he was going to meetings."

He raised his eyebrows. "Are you sure?"

I wasn't sure of anything anymore. "He t-told me," I faltered.

The doctor patted my leg. "I'm sorry, Ms. Robeson. I really am." He turned to Betty. "I'll let you stay, ma'am, another five minutes. Then, I'm afraid I'm going to have to insist my patient get some rest."

"Of course, doctor." He left, but the nurse milled around for a few minutes more, taking my vitals. I wanted to be alone.

"How are you feeling, Faith?"

How was I feeling? Confused? Betrayed? "I-I—" And suddenly, I lost it. Just lost it.

Betty came over and tried to comfort me as best she could with all my tubes and wires. "There, there, sweetheart. It's a lot to take in. But Eli is so sorry, angel. He really is. And—"

I tuned her out. Eli lied to me. He'd been drinking all along. And what about the girl in Albany? Was that all a lie, too? Was anything he told me the truth? Did all his *I love yous* mean anything when he was willing to get behind the wheel with me, roaring drunk?

The nurse looked at Betty with disapproval and cut her visiting time short.

"Eli will be here to see you as soon as he can, now, angel. You call me if you need anything. I left the number with the nurses' station."

I think I drifted off to sleep before she even left.

CHAPTER ELEVEN

E*li*
    Faith's scream filled my head, even months after the accident.

I'd started drinking again the day I went to my Mom's for the first time. I meant to have one drink, to calm my nerves some, but it went down so smooth and easy, I had a couple more. The next few weeks, I started sneaking shots whenever I could, to take the edge off a little, but the night of the accident, I guess I had too many.

We were talking, just talking, about the tickets I won. I thought about how great it would be to go with Faith to the game, and then she said something about the light and I turned to see the bus heading our way as we crossed through the intersection. I'll admit, I was a little fuzzy-headed, like my brain was going, *Humm...what is that big bus doing?* And then it leapt to, *Big bus. Big buses are bad.* I yanked on the steering wheel, sending us into the path of a car.

The next thing I remember, I was waking up in the hospital with the cops. When my scattered brain finally came around to figuring out what happened, they told me Faith was in surgery and things didn't look good. It all seemed so surreal. We were talking about baseball, and the next thing I know I'm screaming out her name, and no one will tell me what's happening to her, and I'm being read my rights. The most painful part was being dragged away from where she was, knowing she was in there hurt somewhere, and I couldn't help her. And it was all my fault.

When I finally got out of jail and made it back to the hospital and up to her room, I cried. I just bawled like a baby. She looked so pale, like you could blow right through her, and she was lying so still. Her cheek was bandaged and tubes and wires ran out of her and things beeped and blinked numbers, and all I wanted to do was climb up into the bed and hold her and tell her how sorry I was.

God, how I hated myself. I hated myself for being whole and uninjured, while she was broken. I hated myself for lying to her and being stupid enough to put her life in jeopardy. I hated myself for being weak enough to get drunk in the first place. And even then, as I sat there loathing what I did to her, my first thought was, *I need a drink to make this all go away. To make me go away. I can't stand to be in my own head and skin anymore.*

I squeezed her hand and held my breath, examining her face for any sign of movement while watching the rhythmic rise and fall of her chest under the sheets, and thanking the Lord she was still with me. When she finally opened her eyes, I flew to my feet.

"Faith! Oh, God, Faith! I'm so glad you're okay." I lifted her limp hand to my lips, dragging the wires and tubes with it, but as I gazed into her face I saw she knew. She knew my deep dark secret; she knew me for who I was. "I'm *so* sorry."

Tears rolled down her face, and she turned her head away and didn't say a word. I searched for the words to make it right, to make her understand the depths of my remorse, but there weren't any that could erase what I did.

"Do you want me to go?" I asked fearfully.

She nodded without turning to me. Everything inside me drained away, leaving me hollow. I kissed her hand one more time, my own tears falling to salt her skin. "I love you. I do," I choked out, and I turned and left.

I went home and drank until I passed out.

For the rest of the week, I got my news from my mom. She and Al would go to visit, and she would update me on Faith's recovery. I knew she was probably petitioning for me for Faith's forgiveness, but I also could see the pity in her eyes when she talked to me that told me Faith was far from forgiving me.

What I had done was tearing me up inside, and a hole grew that was even bigger than the hole that was there before Faith came and filled the emptiness inside of me. Despite the fact I was practically drinking myself into oblivion at night, I was able to do a passably good job at work during the day. I thought about her constantly; everything reminded me of her. At work, I'd remembered the time I fell from the girder, and she nursed me back to health. When I rode the elevator back to my room at night, I thought about the blackout, and how it magically brought us together. Commercials for the tourism bureau ran like a replay of all our excursions into the city. Memories of watching her face light up when she was delighted at each new place I took her, the wind blowing her hair on top of the Empire State Building, the sun lighting her hair as I stretched out on my side, gazing at her as she ate strawberries when we picnicked in Central Park, the funny way she would grimace at herself when she fell when I took her ice-skating at Rockefeller Center... Each memory was bittersweet. I was glad I was able to love her, but wished, in a way that was physically painful, I could have her back. At night it was far worse. I tortured myself with thoughts of her and I together, curled up alongside each other in bed, or of the exquisite way she made love to me. The beauty of knowing just how to touch her to turn her on, and of hearing her call out my name in her need and knowing it was me, and only me, who could satisfy her needs in that specific way.

And to know I threw it all away, so carelessly, when I should have protected it, treasured it, kept it safe and separated from the darkness within me. I despised myself for my weakness and let the longing for her wash over me and punish me for what I did.

A week after the accident, I saw her return home. An unknown car pulled up outside of her building. In the past several days I had become familiar with most of the comings and goings across the street as I waited for signs of her. An older, large, light yellow sedan with a white top pulled up in the handicapped space right in front, and a man got out, who I judged to be about Al's age. A woman got out of the other side and opened the back door, and she and the driver helped the back passenger out. I knew immediately it was Faith, though she walked like a seventy-year-old woman, carefully, step-by-step, as if she were afraid she would hurt herself, or, perhaps, she was still too weak. I watched as they struggled up the few steps she and I had hurried down so many times before. The couple helped her to sit and rest at the top of the stairs, hovering about her protectively. Who were these strangers?

"Eli, man. What's up?" Aaron growled as I stopped in the middle of retrieving a tool for him. He followed my gaze. "Is that Faith?" We watched as the couple escorted her through the door.

"Yeah," I responded, my voice coming out weakly.

For the next couple of weeks, I watched the couple come and go with groceries, or takeout from the diner. Once, I heard Faith's laugh and turned to see the woman with her head thrown back as she laughed. So they must be Faith's mother and father, I concluded, and I began to study them in earnest when they wandered to my side of the street. I should have seen the similarities before. Her mom still wore her hair long, and it was the exact same shade of maple-brown as Faith's, only a tad duller. Her face was sculpted beautifully, like Faith's, but it was her dad's intensely green eyes she had inherited. The gray-haired man cut a handsome profile, his hair still thick and wavy, his skin tanned and pleasantly wrinkled, and I wondered what the big man would think if he'd known it was I who hurt his little girl.

Once I saw Faith sitting in a chair at the window. My guess was her mom put her there, thinking she would enjoy the view, not realizing the view contained me, a painful reminder of all that was taken from her. She did not sit there again.

After about four weeks, I began to see her out walking with a parent on each arm, short walks, at first, but gradually getting longer. I could see for myself, Faith getting stronger, even from across the street. She stood straighter, walked with more energy...and then, one day, she appeared in her uniform.

She walked in the opposite direction than normal, and crossed the street up the block, backtracking to the diner. She was avoiding me. The yellow car disappeared, and this habit of walking up the street was adhered to strictly. A few weeks after she went back to work, she walked out of the diner at the end of her shift, deep in thought, and accidentally, it seemed, her feet took her down the older, familiar path past our building.

"Hey, Faith," Aaron called out. She paused, not turning for a minute, but eventually spinning to face him. "How are you doing?" he asked with genuine concern. I was about fifty feet away, but the wind was blowing in my direction, so I could make out their voices.

She glanced around, not spotting me, as she answered him. "I'm good. Much better, thank you."

"Well, you sure look good," he said in a way that made me cringe.

"Thanks," she responded without enthusiasm, her face turning red. A new, white scar the size of a thumbnail, and curved like one, stood at the corner of her mouth. "See ya." She hustled across the street, but when she got to the stairs of her building, she glanced back and caught my eye. She stood, frozen, for a few seconds, and then turned and ran into the building. I wanted her back so badly I could taste it on my tongue. My chest ached with longing for her as I returned to my work.

The next day, she hesitated as she left the diner, and chose to walk, again, in our direction. Aaron and I happened to be finishing up some work on the ground floor, and he looked up and caught her eye as she passed. "Faith," he said with a smile and a nod.

"Hello, Aaron." Her voice shook a little. She didn't look up; she knew I was standing beside him. The next day, she chose again to take the longer path away from us. My heart and face dropped. I had hoped, maybe, there might be a chance. A chance to rebuild what we lost. But perhaps it wasn't meant to be. I dreamt that night of the accident, and heard her scream, like I had a thousand times over. Then we were together, laying on a blanket in Central Park, and she was looking at me with a sad smile. My finger explored the new scar on her face. Then, I returned to the scene of the accident. The tremendous crash as we hit the glass windows of the department store startled me from my dream, and I woke up in a sweat.

CHAPTER TWELVE

F*aith*
    I wanted to stay away from him, and berated my feet for taking that path. But, still, the sight of him practically took me to my knees. My longing for him was so intense, I could feel my body throbbing. *He lied to you. He did this to you. Scarred you, made you suffer.* But the sad truth of the matter was, I suffered more from his absence than anything else. A thousand times a day, I caught myself phrasing a story about my day in my head to tell Eli when I got home, only to realize there would be nobody to tell the story to, no one to understand.

I was forced to call my parents. I simply couldn't take care of myself during my recovery and there was no one else. Betty and Al offered, but I knew that wasn't right somehow. My parents were surprisingly thrilled to hear from me. They had lost my number over the years, and tried to track me down without success. Nathan had been institutionalized years earlier, and the two seemed more relaxed and happy than I ever remembered them being. They took good care of me, guilty, I think, about all the years I was alone. What was, at first, awkward, turned quickly into a good relationship, and it was hard to send them home when the doctor released me for work.

Eli looked so good. My gaze swallowed up the body that captured me and made me his, familiar to me as my own, but looking thinner, more worn. At night, in my dreams, I had hot, feverish thoughts of him that left me bereft and thirsty. With each day, the accident seemed farther away, and Eli, nearer. I knew it was a matter of time until I caved in, and he must have sensed it, too.

One day, I returned from work, to find a vase of daisies and alstroemeria at my doorstep. I searched the hall for him, my heart pounding, but he was nowhere in sight. I picked up the card, my hand shaking, and read his writing.

Faith-

I know I blew it, but as hard as I try, I can't stop thinking of you. I only wanted you to know I still love you and I always will and I understand what a fool I was.

- Eli

As if by reflex, I drew my breath in and held the card against my heart. Sobs buried inside of me shook me from my core. My hands trembled as I tried to get my key in the door and get inside before I totally fell apart. Suddenly his hand was over mine, guiding the key in. His other hand was bracing me on the other side, his palm on the door and the heat of his body behind me burned.

Before I was fully conscious of what was happening, we were inside of my apartment, the door closed behind me. I turned within his arms, my hands going automatically to tangle themselves in his thick hair. His mouth was on mine, warm, strong, and seeking. My keys hit the floor with a clang. We were both crying.

"Oh, God. I'm so sorry." His voice was in my ears and swimming headily through my veins. His strong, familiar hands encircled my waist as my mouth demanded more from him.

"Eli. Oh, Eli." My loneliness and eternal need for him flowed into my words. I wanted him to touch me, everywhere, all at once. I wanted it to be again like it was between us. Somewhere inside of me a voice screamed, *No. He can't be trusted. He'll hurt you again.* But another voice countered, *But it's Eli. I need him. I want him.* And that second voice won out without much of a fight. It coaxed me as I yanked his shirt out of his pants and stroked the skin of his back. It cheered me as those same hands explored his tight butt and came around to grasp him in front, moaning in appreciation and desire, yanking on his belt. I thought of nothing except having him, over me, on me, inside of me. I had his pants undone and let my hands travel underneath fabric to the flesh, clenching him and pulling him to myself.

He moaned my name on a sigh and I knew in that instant he hadn't been with another woman since the accident, as I hadn't been with another man. He was the only thing that could satisfy me, for whatever crazy reason.

I knew, despite his other lies, he told me the truth about the woman in Albany. He pushed back and his strong hands came to either side of the opening of my uniform at the throat. He pulled it apart and we heard the ripping of fabric, but neither one cared. His hands were on my breasts now, sculpting, kneading, rough, frantic to have me, all of me.

I watched his face as his gaze explored what his hands found. A vein twitched in his cheek and then his mouth was on me, teasing me through the fabric of my bra, the tongue, bringing hot, moist, thrills through me as he kissed the tops of my breasts, and below, where the bra dipped to a point between my breasts. Then it was on the lace again, pulling on my nipples through the silk, sucking greedily as I arched, his strong fingers supporting my back.

As if on cue, he pulled his head back as I straightened up, my hair falling forward, onto my face. He stopped, and I stood, panting, watching his face for signs of explanation for his movements, or rather his non-movements. The furious race of hands and mouth ceased, and we both stood strangely still, like statues. His gaze was fixed on my face and he brought a finger slowly up to trace the scar left from where the piece of the hot dog cart pierced my face. My heart stopped beating as I watched him, and an ache crept over it. I searched him for a reaction. Was he turned off? Repulsed? Fear gripped me and my hand flew to my face to cover my scar.

His gaze came up to mine and he knew my fear. He knew it as surely as I spoke it. He shook his head slightly, in response to my unasked question, holding my hand, with his own, against my cheek. And then we stood looking at each other for the longest time, looking deeply into each other's eyes in silent communion, the only sound in the room our still-labored breathing and the beating of our hearts. Slowly, he bent his head and kissed the side of my mouth where the scar was with tenderness. I closed my eyes and a sob escaped and I began to shake again, so hard if he hadn't slid his arms around me to hold me together I would have flown apart. I put my head down on his shoulder and wept. Wept for all the pain I went through on my own, wept for the nights alone without him, and the mornings, right after the accident, when getting out of bed was a monumental struggle, both physically and emotionally. I wept for those early days, when the scar on my face was still red and raw and I hated to look at myself in the mirror. He held me, whispering my name into my hair over and over again, and saying he was sorry.

Then, abruptly, he released me and turned his back. Had he been forcing himself to accept the new scarred me, and now realized his mistake? He couldn't compel himself to see beyond that imperfection? I felt suddenly, embarrassingly naked and crossed my hands over my chest, taking a step back.

He shook his long mane of hair and looked up somewhere, as if studying the crown molding. "Faith," he whispered, "if I was any kind of a man, I'd walk out that door right now and never come back. I would leave so that I could never hurt you again." And then those huge shoulders began to shake.

I closed the space between us and looped my hands around him tightly, laying my head on his shoulders, and pressing my warm breasts to his back. "Please. *Please* don't leave me again." My voice became small. "I love you. Every day I spent away from you was like living underwater...every movement was sluggish...I couldn't see clearly...couldn't breathe." I stepped back from him, suddenly needing to know. "Look at me."

He turned around reluctantly, and I took another few steps backward until my heels hit the mattress and I stood in the light from the windows. I lifted my tremulous hands and pushed my uniform off my shoulders. His eyes grew wide as he took in the scars from my surgery by my belly button. My confidence began to waiver, and I shivered, despite the feeling of warmth the sun provided to my back as it poured in the room. I raised my hands out to each side of me, laying myself open. "Here I am, Eli. My body is scarred, but we can't change the past. Still, we can make a future together, if you want to—" My voice faltered, afraid of what his response would be.

He hesitated a second, then took two quick, long strides and drew me into his arms, pressing his mouth over mine in a long, possessive kiss. His hands began at my shoulders, passing over my skin, bringing their delightful warmth as they slid over the curves of my shoulder blades to the small of my back, over my hips, removing my panties. He pressed me gently onto the bed and joined me, after taking off the rest of his clothes. He made love to me slowly, inch-by-inch, not hesitating over the new scars as he kissed his way down my stomach, telling me over and over again he loved me. I lost myself to him entirely, surrendering myself to the sensations he created where he touched, or kissed, or licked, luxuriating in the feel of his weight on me, his legs tangled with mine, the sweet smell of him and the taste of his skin. My body was trying to take an imprint of each moment, to hold on to it forever. I feared a time would return when that was all I had again, my memories of us. But I had to be with him, for better or for worse.

ELI

Faith lay in my arms, breathing quietly. I stroked her arm with one hand, the other bent behind my neck, staring at the ceiling and thanking a benevolent God for having given her back to me. My mind played with the images of the past few hours. I thought about how I hid around the corner in the hall, as I did that first time, watching her read my note, my body rigid with tension, hardly daring to breathe. When I saw how moved she was, it was as if my body went to her of its own accord, my hand over hers as she unlocked the door, my face buried in her hair, breathing her in like a drug, my body responding in kind. I thought about the way she stood in front of the windows, the sun pouring over her shoulders, her arms outstretched as if in surrender, so incredibly beautiful it took my breath away.

She had no idea the effect she had on me. She was scared I would somehow think less of *her* because of the scars *I* gave her, when that was so far from my thinking it was simply unimaginable. To not love Faith was impossible for me, had been impossible for a long time. But the scars, they did affect me. Not in the way she thought, but they struck me to the core with what I did to her. Along with the good and perfect images of today mingled images of Faith walking stiffly, in pain, for weeks as she recovered from her surgery. In the days to come, I would see her looking at herself in the mirror, her gaze lingering with unease on that little scar that marred her perfect face, and it would pierce my heart, the heart that belonged solely to her. I clung to her, like a man going down in a maelstrom, living in fear every day I would somehow hurt her again.

I went to my AA meetings religiously, as if that alone would keep me safe from hurting her. I wanted to propose to her, but I told myself I needed six months of sobriety under my belt first.

I didn't make it.

FAITH

The next couple of months were some of the most painful we'd ever experienced. Eli lived with the constant fear he would mess up again, and, although I tried hard not to, so did I. But, he started to do better. He took to working out—as if his body needed it—to occupy his free time, and inspire him to keep his body clean. He jogged with me in the mornings, and saved up for a fitness machine that found a place in the corner of my living room. We fell right into step together, like those six weeks of separation never happened, except for the fact we cherished our time together more, maybe because we did fear it would end.

Then, one day, I worked a late shift and went to pick him up at his place. When Aaron opened the door, I could smell the stench of alcohol. I prayed it was only Aaron, but when I walked in, Eli was leaning on the arm of the couch, moving loosely like some rag doll, with a stupid grin on his face. He had slipped.

Instead of the white-hot rage I expected, I suddenly just felt tired and cold. I guess it was because we'd both half-anticipated it. There was no real shock. I knew in my heart that it was over, then. I loved Eli, and would always love him, but I couldn't help him, and I wouldn't live with this.

"Hey, Faithy." He raised his half-finished glass to me in an added insult. I strode past Aaron without a word. "Oh, come on, Faith." I heard Eli shout over my shoulder, "Don't be mad," he wheedled.

I went into his bedroom and took out a bag I kept under the bed. I started removing my clothes from the dresser, and putting them in the bag methodically, feeling only numb. Aaron stood in the doorway, his beefy arms above his head, grasping the doorframe.

"I'm sorry. I guess he had too much to drink."

Now here was someone I could be mad at. "You *think*?" I said sarcastically. "He's a recovering alcoholic, Aaron." I pronounced each word as if he were moronic, which he was. "*One* drink is too much to drink. Why did you let him do it?"

"I guess because I had plans for tonight I didn't know if he'd want to be a part of."

Whatever that meant, I could make little sense of. I continued to pack, now moving faster with my full head of steam. "I can't be with him every hour of every day and...hey, what are you doing?" Aaron came over and took the pair of jeans I was about to pack out of my hands and laid it on the dresser.

"Come on." He took my hands. "We both know you don't want to leave here tonight like this."

"The hell I don't!" I grabbed the jeans again and he ripped them from my hands and threw them back on the dresser. He reached over and ran the back of his hand down my cheek, over my scar.

"You know, I find that scar totally sexy."

I looked him in the eye. *He must be drunk, too.* "Oh, come on, Aaron. Get real." I tried to get past him, back to the dresser. He grabbed my elbow.

"I am being real here, Faith." He stroked my hair with his big, clumsy hand. "I've always thought that you were *so* hot."

"Okay, this is getting weird. I think I'll leave and come back for my stuff later." I turned to open the door, which had shut halfway, but he reached past me and slammed the door shut and then locked it. "Aaron..." I turned around to say something to him and his other hand came down to pin me against the door. "Aaron." I tried to duck under his arm, but he lowered it, pressing his body against mine to further trap me.

"Come on, baby. Don't tell me you've never dreamed about this."

"Let me go. This isn't funny." I tried to squirm away from him, but as I did, he brought his head to my neck and started kissing me. "Hey. Cut it out!" My heart started beating faster. He reached up under my skirt, pulling my uniform up to my hip and sticking his fingers underneath the back of my underwear. "Aaron!" Panic filled me and my mouth began to sweat in desperation.

"Don't you want this, baby? Don't you want this?"

I realized he was serious. He was drunk, and horny, and way too big for me to defend myself against. Way too big. "Eli!" I screamed. "Eli!"

He stilled for a moment listening. Then an evil grin split his face. "He passed out. Like I thought he would." He brought his hand out from under my skirt, brushing it again along my face. "He's not going to be any help to you tonight," he said steadily. And that's when I knew. He wasn't drunk.

He wasn't drunk at all. He'd planned this out. Planned things out so he could...what?

"Aaron," I said, trying to keep the fear out of my voice. "You need to let me go now." His hand climbed to my neck and he applied subtle pressure there.

"Oh, no, baby. I don't *need* to do anything." And just like that, he whipped me around and on to the bed.

"No!" I screamed, struggling uselessly against his brawn.

"You know, I saw you first. Before Doc or Eli, or any of them. I saw you first."

I tried to make sense of this idiotic statement. Did he really think he could "call" me and I'd be his? He eased off me a little bit, letting go of my hands even, but keeping his legs planted on either side of mine and his pelvis pressed against me.

"Unbutton your shirt."

"What? No." I tried to push him off me again but he grabbed my wrist. He raised his hand and punched me in the jaw. Pain exploded. My head remained turned to the side as my mind whirled. The quilt beside me was becoming stained with the blood pouring from my nose, lip, and mouth. *He hit me.*

"I want to see you unbutton your shirt for me, Faith," he growled through clenched teeth.

I knew he was going to rape me, and I knew there was absolutely nothing I could do about it. My trembling hands went to my buttons. A half-sob escaped. I felt so dirty. It was so wrong. Eli was right outside the door. He could hear us, surely he could hear us. But what choice did I really have? Maybe if I bought myself some time, I'd be able to figure something out.

"Slower. I'm getting off on it. Yeah. Yeah." He grunted, rubbing his groin against me. "That's good. God, you're stacked." His hands were on my breasts, squeezing roughly. "Oh, God yeah, baby." I felt his erection swell and wanted to be sick, then he got up. "Take it all off for me now." He leaned back against the dresser, and I contemplated whether I had better chances of making it to the door, or the fire escape outside the window. I brought my hands to my buttons and started to undo them quickly, trying not to look at the door.

His gaze was riveted on my hands, so I took my chance, I dove for the door, and got it unlocked, then he was on me, dragging me off. I kicked and flailed, but he lifted me up and threw me on the bed with a big grunt and climbed after me. He ripped the rest of my uniform open and grabbed my crotch hard, trapping my wrists with his other hand over my head. He pulled aside the cotton and shoved one thick finger in me. "Ooh. You're hot and moist. You want me."

"Get off me," I screamed, enraged. "*Get off!*" He let go of my hands to fondle my breast and brought his head down to my chest. I beat my fists as hard as I could into his shoulders, but he only grunted more. He dug his teeth into my skin and I screamed in pain.

"Faith?"

"Eli? Eli! Help!" I could hear him outside the door, but his voice was slurred and confused. Aaron plunged his fingers inside me again and again, as hard as he could, actually moving my body up on the bed. I struggled to breathe. He bit me again. Above his sick, animal-like grunting I heard what appeared to be Eli's body sliding down the door. He'd passed out again. Aaron undid the clasp of my bra between my breasts.

"Oh, my God, Faith. You're tits are fucking awesome." I pounded on his big bald head, but I seemed to be hurting my fists more than him. His mouth was on me again, his tongue circling my nipple obscenely before he bit down. I tried with all my might to buck my hips and dislodge him, screaming for help whenever I had breath to. He sat on top of me and started to undo his belt buckle. I reached up and grabbed his balls in both hands, squeezing as hard as I could. "Ooh. Yeah. That's good." I dug my fingernails in and finally got the reaction I desired. "Damn, Faith! That hurts! Be careful with those."

He backed up enough so I could swing my forearm into his crotch. He howled with pain. He raised his fist to hit me, but we both heard someone pounding on the front door.

"Hey. Eli? Aaron? What the hell's going on in there? Faith? Is that you?"

"Chuck!" Chuck Fitzwater, Eli's neighbor.

"Geez, Fitzwater. Mind your own fucking business, why don't ya?"

"No! Chuck! Help!"

"My wife's calling the cops, Aaron."

"Oh, geez." He redid his belt while telling me, "I fucking saw you first, Faith," his eyes glowing. Then he got off me and opened the window and went down the fire escape, leaving me alone.

I lay there for several seconds, panting at first, and then, still as stone, knowing I would begin to shatter in a minute. I squeezed my legs together, feeling inside of me the hot, painful paths Aaron's nails scratched and a dull accompanying ache where I would be bruised later from the force he was using to enter me. My chest was still wet from his saliva, and it was on fire. Tears started rolling silently out.

I took a deep, shuddering breath and pushed it all down, way down, deep down inside of me. And that was when the zombie that became Faith Robeson was born. I got up and systematically buttoned the buttons still left on my uniform. I went to the bedroom door and opened it, and Eli's body came crashing to the floor. Alarmed, I bent over him and checked the back of his head to see if he hurt himself, but he seemed okay. I laid my hands on his chest. It rose and fell and my concern for him turned to something hard, and cold, and bitter. I got up and walked away from him, leaving him lying in the doorway.

I recognized now the pounding on the door never ceased. Chuck was calling out my name. "Chuck." My voice was raspy.

"Faith. Faith. Are you okay?"

"Yes. I need to clean myself up a little before I open the door, okay?"

"Sure. But you're okay, aren't you?"

"Yes."

"What about Eli and Aaron?"

"Eli...is fine," I replied, looking over to where his feet were sticking out into the hall, illuminated by the light from his bedroom. "Aaron is gone," I added flatly.

"Okay," he said hesitantly. "Well...I called the cops. They should be here anytime. I'll wait right here until they get here."

"Okay." I went into the bathroom and washed the blood from my face. My nose was swollen and red, my lips were split, and when I rinsed my mouth out, blood oozed from my gums. A couple teeth were a little loose, but I figured they'd tighten up eventually. I went back into the living room and sat on the couch. I stared at the beer bottles and glasses on the table blindly, sitting on the edge of the cushion, my back straight. I imagined reliving it all with the police, speaking the words, and nausea rose to my throat. I would not do this tonight, I decided. I got up to leave and had my hand on the doorknob when Eli groaned. My heart did a little lurch, and I ran over to him, but he was still out cold. I worried he would throw up and choke on his vomit, so with a struggle, I got him onto his side. I let my hand rest on his face for a minute, and choked back a sob. Then I got up and walked away.

I opened the front door and walked by Chuck Fitzwater—who appeared to be pacing the hall—without lifting my head. I took the stairs.

"Faith? Faith, wait. The police are coming. You need to talk to them."

When I didn't respond he got desperate. "Joyce!" he screamed for his wife.

I kept heading down the stairs. He leaned over the railing, yelling to me as I circled ever-lower beyond him. "Faith...you're going to be okay now. They can help you. You have nothing to be ashamed of."

That was the last thing I heard before I banged the exit door open. I had nothing to be ashamed of. Then why did I feel so dirty? I opened the door to the used car I bought after the accident as the police car pulled up, parking right in front of me. I got into the car and watched the policemen amble out, as if they had all the time in the world, laughing and joking with one another as one of them passed through my headlights in front of me. I stared at them with loathing from behind the screen of my hair that I had let fall forward in front of me. I pulled away and drove home.

I took the stairs up to my place and was unbelievably grateful to not run into anyone. I threw my ripped uniform and panties into the chute leading to the incinerator and then pulled off my bra and shoes and stockings and threw them in as well, staring into the dark abyss for several seconds before walking away. Naked, I went to the bathroom and showered until the water went cold, and showered some more. I ended up lying in the bathtub for the rest of the night. I don't think I ever slept. I was cold, only covered by a towel, but that knowledge lived only on the periphery of my mind. I never really cried, but tears ran silently down my face.

I knew the magic of the love that was Faith and Eli's was gone, and I mourned for it. I knew in the days to come that would hurt far worse than Aaron's fist, his teeth, or his violating fingers. In the morning, I went to the closet for a clean uniform and had to run back into the bathroom and throw up. It took me twenty minutes to work myself into a place where I could pull that pink fabric over me without retching. My eyes stared back at me blankly from the mirror as I rubbed foundation over the cuts and bruises. I was still swollen, but I convinced myself no one but I would be able to tell. I put my hair up carefully, securing it with a banana clip, and walked robotically to the diner. I had trouble focusing on my first couple of orders, but soon, routine saved me, and I was able to go about my job competently, if not well.

I was stunned when they walked in.

CHAPTER THIRTEEN

E *li* I was watching the game with Aaron, waiting for Faith to get off work. It was a close match between the Raiders and the Steelers and I was enjoying the intense action of a good football game. Aaron walked in with two beers and set one down in front of me before going to his seat.

"Hey, man. I don't drink any more, remember?" I said, irritated.

"Oh, yeah. Sorry, man. Leave it there. I'll drink it later." He was chattering more than usual. After the beer sat there a while, I started to feel jumpy. My gaze was drawn to the familiar brown bottle, and I watched a drop of condensation drip all the way down to the table, my mouth watering. *Dammit,* I thought crossly. *Why did he have to do that?*

Aaron got up about a half-hour later and went to the kitchen again. "Want a Coke or something?"

"Yes. Yes," I said with relief, although, without Aaron in the room, the beer seemed even more tempting. It was as if I could hear its siren singing to me. Luckily, Aaron finished in the kitchen reasonably quickly and came back and set a Coke down in front of me.

"Thanks." I took a big swig and swallowed fast, before I even realized the rum was in there. "Hey. This has rum in it."

"Oh. Sorry. I must have given you mine. Here." He handed me the other glass then jumped out of his seat cheering for a great run, and I hopped to my feet along with him. We both were rooting for the Steelers, so we high-fived each other before sitting down. I took a drink of my soda.

"This one has rum, too."

"You're kidding." He tasted it. "You're right. I must have accidentally poured some in both. I'll get you a new one at halftime."

By halftime I was shit-faced.

When I woke up, Aaron was lifting me into my bed, which was kind of strange. He usually left me passed out on the couch. Through my blurry vision, I caught him wiping the side of the bed with a towel. Aaron cleaning? I must be hallucinating. In the morning, I saw blood there, and decided I must have had a bloody nose. I got those sometimes.

The next morning I stumbled out of my bed, my head screaming louder than the baby next door, and into the kitchen. Aaron sat hunched over a cup of coffee. He eyed me when I came in but I didn't say anything at first.

"Thanks for getting me into bed."

"Sure. Sure."

I stopped suddenly, with a glass in my hand, ready to put under the faucet. "That's strange that Faith didn't come over last night."

Aaron looked like he was going to choke on his coffee for a minute, then he grinned. "Yeah."

"I wonder why she didn't. She didn't call or anything."

"Uhh...she did call. She said she was tired and she was going home."

"Oh." I was relieved she didn't see me.

"Hey, you wanna go get some breakfast over at the diner? My treat."

"Well, if you're treating, sounds great." I returned his grin. "Just let me get some aspirin and a shower."

When we walked into the diner, I automatically went to a table in Faith's area. She was busy in the back, but when she came out and saw us, she froze with her mouth hanging open. I assumed she was glad to see me. She moved toward us slowly. Aaron was grinning at her in a strange way, and I looked back at her and her jaw was tight. She walked straight over to Aaron and threw the ice water she had in her hands all over him.

He jumped up, cussing, and she ran from the table. I ran after her.

"Faith? What the hell?"

Dino jumped into our path. "Faith!" the big man bellowed, repeating me. "What the hell did you do that for? I should can your ass."

"That's okay, Dino," she said, ripping her apron off and throwing it at him. "I'll save you the trouble. I quit."

She stormed out, and I followed, just as shocked as I would have been if she threw the ice water on me.

"Faith," I called after her, but her anger had propelled her halfway down the street.

"Leave me alone." I ran to catch up with her and grabbed her elbow as she reached the corner. She turned on me and started flailing like a wildcat, hitting and scratching indiscriminately. I was blown away.

"Faith. What the hell is wrong with you?"

"What the..." she repeated, her voice an outraged scream. She pulled apart the top of her uniform and I could see deep bruises and bite marks all across her chest.

"*This* is what the hell is wrong with me." She sobbed.

Confused, I reached out my hand to her and she backed away, fear in her eyes, along with the anger. "*No*! Never again." She turned and marched across the street even though the light was still red, dodging cars, their angry horns creating a cacophony.

What happened? Did someone jump her on her way out to the truck after work last night? I always worried about that, but Dino promised to walk her out.

Then my mind filled with rapid-fire images, Aaron's evil, triumphant grin when he looked up at Faith, her look of betrayal when she saw me, the water splashing everywhere, the bruises, the blood on the sheets...it was Faith's, not mine.

"Faith!" I screamed, nearly getting hit by a cab as I chased after her. "Did Aaron do that? Did Aaron do that to you?"

She turned around and looked at me, incredulous. "You don't even re-member?" she shrieked, her voice cracking. Her uniform was still open to her bra and the red, angry bite marks stared back at me, mockingly.

"Oh, my God." Aaron did—what?—to her while I was passed out in the living room? "Oh, my God!"

"It's over, Eli." The words vibrated in the air. "*This* is over," she added with a cold finality. She pulled her uniform back together and held it with one hand, trying to restore some dignity. She glanced about, noticing the people on the street who stopped to stare, and turned around and disappeared into the building as I stood, staring lamely after her.

When I got back to the diner, Aaron was gone. He didn't show up for work the next few days either. That night I couldn't sleep in my room, the room where he... On the couch, I had a nightmare that in reality was a memory. I was stumbling down the hall, and Faith screamed out my name. I called to her, but I felt confused, off-balance. She was crying. My God, what else did I hear? Sounds of him, hurting her, touching her, while I did *nothing*. She'd needed me, and I let him violate her in unimaginable ways. I hated Aaron.

But mostly, I hated myself.

Unable to sleep anymore, I got up and packed my things and took a bus to Chicago, hoping to leave behind my nightmares, and choosing to give up everything that was good in my life.

But a change in locations didn't lessen the pain.

FAITH

I spent the next two days locked in my room. I didn't cry. I didn't think of Eli. I didn't really think about anything at all. Not once did I have a desire to look out the window. I spent most of the time sitting on the edge of my bed, clasping and unclasping my hands. I threw all of my uniforms down the chute and imagined the flames of the incinerator licking them up and destroying them. I forced myself to eat some crackers. I slept finally, some.

On the third day, Glo came to my door to offer me my job back. I let her in.

"So, Faith..." She looked around my place absentmindedly, trying to come up with something to say. "Look," she said, finally. "Eli told us what Aaron did to you, and I would kill him myself if I could."

I didn't say anything.

"Eli was so pissed. It took Dino threatening to call the cops to get him to settle down." She played with her hands, rubbing them over and over again. "You know, 'cause Eli's had trouble with the law before and all..." Her voice trailed off. She reached out and grabbed my hand, squeezing it. "You okay?"

I gave my head a slight nod and the tears I held back rose dangerously close in my eyes.

"Let me see it."

I looked up, not understanding.

"Let me see what Aaron did to you."

I balked at first, then I simply lifted my sweatshirt. The bruises had started to turn an angry yellow, but the bite marks were still a vibrant red where he'd broken the skin.

She gasped. "Holy shit, Faith! That bastard did that to you?"

I nodded, my throat tight.

"Did he rape you?"

I shook my head vigorously.

"But he tried to, didn't he? That son-of-a-bitch!" She sat still for a long minute, then, took my hands again. "They're gone now. Both of them. I heard Aaron went back to his folks' place for awhile. Some of the guys at the site found out about things and planned to go bash in his skull, but Mr. Drew talked some sense into them, I guess. And Eli—" she watched my face for my reaction "—no one knows where he went. He just left."

To my surprise, the news filled me with a sense of relief. I didn't think that I could bear seeing him again.

"You're not coming back, are you?"

I shook my head. "I c-can't," I whispered.

"Okay, then," she said rising. "But just 'cause you don't work there, doesn't mean you can't stop by now and then." But we both knew I wouldn't. She gave me a long hug and left, making me promise to call her if I needed anything.

When she left, and the apartment was quiet again, I wondered about her having a heart after all. Somehow that little bit of kindness awoke me from my stupor. I borrowed my neighbor's newspaper from the hall and looked at the want ads. I cleaned myself up, and went to apply for a sonogram technician's position offering on-the-job training. They hired me right away. I got to wear scrubs, rather than a uniform dress, much to my relief, and I found I could disappear completely in the ambiguous outline of the scrubs. I wore my hair up every day, wore no make-up, did my job quietly and efficiently, and then went home.

Six months later, another technician asked me out. Brendon was cute, with short-cropped black hair, dark eyes, and that sexy eternal stubble on his face. He was a few years younger than me, and seemed sweet. I told him no at first. But he would come and sit with me at lunch. One day he reached across the table at lunch and took my hand.

"When are you going to give up this silly charade of not being attracted to me and let me take you out, Faith Robeson?"

I couldn't speak. He rubbed his thumb across the top of my hand for several seconds, looking into my face. He squeezed it with a quiet sigh and was going to withdraw his hand, but I clutched it. "There is hope then?" he asked good-naturedly.

I laughed. He started to find me each day to walk me down to lunch and started to loop his hand over my shoulder as we talked. It seemed right, comfortable, and I found myself relaxing. Some of his friends joined us one day. They were nice, and funny, and I laughed for the first time in months. Brendon joked and teased me, and even pulled me onto his lap one time, brushing his lips over mine and laughing.

"So, how long have you two been going out?" his friend, Simon, asked.

Brendon looked at me, a smile still on his face. "We're not going out. Faith's not into me, I guess." He winked in my direction, but I could see a sadness behind his eyes.

When we were walking back upstairs later, Brendon was holding my hand and being uncharacteristically quiet. I surprised myself by saying, "You know, Bren, what you said earlier, about me not being into you? It's not true." I looked straight ahead, although I saw his head snap up out of the corner of my eye.

He hesitated, weighing his words. "Would you go out with me tonight, then?"

I let a smile curve my lips. "I'd have to check my schedule...but I think I can do that."

"Come here," he said excitedly, pulling me into a stairwell. Before I knew it, his lips were pressed to mine, warm, soft, inviting. I brought my hands slowly behind his neck and surrendered myself to the kiss.

We went to the theatre that night, to a movie the next, out dancing a few nights later. Brendon had a few drinks, which helped him to relax more on the dance floor. He was actually an excellent dancer and I was beginning to really enjoy myself. He grabbed my hips and swayed with me, his eyes getting heavy as he gazed down into my face. He kissed me, and this time with a different tenor than his previous kisses. It was hot and imploring, and my head spun. "Let's go back to my place," he said, his voice husky. I nodded tentative-ly.

Brendon lived in a new high-rise near the hospital where we worked. His place was nice, with high ceilings and one lengthy window with a view of the city lights. It consisted of one long room, in a line, that served as a living room, dining room, and, one sectioned-off area, as a kitchen, with a bedroom and bathroom off to one side. The kitchen was three times the size of mine, with one wall that was floor to ceiling bricks, and a bar where you could eat on stools facing the kitchen. The living room had one deep black suede couch and two over-sized chocolate brown chairs with a low, black coffee table. He dropped the keys on a table inside the door and immediately grabbed me.

His mouth explored mine greedily, and then he pulled me close to moan in my ear. "I've been waiting so long for this." The rough stubble of his face against my cheek sent tingles through me as he kissed my neck. He untucked the sheer white blouse I was wearing from my jeans, and slid his hands be-neath the fabric, exciting us both where he let his hands skim over flesh. He brought them up to rest flat on my chest, gently parting the fabric of my blouse and twisting a finger through my bra strap. He looked up, searching my eyes intensely, his own dark eyes misty. "You are so beautiful." He kissed me and then brought his head down to my chest, kissing my skin there. I went absolutely rigid, the blood draining out of me. Memories flooded back with such intensity it was as if I expected Brendon's teeth to sink into me at any second. He lifted his head. My skin was cold and my breathing erratic. He must have seen the fright in my eyes. "I'm sorry. I'm rushing you. We'll take our time. Come over here."

He led me to the couch. "Would you like a drink? Maybe some Bailey's or something?"

"Sure."

He poured our drinks in the kitchen and brought them back to me. He drank his down quickly and set his glass on the table, taking my hand and caressing it as we talked about work. At one point, he reached over to play with my hair. "You know, you look a lot better in street clothes than you do in scrubs. Not that you don't look good in scrubs," he added quickly, "but, you look *really* good in regular clothes." He slid my cross back and forth on the chain at my collar bone, and then reached up behind my neck to pull me in again for a kiss.

I tried not to think about Eli, but it was nearly impossible. And I hate to admit it, but I was imagining him kissing me as Brendon did, and that helped me to loosen up. I set my half-finished glass down next to his and guided his face again to mine. He leaned in and I lay against the arm of the couch. His hands again went under my shirt and slid up to cup my breasts. I tensed a little, but told myself to relax. Brendon wasn't going to hurt me.

He stood and held his hand out to me. With his hand behind his back, he led me, to his bedroom without saying anything. I didn't notice anything about the room, because I was having trouble breathing. The fear gripped me so strongly it was like being choked. He stopped by the bed and kissed me again, bringing his hands up to unbutton my shirt. I held my breath, screaming in my head every time a button came undone. I flashed back to the way Aaron watched me unbuttoning my shirt as he had ordered, getting off on my humiliation. I closed my eyes. When Brendon pulled my blouse off, I freaked out.

"Stop. Stop!" I shrieked wildly, taking my blouse and clutching it to my breasts. I was shaking uncontrollably.

"Faith?" He stepped toward me.

"No, don't!" I backed up so quickly I tripped and fell to the floor. Brendon bent to help me but I threw up my hands defensively and tried to scoot away from him. To my utter embarrassment I began to sob. I turned my face from him, my arms still held up to block him from me.

He knelt down beside me, his face creased with worry. "What did I do wrong? I'm sorry. I didn't mean to...to..." He seemed at a loss, unsure of exactly what he did wrong.

I sat and scooted until my back was against the door, sobbing uncontrollably; I clutched my knees to my chest and put my head down. I wanted the world to swallow me up right there. "Oh, God. I'm so sorry," I moaned miserably.

"No. No." He sat next to me, his back also against the door, and tentatively put his arm around me. The immediate fear over, I bent into him and laid my head on his shoulder, still weeping loudly. "Hey, hey...shhh. It's okay." His voice was soft and comforting. I started to get a grip finally.

"I'm sorry, Brendon. I just...I...can't..."

"You're not ready. I was putting too much pressure on you."

"No. It's just—" I hadn't told anyone at work about it, or talked to anyone besides Eli and Gloria about it either. "—a couple of months ago, I was...attacked...by someone I knew."

"Oh, geez. I'm sorry. I—"

"No. You've been very patient with me."

"I had no idea."

"Of course you didn't." I sniffled.

He reached up and brushed away a tear. "We'll take things really slow then. One step at a time...only what you're comfortable with...okay?" He lifted my chin with his hand and I nodded.

"I feel like such a...fool."

He smiled. "There's no need to feel like that. I think you've been very brave."

"You do?"

"Yes. How about I drive you home and you get a good night's sleep, and I'll take you to Shakespeare in the Park tomorrow."

I smiled. "I'd like that."

When we got to my place, he walked me to the door and kissed me sweetly before leaving. The next day, he sent me a dozen yellow roses with a card that read:

Here's to fresh starts.—Bren

We had a great time at the play the next night, and we continued to spend most of our time together over the next few weeks. One day at lunch, he invited me over to his place for dinner. Remembering Eli's culinary skills, or lack thereof, I was hesitant.

"You can cook?"

"For your information, I'm an excellent cook," he said with a grin, tweaking my nose.

And he was. He made a fantastic Carbonara, with a nice salad and crusty French bread.

"That was delicious."

"I told you. And for dessert, I made cheesecake."

"Ooh. Now I really am impressed. You did make it with cream cheese, not Swiss cheese, right?"

"Huh?"

"Never mind."

After dessert, we retired to the couch and snuggled up to finish off our glasses of wine.

"This has been an awesome evening, Bren. Thank you."

"Anytime, beautiful. How about a dance?"

"A dance?" I laughed.

"Yeah. Come on." He pulled me off the couch and walked over to the stereo to turn it up. Some sultry jazz number was playing, and we swayed to the music together. He brought my hand to his mouth and kissed it, holding me close. We made our way over to the light switch, and he turned it off, still able to see by the light of the candles we left burning on the table, and from some residual outside light. He held his hand up so I could twirl under it, and then brought me in close again. He had his hands on my hips and he moved his with mine in a way that made my heart race. He stared into my eyes and the wine rushed to my head.

I thought about how sweet and understanding he was since the night I freaked out, never pushing me, always the gentleman. I reached up to pull him down for a kiss, unbuttoning his shirt as I did and running my hands across his chest. I kissed his chest, then, feeling freer, I pulled back and slowly unzipped my black sweater. His eyes opened wider as I shed it. He pulled me in by my hips, and we moved together again with the music, his eyes smoky as he watched me move. I don't know if it was the wine, or the way he was watching me that made me feel empowered, but I arched backward, with his arms around me, and swung my hair from side-to-side. I laughed, low in my throat, and then straightened, my face inches from his. I nibbled on his lip and then arched back again.

He laughed then moaned. "Oh, baby. That is *so* turning me on."

I straightened again. "Is it?" I asked mischievously. I moved back and un-did my belt buckle, while staring him in the eye with a wicked grin. I stepped out of my jeans and walked around him slowly, trailing my fingers around him with my arm extended as I did. I was enjoying myself, and I was pretty sure he was having fun too. On my second trip around, I stopped behind him and reached around to his groin, pulling him to me. "What about that, Brendon?" I whispered in his ear seductively. "Is that turning you on?"

He groaned. "You have *no* idea."

I circled around to the front again, biting my lip. "Oh, I think I do." I yanked his shirt off his shoulders and tossed it aside. He looked at me thoughtfully, but I was fully into my role of temptress. I grabbed his hips, then, shimmied down to squat in front of him, my hands now on his butt, my mouth perilously close to a very sensitive area. His whole body was tensed, and I was getting off on my power to seduce him. I came back up slowly, and walked my nails slowly down his stomach. I yanked on his belt with a violence that nearly sent him over the edge, and then led him by his belt into the bedroom. I pushed him onto the bed, and then climbed on top of him. His hands went under the fabric of my lacy black boy shorts and he squeezed my flesh.

"Faith, you are, hands down, the hottest woman I have ever—"

I buried his statement with my mouth, then swung my leg off him and grabbed him between his legs, hard. He sucked in his breath, but relaxed as I began to stroke him. He lifted me up and tossed me onto the pillows where I bounced with a laugh. I sat on my elbows as he stripped down the rest of the way, my hair wild, one bra strap off my shoulder. He came over to me and started kissing my stomach and I threaded my fingers through his hair while he did it. He ran his tongue along my waistband with such expertise I released a moan. That fueled him, and he tore off my panties, swinging on top to penetrate me. His hands were on my breasts at first as he pulled himself into me, then he bent over me, watching my face as he took me higher. He bent lower to kiss my neck, and panic seized me. The weight of his body on me was now too familiar, too close; I felt trapped.

"No," I said weakly, no air behind my voice. He continued to move on top of me. "No," I said louder. And then I was hitting him. Pushing and clawing at him in desperation. "Get off. *Get off!*"

"Faith? What?" He screamed as I knocked him off to one side. He reached over and yanked on the lamp. I was crying in frustration and embarrassment. He ran his hand through his hair agitatedly. "Damn. You're a freaking headcase!" I jerked back as if he struck me. I rolled out of bed and grabbed my panties off the floor. "Where the hell are you going?" he yelled after me as I rushed from the bedroom.

When he got to the living room, with his pants back on, I had already pulled my sweater on and I was hopping up and down, trying to pull my jeans up.

"Faith, wait," he said, more calmly. "Don't go."

I sobbed once, and then ran out the door. I looked back down the hallway while I waited for the elevator, willing the doors to open, tears running down my face. He stood in the doorway, leaning one hand on the frame. "Come back. Come on. We'll talk about this."

The door dinged open and I got on board without looking back. When the doors closed, I slid down the back wall of the elevator and covered my face with my hands and let the tears come. I barely had time to pull myself together when the doors opened on the ground floor. Though taken aback at first by my disheveled appearance and questionable emotional status, a kind doorman called me a cab. As I was getting in, Brendon rushed out, having pulled on a thin, gray sweater. "Come on. Don't leave like this." I closed the door of the cab and he pounded on it. "Dammit, Faith. You can't get me all worked up and leave." The cabbie pulled away and I looked back to see him pacing, running his hand through his hair.

When I got back to my place, my phone was ringing. I picked it up. "I'm sorry. I was way out of line. Maybe we could—"

I hung up the phone.

The next time I saw him at work, he apologized profusely, saying he was a gigantic jerk and begging for my forgiveness.

"It's okay, Brendon. I shouldn't have...done what I did."

"No. The fault was all mine. I should have been more understanding."

"Well, why don't we just say it wasn't the best moment for either of us."

He asked me out again, and I told him I didn't think it was such a good idea. I think he was relieved.

CHAPTER FOURTEEN

M*ax* New Year's Eve found me in the same place. I had hooked Amber up with a plastic surgeon friend of mine; unintentionally, in more than one way. She told me she wanted a boob job, and then she let the good doctor, how should I put it? Play around with his work a little. As a gesture of gratitude for her recent tumble with her surgeon, Amber invited me to her party again.

Coming back to Faith's building had me rattled, and I slunk off to the balcony again with a pilfered bottle of Dom. I was well on my way to oblivion when my hostess found me out.

She had me light her cigarette, then looked at me curiously through the haze of smoke she blew. "Max, darling, you really should come back in, it's cold out here."

"Yes. Well...I will shortly. So, where are Faith and Eli?" I asked as nonchalantly as possible.

"What? Haven't you heard? Eli left months ago."

"Left?"

"Yes, Max, left. As in, bye-bye. No one's heard from him since. Oh." She caught sight of some young stud who looked to be about twenty years her junior. "I've got someone I *need* to talk to." She crushed her cigarette out on the ledge of the balcony.

I smiled at her. "Good luck with that."

She came over and feathered her lips over mine seductively. "Oh, I don't need luck, love. Don't you remember?"

"I remember." I laughed, and she hurried off. I took a long swig directly from the bottle, and tilted my chair back to think about this new information. Eli left Faith? Was he out of his freaking mind? Before I even had much of a chance to contemplate it, the door flew open, and out she rushed. This year she had on a knockout of a black dress with a sparkly necklace hanging halfway down her bare back. Her arms were bare, the dress with sheer layers of petals at her shoulders, veeing in the front, and fanning out from her waist. She leaned against the railing and covered her mouth with her hand and started to cry softly.

I slowly rose and crossed to put my hands on her shoulders. "Faith."

She whipped around, but instead of hiding the tears in her eyes, when she saw me, she let them go, burying her face in my chest. After a while, when she calmed down some, I asked her, "Do you want to get out of here?" She nodded. "Okay. Stay behind me. I'll make a beeline for the door and then you won't have to answer any questions."

After negotiating the crowded room successfully—everyone was too wrapped up in their booze to even notice us—we got on board the empty elevator and I couldn't help but think about the time Eli and Faith got trapped in it together, so long ago now, it seemed. "Do you want to go to the diner and get a cup of coffee?" She nodded, still sniffling some, with her head down. I put my hand over her shoulder and we rode the rest of the way down in silence, though my heart was pounding in my chest just being near her again.

Once we hit the street, she seemed to relax a little, reaching her hand up to where mine rested on her shoulder and giving it a squeeze. I looked down at her and she smiled up at me sheepishly. Her hair was held loosely at the crown of her head, and a number of tendrils curled softly around her face.

"You look good, Faith."

She stopped and stood in front of me, reaching up to lay a hand on my face. "So do you, Doc. I've missed you." Her voice was wistful, but she had no idea what she was doing to me. My heart gave that old, familiar twist Faith created for it, and I fought back the urge to kiss her. We walked again, crossing the street. Faith looked up toward the diner.

"It's been a while since I've been in here."

"You don't work there anymore?"

"No. I'm a sonogram technician now at Bellevue."

Now it was my turn to stop dead in my tracks. "No, shit? That's where I'm in residency."

She flashed me an electric smile. "You're joking." Thunder rumbled faintly. It was an unusually mild last day of December. We hastened our steps to get inside before the rain started falling.

I held the door open for her and she walked in to the twinkling of the door's bells. We chit-chatted over nothing serious, catching up on each other's lives over coffee. Dino and Glo stopped by to say hello, both expressing their desire to see more of us. When they asked after Eli, Faith practically flinched. *Gone, but not forgotten.* After they left, I looked over at Faith, who seemed to be studying the inside of her coffee cup intently, and judged the time was right to take the conversation to a more serious level.

"Are you going to tell me why you were crying earlier?"

She started, surprised from her thoughts by my question, and then looked off, somewhere beyond my shoulder. "It's a long story," she answered evasively.

I spread my arms over the back of the booth, settling in. "The night's still early."

She glanced around. "Yeah, but I think Dino and Glo are trying to close up."

I stood, offering her my hand. "Then let me walk you home."

When we headed out, the fleeting rain showers had quit, leaving the city bathed in a silvery glow. We walked as we had before, unhurriedly, my arm around her shoulder. The temperature had dropped a little bit, so I took off my coat and slid it over her shoulders, despite her protests. At the corner, she stopped and looked up at me.

"Are you tired, Doc?"

"Not at all. Why?"

She glanced up at her dark apartment window. "I don't feel like going home yet," she said, her voice giving away her fragile state.

"You want to go back to my place for a night cap, and welcome in the New Year together?"

She hesitated a second, then nodded her head. "I think I'd like that."

"My car's up the street a ways."

"This is yours?" she asked when we reached it, admiring my sleek, new, black Mercedes-Benz.

"Yeah. You like it?"

She ran her hand covetously over its smooth paint job. "What's not to like?"

I watched her gorgeous face in the car window's reflection. *I would give you this and so much more, if you'd only let me.*

When we got to my place, she was equally charmed by it. "Oh, Doc. This is great." She practically skipped to my window. "It's beautiful."

"That's my favorite feature, too," I responded with a laugh. "Champagne?"

"Do you have some on hand?"

"Of course."

"Oh," she said as if just thinking of something. "You were probably planning to bring someone else back here tonight. I should leave." She made to scoot out the door, but I grabbed her hands.

"Only because I never dreamed I'd be so lucky as to run into you tonight." I brought both of her hands to my lips and kissed them.

"Still a charmer, aren't you, Doc?"

"I do my best." She followed me over to the kitchen, admiring all of my fancy gadgets as I wrestled the cork out. She jumped when it popped and laughed as it foamed all over the place. Filled with mischief, I shook the bottle a little, sticking my thumb over the top and spraying her a tiny bit.

"Oh. Stop," she cried out, laughing.

"Sorry about that."

She passed her hand over her chest, mopping off the champagne and flinging it at me. The sight of those suds dripping down her cleavage filled me with desire and it must have shown on my face.

"What? I must look a mess." She laughed, pushing back a strand of hair that got wet.

"Not at all," I returned, my voice sounding odd in my own ears. I turned around to remove some flutes from a hanging wine rack, telling myself to get a grip on my emotions, which were perpetually at the surface whenever she was around. After pouring I turned back to hand her a glass, and she was closer than I expected. She took the glass from me, and tapped it against my own, as I had become unexplainably speechless. We sipped our champagne, looking silently into each other's eyes.

"Can we go sit in front of the window?" she asked abruptly, as excited as a kid when the last school bell of the day rings.

"Sure, whatever you want."

On her way to the window, she noticed a sculpture I'd made of an Indian squaw, only it wasn't really an Indian squaw, it was Molly O'Shea, whom I doubted had a drop of Indian blood in her, but who made me think of an Indian when she made love, loudly, and passionately, like a Comanche giving his war whoop. Faith walked around it in a circle, trailing her finger along its base, studying it intently. I couldn't have felt more self-conscious if I'd been standing there on a pedestal myself in the nude.

Her cat-like eyes flicked up from the statue. "She posed for you?"

"Not exactly." I looked down and traced a finger along a curve myself. "I kind of did it from memory and imagination," I added, not wanting to get into the lurid details.

She nodded, accepting the answer with her usual ease. "It's beautiful, Doc. It really is." I could tell she meant it, as she continued to gaze at it rapturously.

I shrugged. "I kept it because it was the first one I made that won a prize."

She looked at me with a newfound respect. "I had no idea you were so talented."

I felt pleased with myself, but awkward and decided to joke it off by taking her hand and kissing it devilishly and stating, "Madam, you have *no* idea."

She smiled at me broadly, while at the same time blushing.

I grabbed some pillows from off the couch, and a blanket from off the bed, and lay them on the hardwood between my desk and the window. The rain had turned to huge drifting snowflakes, but I hardly noticed, only seeing them reflected in her eyes. She sat close to me, with her long, luscious legs curled to one side.

"Doc, why did you leave? I never got a chance to thank you for...helping me...that night, in Albany..."

"Ahh..." I studied her face, judging whether or not to tell her the truth, or some fraction of it. "I found it difficult to see you back with Eli after...what he did."

"But that was all a misunderstanding."

"Okay. Well, maybe I simply found it hard to see you back with Eli at all."

She looked down, watching the golden bubbles rise to the surface of her drink. I reached over and touched her face and she looked up quickly. I trailed my thumb over the scar that danced on the edge of her smile. "How did you get this?"

Her face flushed under my hand. She looked down again, contemplating her answer. "You won't like it," she said finally.

"Tell me," I insisted.

"We were in a car accident."

"You and Eli?"

"Yes."

I could tell she was hiding something. "He was drunk," I concluded, my voice tight.

She nodded. "And the worst part was I thought he'd quit. He attended AA meetings, but..." Her voice trailed off.

I was silent, twisting the stem of my glass in my hand. I looked at her intently. "How bad was it?"

"Bad," she answered, her voice barely a whisper.

"Your injuries?" I asked, clinically.

She looked out the window without speaking at first. "Broken ribs, a perforated abdomen, bruised liver..."

I interrupted her litany of injuries. "And you took him back." I jumped to my feet, pissed at a man who wasn't around to receive my anger.

She started to get up. "Maybe I should go."

"No, Faith. I'm sorry. I'm being stupid. Don't go," I added, with a hint of desperation.

But she stood anyway. "Maybe this wasn't such a good idea."

"Faith." I grabbed her shoulders, and party-blowers sounded from all around us. We stood for a long while, awkwardly as the noise died out and the snowflakes fell silently outside. She stretched up on her tippy-toes and kissed me softly.

"Happy New Year's, Doc," she whispered, her voice strained. She turned to leave, but I pulled her back, roughly, into my arms, crushing my mouth over hers. At first, she remained stiff in my arms, but little by little she melted into me, forming her slender body to mine.

I trailed my lips down her shoulder, tasting the sweet, sticky champagne still clinging to her skin. My body quivered next to hers, my need for her setting me on edge.

She pushed away gently, but kept her hands on my arms. Her eyes remained closed, but the pain was etched on her face. "Doc, I can't do this...*yet*..."

That three letter word saved me. "Okay, I understand."

"I'm still trying to get myself together."

I reached up and ran the back of my hand across her cheek. "You know, I've thought about you the whole time I've been away."

Her mouth opened, and her eyes grew wide. She blinked several times then placed her hand over mine where it rested on her cheek. She turned and kissed the inside of my palm. "You've always been so good to me." The warmth of her lips sent shockwaves through me, but she turned away and looked out the window, her back to the room.

"I tried seeing someone else, after Eli was gone, but...it didn't work out that well."

"Why?" I asked, though I knew the answer.

"I...I wasn't ready. I know it's been over a year now...I should move on. It's just...hard."

I put my hands on her shoulders and gently turned her to face me. "I've waited this long, Faith, I can wait a little longer."

Her eyes were damp. "I'm so terribly lonely. Would you hold me, Doc? Would that be okay?"

Okay? It was what I'd wanted to do since the first moment I'd laid eyes on her. I smiled. "I think I can handle that." She took my hand and led me over to the couch. I can't even tell you the number of fantasies I had on that short walk. Her leading me to the bed instead, seducing me in any number of ways...

When we got to the couch, she kicked off her shoes and sat. "Is it okay if I let my hair out of these pins?"

"Whatever you want." I still stood in front of the couch, my hands stuffed in my pockets for fear I wouldn't be able to control them. She removed her clips, and set them in front of her on the coffee table and shook out her hair, innocently, I'm sure, but still, highly provocative.

"Aren't you going to join me?" She patted the couch next to her, and I kicked off my shoes, too and quickly sat. She considered me, her head tilted to one side a little. "Are you sure you're okay with this?"

"Come here," I answered her quietly, raising my arm so she could duck under it. She leaned into me, closed her eyes and relaxed as I stroked her arm. After a bit, she seemed to nod off. I stretched carefully, trying not to disturb her, and pulled the chain on the lamp, bathing the room in darkness, the only light filtered in from outside.

"Do you mind if I take my stockings off?" she mumbled sleepily.

"N-no," I answered slowly.

She pulled her dress up slightly and I could see the lacy tops of her thigh-highs.

Without any sense of pride, I slid out from behind her, stretching her over so she lay against the arm of the couch, and knelt on the floor in front of her. Her eyes opened wide in the darkness.

"Let me."

She hesitated, then nodded her head slightly and I put my hands on opposite sides of her right knee. Slowly, I slid my hands up her thighs, relishing the feel of the silky stockings, and then her skin. I slid my hands a bit farther, until my fingertips touched the crease where her legs hit her torso. I looked over at her as she lay absolutely still, watching me. My mouth was dry. Without moving my hands, I leaned forward and slowly brought my lips to hers. Her mouth opened to mine easily, her lips holding me in their tantalizing grip, and then I pulled away, knowing I was on the edge of my control. I moved back, resting on my heels as I painstakingly rolled her stocking down, and off her lovely heel. She shifted a little so I could reach her other leg. I rubbed her foot, and calf, and then moved up on the couch.

"Max..." Her voice strained as she issued the warning.

"It's okay," I pleaded, hating my weakness. "I won't do anything." She rolled over so she was flat on the couch, but she didn't say anything else. I rubbed her leg again, always pushing my restraint to the edge. I lifted her leg to my shoulder and her dress fell to her waist. I brought my hands again to the very top of her leg, and caressed her, inches away from her center where heat emanating from her. She bent her leg to accommodate me and her heel slipped over my shoulder, but she didn't seem to mind. I moved back again, slipping the stocking down, slowly, slowly, kissing the inside of her leg with each successive inch. She quivered and took a sharp breath, and I had to stop to gather myself. With a moan, I sank on the couch behind her. She moved so I could slip my arms around her. My lips went to her ear and I said, without thinking, "Faith, baby...I'm sorry...I want you *so* badly."

She rolled into me and I rose up on one elbow. Her lips were warm against mine as she whispered, "I want you, too...but I'm not ready. I don't want to hurt you."

"Oh, for God's sake, Faith, hurt me already," I groaned.

She laughed, a delightful shiver of music. Then said seriously, "I won't do that. I respect you too much."

I brushed the hair from the side of her face, running my socked foot over her incredible legs. "That's what they all tell me," I said with an exaggerated sigh.

"Yeah, right." She laughed, swatting me lightly in the chest. Then she straightened a little and caught my lip in her teeth, bringing her hands up to tangle in my hair and pull me down, her kisses coming more quickly, pulling me into her.

"Faith..." I said against her lips. "If you keep doing that, I don't know how much longer I'll be able to remain a gentleman."

"Oh, I'm sorry," she said unconvincingly. I fell behind her and drew her in, pressing her against me from top to bottom. I pulled her hair back and kissed her neck lightly. "You taste like champagne."

"Is that a good thing?" she said playfully into the darkness.

I laughed, low. "I never knew you were such a tease."

She rolled to look up at me with concern. "I don't mean to be a tease...is that what I'm doing? Do you think I should leave?"

"If you tried to leave right now, I'd have to run out in the hall and tackle you, and that would embarrass us both." I tapped a finger to her lips, then, kissed them quickly. "You aren't a tease."

She rolled back and rested in my arms, quiet for several seconds. "I may have meant to tease you a little," she admitted.

I laughed. "Shut up, Faith."

I could feel her smile in the darkness as she snuggled closer. We fell asleep peacefully, in each other's arms.

When the rising sun pinked my huge window we woke.

Sensing I was awake, she turned. "Hi," she said with a sleepy smile.

"Hi." I ran my hand down her silky arm. "You know..." I said slowly, "your reputation is ruined now. You might as well sleep with me."

Her smile broadened. "Does that work with all the ladies, Theobold?"

I kissed her lightly. "Can't blame a guy for trying." I climbed over her and hopped out, turning to offer her my hand. She slid up gracefully, her curvaceous, bare legs coming off the couch. She still wore her party dress, the sheer fabric petals flowing temptingly over her shoulders. She looked as beautiful as when I first saw her on Amber's balcony. I pulled her to her feet with one swift move and grabbed her around the waist. "You look *good* in the morning." She smiled beguilingly and gently pushed off me.

"I've got to go. I have to work today." She lifted her leg behind her, leaning on my arm for balance, and slipped her sexy black heel on without her stockings.

"I'll drive you."

"No, that's okay." She slipped the other shoe on. "I'll catch a cab." She grabbed her purse and rushed toward the door. I picked up one of her stockings that somehow landed draped over the back of the couch.

"What about your stockings?"

She smiled at me from the door. "You keep them...for next time." She slipped out and was gone. I brought the stocking to my face, rubbing my whiskers with the silky fabric and smelling her fragrance. I flopped on the couch with a sigh. "God, I love that woman."

CHAPTER FIFTEEN

E*li* The Chicago smog choked me, turning the sky a dismal gray. I trudged up the trashed out stairs of my rat hole of an apartment building with a cup of coffee. When I got into my room, which I realized was not much bigger than most people's walk-in closets, I pulled out my books and got to work. I'd gone back to school. I was studying architecture by day, and bartending by night, something my AA sponsor was not at all happy about. But, it paid the bills, and seeing all the drunks at closing was enough to keep me clean and sober for a long time. What a bunch of idiots. I cursed under my breath as I spilled coffee on my notebook, ripped the page out, and copied my notes from it before wadding it up and tossing it on the bed. I tried to concentrate on my History of Architecture book, but before long, I was staring out my grimy windows at nothing, thinking about Faith again.

It was strange for me to think she hadn't been to my apartment, as she was constantly there in my thoughts. I went to sleep thinking about her; I woke up thinking about her. Stuck in the frame of my cracked dresser mirror I had a tattered picture of her. I looked at constantly, wondering what she was doing at whatever time of the day or night I was thinking of her. I wondered if she got her job back, or if she was doing something else. I wanted to call her, but that sort of defeated the purpose of staying away.

I thought about Aaron, too. And how I'd like to kill him. When I thought of him doing those things to Faith...it made me sick. When I imagined him taking his meaty hands to someone I loved more than anything, someone who would have never hurt a soul...when I imagine him touching her body intimately, and how she must have felt, scared, humiliated... And I long ago figured out Aaron set me up, got me drunk on purpose, though I took full responsibility for it. He didn't shove it down my throat after all, but he knew my weakness, and played on it to hurt Faith. My sponsor told me I wouldn't get better until I forgave him, and I knew it was true. I also had to forgive myself for having left her alone with him. That was even harder.

The phone rang. It had to be my mom. She was the only one who had no sense of the proper time to call somebody. I answered without introduction, "Hi, Mom."

"Eli. Oh...you were up weren't you?"

"Yes, Mom. I was up." I flopped on the bed, smiling broadly, tossing my crumpled ball of paper up in the air and catching it as I listened to her talk about Al's latest bowling scores.

"How are you?"

"Okay," I said, trying to mean it. "I'm still clean."

"That's excellent. I worry about you surrounded by all that alcohol."

"You and my sponsor both."

"When are you coming home?"

I sighed. "We've been over that, Mom. This is home now."

"Have you met anybody?"

I thought about the girl I'd brought home the other night. Now that had been a complete disaster. She was cute, and nice, witty, and intelligent, and...not Faith. I knew by now Faith had probably found somebody. Part of me hoped she had, she deserved it. But, as for me, I'd come to realize there was no one for me but Faith, and that was over.

"No." I sighed.

"Well, surely you meet some pretty girls in that bar of yours."

Hell yes. The place was near campus and was crawling with little coeds who wanted nothing more than to waste Daddy's money getting drunk and getting laid. I was propositioned on a nightly basis, sometimes in new and creative ways. One girl hid in the bathroom and came out after closing while I was cleaning up, buck naked. She offered to screw me on the pool table and the next night her friend wanted to go down on me behind the bar while I served. On more than one occasion, I had considered taking them up on their offers, but as soon as my lips touched theirs, the deal was over. I just couldn't do it.

"Mom, do we have to talk about this?"

She hesitated. "No. I guess not. If you don't want to."

"I don't want to."

"Okay." She sighed. After a pause she said, "I saw Faith today at St. Mary Margaret's."

I sat so fast I got a head rush. "You did?" I asked, holding my hand to my forehead. "How'd she look?"

"She looked lost, Eli. Utterly lost."

I closed my eyes. Even away from her I managed to hurt her. When I found my voice, I asked, "What's she doing nowadays? Is she still at Dino's?"

"No. She's working at the hospital. Bellevue. She's a technician of some sort...a sono—what do they call those baby pictures?"

It took a minute for me to figure out what she was talking about. "Oh. A sonogram technician." I thought about Faith nursing me after my accident, and about the way her eyes lit up whenever a baby was near. "That's good. That's good. She'd be good at that." It warmed my heart to think of it. I got out of bed and took her picture from off the dresser, staring into her beautiful face. An urge to drink came rushing over me so powerfully I almost shook. I needed a meeting. "Sorry, Mom. I've got to go."

"Oh, okay."

"Thank you for calling. I love you, Momma."

"I love you, too, son."

I set the phone on top of the dresser. I knew she wanted to see me settled, see me happy. It had as much to do with her guilt over the past as it did her maternal instincts. I grabbed my green flak jacket and headed to the Salvation Army Center. They had a meeting at eight.

FAITH

Max Theobold. He's like my own personal guardian angel.

New Year's at Amber's was another painful reminder of Eli's absence. I thought I was finally getting beyond the public outburst stage, but it was like a case of déjà vu gone bad. Everything the same, except the one important thing; Eli was absent. Amber opened the door, looking through me as usual, and quickly left me alone on the doorstep. I stood awkwardly, remembering I had entered on Eli's arm just two years before. So much had changed since then...Eli's fall and recovery, the car accident and our breakup, and the night Aaron attacked me, followed by months on my own, and the ill-fated attempt at a relationship with Brendon. Through it all, Eli was never far from my thoughts, and never more so than on that New Year's Eve.

I guess I was feeling a little sorry for myself when I stumbled out onto the balcony and was discovered by Max. At first it was overwhelmingly comforting to see him, but as the night wore on, I found my feelings for him started to change.

I'd always thought of Max as a sort of mischievous teddy bear, caring, with an endearing sort of impishness. He was certainly attractive. Though he was shorter and stockier than Eli, he was as well-built in many ways. His brown eyes didn't have the same explosive effect that Eli's green eyes did, but they were so expressive, they moved you. They could twinkle at you and make you giddy, or soften and touch your heart. Certainly they contained a level of intelligence, but always cut with a generous portion of good humor.

And there was something else about Doc, a certain, indescribable something, that drew me to him. Maybe it was simply that strange mixture of qualities that made him up, self-assured, but just shy of cocky, big-hearted, but not the kind of guy who'd let you take advantage of him, worldly, yet in many ways still innocent, strong, but still vulnerable. It was that ease with which he flirted with heartache that scared me most, because the thought of hurting him was unbearable.

He'd been so sweet, shuffling me out of Amber's and taking me to the diner. He had this wonderful ability of knowing when to ask questions, and knowing when not to pry and I adored him for it. When he suggested going back to his place, I jumped at the chance to spend some more time with him. Being with him reminded me of the old days, when Max and Eli and I would joke around and have fun, and I needed that so much.

But, when he kissed me... It was not at all like it was with Brendon; all thoughts of Eli were vanquished when Max's lips met mine. It was only when I left him I would begin to feel so horribly guilty. He was Eli's friend, and even though it was well over a year since Eli and I had been together, and I had no idea whether I would ever see him again, I still felt I owed him a degree of loyalty.

But at times when Max looked at me I found my heart in my throat, my pulse beating quicker. If I were being truthful with myself, I would admit I wanted him to kiss me that night in his apartment. Still, when he pulled me in and pressed his lips to mine, I couldn't, at first respond; and then, I couldn't *not* respond. It frightened me, how quickly I fell into loving him. Was I just that lonely?

When I left that morning, I was feeling happier than I had for a while. That was, for the first few blocks in the cab. It was the warm feeling Doc always gave me. He made me feel safe, loved, taken care of. He would listen attentively to me if I had something serious to discuss, but most of the time, he simply kept a perpetual smile on my face when we were together.

But the closer we got geographically to my past with Eli, the more I thought whatever feelings I was developing for Doc were just plain wrong. By the time I pulled up to my building, my heart was heavy, and I was chewing on my fingers.

When I got back to the apartment, a message was waiting on my machine. I guess with the snow a lot of people cancelled their appointments and they wouldn't be needing me today. An unexpected day off.

I took a shower, but as I stood with my eyes shut, letting the steaming water run down me lazily, images of the previous evening played in my head. I could almost feel the way his sure hands made their tormenting way up my leg as I wondered where he was going to stop, praying both that he would and that he would not. I had been immobilized by the desire he ignited in me, and if he had made even the smallest effort to seduce me, I'm certain I wouldn't have been able to resist him.

I stepped out of the spray of the water some, so it only hit my back, and as I did, my eyes opened, and my lips began to curve into a smile as I thought about how he teased me in the morning, telling me I might as well stay as my reputation was ruined anyway. It was this lighthearted way he approached what I knew was serious to him that made me love him all the more. I turned and put my face in the stream, closing my eyes again and recalling the way his lips had grazed my inner thigh, the heat of his breath, the moisture of his mouth, the mixed sensation of sharp teeth and tantalizing tongue. I moaned, leaning with my forearms pressed against the tile under the shower head, wishing he were with me, touching me again, making me feel beautiful and desired and alive.

After I was finished, I got dressed and left the apartment, finding its emptiness suddenly disheartening. I wandered up the street aimlessly, again feeling uneasy about my emotions when it came to being with Doc. I never expected myself to be with anyone besides Eli, but now I let my imagination wander and thought about whether or not I could possibly be happy with Doc.

Looking up, I found myself at the foot of the steps of St. Mary Margaret's, the church where Eli had attended AA meetings. Staring up at the crosses in the lead and glass doors that opened into the church, I felt strangely drawn there. Stepping forward, I opened the heavy doors, releasing the melodious organ music so it flowed through me as I walked in like I was in some sort of trance. New Year's Day services were underway and I snuck into a back pew and listened to the priest talk.

It had been many, many moons since I attended a church service. My parents stopped going when Nathan's erratic behavior became a concern. The soothing voice of the priest and the quieting hum of the choir calmed and filled me until, before I knew it, the congregation was being dismissed. As people gathered their belongings, my eyes roamed over the crowd and I made contact with another pair of wandering eyes. Eli's mother, her mouth hanging open. Betty Archuletti nudged Al and gestured in my direction, but before he could pinpoint me, I hurriedly exited my pew and dashed toward the back. I couldn't face her. Surely she blamed me for her having lost Eli a second time. I wasn't the only one his absence affected after all. But the crowd in front of me was in no such hurry and people chit-chatted about "the big game" against their rivals, St. Bede's, which, from the tenor of things, I understood to have had a victorious outcome for the St. Mary Margaret Crusaders.

"Faith. Faith, wait." Betty bustled toward me, weaving through parishioners like a seasoned veteran.

I cringed, dreading what would surely be an ugly confrontation in a public place, but when I turned around they were smiling at me. Despite that fact, I almost cringed when she threw her arms around me, as if expecting a blow.

"How are you? We haven't seen you for so long. What have you been up to? Did you change your hair?"

Unsure of where to start with the flurry of questions, I decided to begin with the last, and least complicated. "I did get it cut differently." She fluffed my slightly shorter hair which now contained a few subtle layers framing my face.

"It looks good, honey. Don't you think so, Al?"

"Oh, yes. Quite attractive." He smiled brightly.

I ducked my head. "How have you two been?"

"Oh, great," she replied at the same time as Al answered, "Fit as a fiddle."

"Good." I glanced awkwardly about as people passed us. After a pause Al and Betty exchanged glances.

"Still at the diner?" Al asked finally.

"No. I'm a sono-technician now at Bellevue."

"Oh, that's nice, dear. Did you go back to school, like Eli?"

"Go back to—" The sound of his name broke my focus. "—school? No. No, I didn't. Eli...went back to school?"

"Yes," Betty said, proudly, almost clapping her hands in her excitement. "He's studying architecture."

"Architecture...that's fantastic. I always said he'd be a great architect." I had to share his mother's enthusiasm. "I'm kind of surprised you're talking to me," I blurted out.

She looked confused. "Why wouldn't I want to talk to you?"

"Well—" I stammered, feeling my face flush, "—I was worried you would resent me for...chasing Eli off."

"Resent you?" She grabbed my hands. "No, Faith, not at all." She peered earnestly into my eyes for a minute, then looked down and added quietly. "I know Eli has his problems...but *you*—" She squeezed my hands, annunciating each word. "—*you* were the best thing that ever happened to him." When she looked up again she had tears in her eyes to match the ones in mine. She hugged me and I fought to control my emotions.

Al patted us on the back. "Now you ladies stop that or you'll have me bawling like a baby." I glanced up and to my surprise tears were in the dear man's eyes, too.

Betty and I laughed, and she released me to take her husband's hand. She turned back. "We'd love to have you over for dinner some time." She must have seen a look of panic in my eyes. "We won't even bring up Eli's name if you don't want us to."

I smiled, relieved. "I'd like that." We exchanged hugs all around, and then the couple took off, holding hands. I thought about how nice it was that Betty had a second chance at love.

When I got to the street, I couldn't face going home yet. I turned and headed up the street in the opposite direction. It had begun to snow again, this time minute flakes that were blowing into my face and eyes. I bent my head and trudged up the street, thinking about Betty and Al, and Eli...and Doc. Was it possible *I* could have a second chance at love? I walked and walked, and when I looked up, finally, to get my bearings, I realized I was only a few blocks from Doc's. My feet kept walking automatically, and my heart started feeling lighter. When I got to his place, I trotted up the stairs, all ten stories' worth, and knocked on his door. As I stood waiting for him to answer, I started feeling anxious. What was I doing? I couldn't have a relationship with Doc. Doc was my friend, my cohort, my comfort. What if I messed that up?

I turned back around and ran down the hall, bursting into the stairwell. Without letting up, I scrambled down the stairs, practically sliding across the landings in my haste. I was so intent on my escape, I didn't hear someone coming up.

CHAPTER SIXTEEN

M*ax* My morning jog was enjoyable despite the chill in the air. I'd allowed my mind to wander to thoughts of Faith without censure. Ever since I met her, my womanizing days came to an end. When my habitual flirting occasionally drew attention from some woman, I was quick to end it. I came to realize that was not what I wanted any more. I wanted someone like Faith. And now she was free from Eli, I was determined to make her mine. I could tell it was going to take some time. I was willing to put money down whatever caused the two of them to break up messed her up inside pretty good; I could see it in her eyes. I chuckled as I remembered her parting comment, to save her stockings for the next time. Wouldn't I love that?

These thoughts filled my mind as, low and behold, the love of my life came barreling around the corner of the stairs and almost made me do a header down the stairwell. "Hey. Hey." I grabbed her forearms to steady her and her green eyes flashed up to mine. Pain was in them, and I pondered whether to explore it, or lighten the mood a little. Trying to read her, I opted for the latter. "So, you've reconsidered then?"

She looked at me confused.

"My offer. You know...to make your stained reputation worthwhile?" Her face flushed and she dropped her eyes and squirmed a little, like she always did when I teased her. I slipped my hand over her shoulder. "How about keeping me company while I make myself some breakfast? Are you hungry? Have you eaten?"

"No, actually. I'm starved." She relaxed and gave me a weak grin.

"Well, we can't have you passing out in the stairwell. Come on up." We fell into step together. "Why are you in the stairwell to begin with?"

"Um...I have this thing about elevators."

"Oh, yeah. Eli told me that." I immediately regretted mentioning his name as she became quiet again. I looked at her profile. She was wearing a sweater and down vest and a multi-colored knit cap pulled down over her ears. Her hair, which was always this incredibly rich color of golden brown, tumbled out of the cap and curled softly below her shoulders. Her skin was creamy, off-setting her thick, black eyelashes, and her cheeks had a rosy tint to them from being outside in the cold. Her nose turned up a tad, and right now she reminded me of one of those idealized drawings of children that used to be on the Charmin toilet paper packages.

When we got upstairs, I let her in and immediately went to the kitchen, droning on and on endlessly about nothing in particular, and making her laugh now and again as I cooked. She sat on one of the stools looking into the kitchen and listened, adding a bit here and there, but mostly letting me talk. As I waited for the eggs to cook, I came back over and leaned on the counter between us. "You're quiet this morning." She glanced away then raised her sensational green eyes to mine.

"Am I?" I could see she forced her smile. "I don't mean to be."

"You don't have to pretend with me, babe," I said quietly. "If you're upset, and you want to talk about it, fine. If you don't, that's fine, too."

She sighed, playing with the stocking cap she had removed from her head and set on the counter. "Doc, do you think it's strange that I'm still hung up on...Eli?" She couldn't even say his name without wincing. She didn't lift her head.

I looked at her thoughtfully. "I guess I'd have to know the reason for your breakup to be able to properly judge that."

She pulled on the yarn of her stocking cap with her long fingernails for several seconds without responding, coming dangerously close to unraveling it. Just when I'd decided she wasn't going to talk about it, she spoke up. "Something...*really* bad happened." Her voice was small and quivered like a tightrope walker. "I was upset. I told Eli it was over. And he moved to Chicago without saying goodbye, which was my fault because I told him to go..." Her voice trailed off. She still worked steadfastly at destroying her hat.

I covered her hands with my own. "You loved him, Faith. That doesn't change because he's in another place."

She swung off her bar stool and paced behind the counter. "Yeah, but it's been *over a year*. What's wrong with me?"

I came around the counter. "Nothing's wrong with you. Some loves just...don't die." And didn't I know it.

She stopped pacing and looked at me for a second, then unexpectedly rushed into my arms, laying her head down on my chest. I dropped my hands over her with a sigh and laid my cheek on top of her head. I closed my eyes and breathed in her heavenly scent. Too quickly for me, she pulled away, blinking tears back as she looked up at me.

"Thank you, Doc. Thank you for always managing to be here for me, and always knowing just what to say."

For a man who was supposed to know the right thing to say, I was suddenly speechless as I looked into her eyes. The moment spun out for a second; then I hastily pulled her into my arms for a quick squeeze. "Now, I better get our eggs before they burn." I left her and returned to the kitchen, rolling my eyes at myself with a disgusted sigh. I filled our plates and brought them out to the mini dining room table that sat on a swatch of burgundy carpeting under a chandelier my landlord let me install.

"These are great." At first, she dug in with relish. After a while, though, she was picking at a piece of egg on her plate, rolling it over and over again. She had become quiet once more.

"Faith?"

"Hmm..." she answered distractedly, not looking up from her egg boulder.

"Can I ask you a question?"

She finally noted my serious tone and set her fork down, only to start drumming her fingers lightly on the table. But at least she was looking me in the eyes. "Yes."

"The really bad thing that happened...was it the car accident?"

She blinked. "No. It was after that."

I absorbed this information. "How did you know he was drinking before the accident?"

"They told me in the hospital."

I hesitated, my elbows on the table, fingers interlaced. "Was Eli injured?"

"No," she said with a look of concentration as she remembered. "I thought so at first. He was passed out. But it was from the alcohol, not an injury, and the blood all over him was mine."

Despite being a surgeon, the image had the eggs surging in my stomach. I turned my head with a grimace, a small noise of disgust escaping my lips as I slammed my hand on the table. Her eyes flashed up to mine and I realized I frightened her. "I'm sorry," I said with more calm than I was feeling. I phrased my next question carefully. "Did you know he had been drinking when he got behind the wheel?"

"No. Even looking back, there were no clues. He seemed fine, absolutely fine." She frowned. "He did ask me if I wanted to drive, though, which was unusual...I guess I should have figured it out. But he was going to meetings. I thought it wasn't even a possibility. I guess it's always a possibility with an alcoholic, but I thought I'd recognize the signs." She shook her head, still disbelieving. "He seemed fine." She clutched the tablecloth in her hands.

I laid my hand over hers again and she relaxed it. "Oh. Sorry."

I shook my head. The tablecloth was of no consequence. "When you found out," I started, determined to have my answer, "you just...*forgave* him?"

She shook her head. "Not at first. I couldn't even look at him at first. I called my parents to take care of me during the first days of the recovery, and I spent six weeks on my own. But when I returned to work, I would see Eli on my route. I went the other way for a while, to avoid him, but I thought I was being immature or something, so I deliberately walked by the site." She sighed. "Eventually he asked for forgiveness, and I gave it to him."

She looked up and must have seen the coldness in my eyes because she stood abruptly. "I know that isn't what you wanted to hear, Doc," she snapped. She was so raw in those first few days, anything would set her off. "You think I'm a fool, and you're probably right." She snatched up her plate, and started heading to the kitchen, but I jumped up and grabbed her elbow.

I took her plate from her and laid it down on the table. "I don't blame you. I understand what it's like to be a fool for love." *Only too well.* "I admire your loyalty to him. I don't think many people would be able to be that forgiving." Finding myself becoming angry again, I collected her plate and mine so I didn't have to look at her. "I know *I* wouldn't," I couldn't help but grumble. She followed me into the kitchen, where I, very businesslike, with suppressed fury, scraped the food down the disposal and rinsed the dishes off to put into the dishwasher.

As I closed the dishwasher, her arms slipped around me from behind. She rested her head between my shoulder blades. "Please don't be angry with me."

I sighed, letting the anger drain from me with the air. I turned in her arms and cupped her face to raise it so I could speak directly to her. "I'm not angry, honey. Not at you." Doubt shrouded her eyes. "Listen...you said work cancelled out on you. What are you doing for the rest of the day? Do you want to catch a movie or something?"

She looked thoughtful. "No. I've got a lot on my mind. I think I should go home and sort through it."

"Okay, but while you're thinking, add this to it." I kissed her, letting one hand go to her waist, the other under her hair, cradling her neck. She responded, pressing me back against the counter and sliding her pleasantly cold hands underneath my running shirt. The kiss was long and heartfelt and began to accelerate into areas from which, had it gone on much longer, there would have been no return. We pulled back simultaneously. We looked at each other for a long second, and then I shook myself. "Do you want me to give you a ride home?"

"No, the air will clear my head, which needs clearing, by the way, after that kiss." She smiled at me slyly and I was thrilled the kiss affected her so. "Thank you for breakfast," she said over her shoulder as she went to retrieve her worried hat and vest.

"Hey, I'll be happy to make breakfast for you anytime," I rejoined suggestively. She turned and gave me a cute smile as she pulled on her gloves, and even from across the room, she sent me into orbit. She walked back to me slowly, and my body tensed, but she gave me a quick kiss and left, throwing a "bye" at me on the way out.

My hands released their sweaty hold from the counter, and I decided the shower I planned for after my run had probably better be a cold one.

FAITH

Monday morning rolled around and I was glad to have work to distract me from thoughts of Doc, or so I thought. I was escorting a patient out when Brendon came up to me. "There's a doctor outside who wants to talk to you." He had a strange look on his face which made me nervous. Had I screwed something up?

But as I rounded the corner I caught sight of Doc leaning casually on the front desk, talking to the receptionist. When he saw me, he stood, beaming as he held two takeout coffee cups aloft. "Break time?"

I looked at Brendon, silently asking him to cover me, but his eyes were focused on Doc. "Hey, Bren...mind if I go on break now?"

He looked back at me, his face tight, but muttered, "Sure. Whatever."

When I came out the door to the reception area, Doc very naturally put his arm over my shoulder. He whispered in my ear. "Who's that kid behind the desk? Tall, Dark, and Scruggly?"

"Who? You mean Brendon?" I whispered conspiratorially.

"Yeah. The one that's still staring at us," he said, throwing a look over his shoulder.

"Oh," I said, glancing back, too, a little worried. "He's the guy I told you I dated...only it didn't work out. And he's not a kid," I added defensively. "He's only a few years younger than me."

"Really?" Doc replied, and he let his arm drop down to my waist, undoubtedly on purpose, and nuzzled my ear. "I don't like him."

I giggled and squirmed because he was tickling me, but that only seemed to encourage him more, until he was in danger of spilling our coffees. He came to meet me several times that week, and he never put any more pressure on me than to chat over my break time. When Friday rolled around, though, he looked at me over his coffee cup seriously. He had on scrubs because he'd been in surgery all morning and he looked beat. "Are you going to let me take you out tonight?" It was a question I'd been both longing and loathing to hear him ask.

"I'm not sure if I'm ready."

His beeper went off. He glanced at it and stood with a frown. "I've got to go."

"Everything okay?"

"Yeah. It will be," he returned vaguely. "My driver will be there to pick you up at seven. You have until then to get ready to date me."

"Driver? Where are we going?"

He bent over with a smile, giving me a peck on the nose. "You'll see."

"What am I supposed to wear?" I yelled after him, becoming excited despite myself.

"It won't be a problem," he threw over his shoulder.

"What is *that* supposed to mean?" I said to the empty table.

But when I got home, I discovered what he meant. Propped outside my door was a gigantic, white box tied with a red ribbon with a smaller white box on top of it, and one the size of a shoe box next to it. I bit back a smile, scooped my packages up and headed inside. I looked at the big box for a minute, running my hand across its top in goose-pimpled anticipation before tugging on the ribbon ends. When I pulled the lid off, I stared for several seconds before reaching in and carefully pulling out an exquisite, black, full-length ball gown with a huge, satin, gold sash. "Ooh," I gasped with awe and delight. I ran over to my bathroom mirror with it, letting the box drop to the floor. I held it up in front of me and posed, checking it out from every angle. I looked at the bright-eyed girl in the mirror. It had been a while since I'd seen her. Remembering the other, smaller box, I went back to pick it up and pried off the lid. Inside were my thigh-high stockings, freshly laundered, with a note, scrawled in Doc's erratic handwriting.

For the next time.

I laughed out loud and opened the shoe box. Nestled inside were the most gorgeous strappy, little heels that I had ever seen. I couldn't help but squeal again and danced over to my dress happily. I took a long, luxurious shower that almost washed the day away. When I got out, I lathered on moisturizer and pulled on the dress. It had a long-slit that I thought at first was too revealing, but after awhile, I told myself I was being too prudish and that I looked hot. Then I laughed at my own vanity, feeling lighthearted.

It fit amazingly well. I went to pull the stockings out of the box, and found under them a beautiful necklace and earrings. I put the necklace on and then ran to the mirror to see how it looked. I gave a tiny gasp of pleasure. The stiff, V-shaped design hung perfectly across my collarbone, a series of intertwined almond shapes that came to a point that suspended a tear-drop shaped, shining, amber-colored jewel. I trailed my fingertips over it. It looked like it was designed especially for the dress, which was off-of-the-shoulders and veed down to mirror the necklace. The wide, gold sash gave the dress a distinctive flair.

I put the earrings on. They were longer than I usually wore, but I had to admit they looked great with everything else. I pulled my hair up in the back and decided the up-do was definitely the way to go, accenting all the miles of skin from the nape of my neck to where the dress plunged behind. I fussed with my hair, finding a rhinestone comb that I bought on a whim and never wore and stabbed it into my thick tresses. I was still fiddling with it when someone knocked on the door. Glancing at my alarm clock, I saw with distress it was, indeed, seven. I grabbed my purse from off the counter, shoving my lipstick in it and calling, "Coming," while giving myself one last critical check.

When I got to the door and yanked it open, I gaped at the man on my doorstep. He was dressed in a sharp, black-on-black tuxedo, crisp, form-fitting, with a black chauffeur's cap set at a rakish angle. At first Doc seemed to stick to the script he wrote for himself. He had his legs spread, his hands behind his back, at attention. "Ms. Robeson?" he asked formally, keeping his face poker-straight. "I'm here to..." but when he glanced down at me, he seemed to suddenly swallow his tongue, "...to...." His voice faltered, and he gave up. "Wow! When I saw that dress I thought...but I had no idea...man!" A big grin lit his face. "Do we really need to go anywhere?" he asked, pushing us both back into my apartment, his hands on my hips, managing at the same time to close the door behind him.

I laughed and pulled his cap down over his eyes a little. "Do you always get this fresh with your clients, driver?"

"Only the gorgeous ones." I squirmed out of his grip, but he made a lunge for me, which I tried, unsuccessfully, to dodge. "Why do you think I bought you those impossibly high heels? I knew you wouldn't be able to escape from me." He pulled me in to kiss me passionately, but his kisses soon became tenderer, touching my heart more than moving my body. He pulled back, looking me deeply in the eyes. "I've missed you this week." I could tell by the way his chocolate-brown eyes melted that he meant it. And he did it again.

Turned my heart inside out. Playful one minute, and then sliding into serious without even a warning, catching me completely off guard.

"I missed you, too." I was a little uncomfortable saying it, although it was true. "Where are you taking me?"

He chuckled. "So, the lady gets straight to the point, does she? What would you think about joining me at a charity dinner to raise money for cancer research? It's supposed to have a good band. But, if you'd rather not, we could do whatever—"

"No. That sounds wonderful. And you already bought the tickets, didn't you?"

"Yeah, but if you'd rather—"

"It's a great cause, and maybe I could lose my date and climb into the backseat with my driver for a little while," I teased.

"Your wish is my command, madam," he said smoothly, tipping his hat to me. I looped my arm through his and he started to lead me out.

"Wait. I haven't even thanked you yet. This dress is amazing." I swept my hands over the elegant folds of the skirt.

He kissed my hand. "The dress is beautiful. *You* are amazing."

My cheeks flushed. "In any case, it was very thoughtful, and I probably shouldn't have kept it, but...I love it."

"Of course you should keep it. It was made for you. Now, not another word." He closed the door behind us and took my key to lock it for me. I felt like a princess, being escorted out in a ball gown on an otherwise run-of-the-mill Friday evening. The weather was playing along with us, and stayed somewhat mild, although the nip in the air promised the cold weather would not be held at bay forever.

On the way to the hotel, Doc kept up the charade by putting me in the back seat while driving, his eyes twinkling as he talked to me in the rearview mirror. I have to admit, it was quite a turn-on to only see his eyes, and eyebrows and the bridge of his nose underneath his cap. When we got to our destination, he insisted on going around to open the door for me, rather than letting the valet do it, and handing me out of the car. He watched me as I climbed out and then flung his cap into the back before whispering in my ear as we walked up the carpet leading inside, "Maybe this wasn't such a good idea. Every young, eligible doctor in New York City is going to be in here, and lady, with those legs, they're *all* going to want to dance with you."

"Well, unfortunately my dance card is full." I smiled back at him. It was strange how easy it was to fall into this whole Max and Faith thing. A week ago, he'd been an old friend I hadn't seen in years. Now he was...what exactly? As we drew closer to the building, under the protection of a covered walkway, a doorman scurried to hold the door for us with a little bow. Inside the foyer was filled with stately-looking men and women, laughing gaily at private jokes as they waited in line to be escorted to a table. I glanced around. I never attended anything remotely like this in my entire life. The closest thing I'd come to it was my cousin, Charlotte's, wedding, and, even in that, the groomsmen were only wearing suits, and the bridesmaids, dresses of their own choosing.

"What is it, Faith?" Doc asked as we were about to be seated.

"What?" I answered distractedly, my eyes flitting around the room, looking for cues as to appropriate behavior on such an occasion. A full orchestra dressed in white tuxedos played some timeless tune I recognized but couldn't name.

"Is something wrong? Your hands are shaking."

"Oh. Well...I guess I'm a little nervous. I'd be nervous *serving* at a shindig like this, let alone being a guest. Don't forget, I'm used to passing out grits and country-fried steak."

"But you did that with such style and grace," he teased.

"Obviously you weren't there the day Glo tripped me and I fell right in front of Eli and... Well...I'm not always so graceful." Just thinking about it filled me with guilt and sadness. He seemed to notice as he reached across the table and took my hand.

"Let's dance." He stood, and I looked around, my heart ratcheting up a notch.

"But no one else is dancing," I whispered loudly, in a panic.

"Not yet, but they will be." Disregarding my protests he ushered me out onto the dance floor and pulled me gracefully into his arms. We swayed easily together to the music, and my smile began to thaw from my fear-frozen face. "You dance beautifully," he said, his voice deep.

That's when I realized I was dancing. "I-I'm following your lead." We were the only ones dancing, but somehow I didn't seem to mind. After a few minutes, a distinguished looking, white-haired gentlemen and his diminutive wife took the dance floor, nodding to us with a smile.

I looked back at Doc. "You have a certain magic about you. Did you know that?"

"Do I?" he said, seeming genuinely surprised.

"Yes, you do." I reached up to trail a finger over his lips. He grabbed my hand and brought it to his lips again, kissing it as he looked into my eyes. Then he extended his hand so I could spin beneath it. Things were always so easy with him, no complications, no worries. No chasm of darkness waited to swallow him up, as I always sensed with Eli. But it didn't make me love Eli any less. I pushed the thought from my mind as Max led me back to the table.

We were the last couple on the dance floor. In fact, I think we were still there when the whole string section packed up and headed home. As the last note hung in the air, he kissed me sweetly and I responded, "This has been a wonderful evening. Thank you."

"You still wanting to make it with the driver?"

"I don't know. First I have to ditch my date." He smiled, sliding his arm around my shoulder.

"Good night. Thank you." We waved to the last of the band members on our way out.

When the valet brought the car up Max grabbed his hat out of the back and held the door for me, with a grand sweep of his hand. The valets grinned and sat back to watch us with interest. Max climbed in the front adjusting the rearview mirror so he could see me better. "Where to ma'am?"

"Home, James."

He smiled, but I caught a flicker of disappointment in his eyes. He was hoping the night would continue...and, I found, I was thinking the same thing. I thought about it all the way home. When we got to my place, he parked in front of my building and got out to again open my door. "May I see you to your door, madam?"

I looked at him as if contemplating this, but in truth, I had already decided. It gave me an opportunity to study his face. He was trying not to get his hopes up, in case I should refuse him, but the tension showed as he waited.

Along the jawline, and evident in the way one of his cheekbones twitched a bit. I reached out and straightened his tie and then pulled him toward me by it and kissed him. "I'd like that." His smile relaxed his whole face and I realized he had been holding his breath.

On the way up in the elevator, he stood behind me in the back, a hand on each shoulder as a few people piled in after us. As the elevator climbed, I could feel his breath in my hair and he leaned in at one point to brush his lips gently up my neck, knowing the other people in front of us were involved in an argument and oblivious to us. I bit my lip so as not to let a moan escape, but my body melted against his and my hands reached back automatically to hold on to the sides of his legs. When we reached my floor, we rushed passed the couple.

As soon as we were inside the door, his hat hit the floor, and he whirled me around to press me against the door, our mouths searching for each other hungrily. He outlined my figure against the door, his hands running over the silky fabric covering my hips. His mouth traveled down my neck and he whispered my name urgently.

My mind was screaming, *Yes. Yes. This is right. Doc can make it all better. He makes you happy. You can be happy with him* .My eyes were closed as I concentrated on his lips on me, his hands now sliding up to my breasts, mine clenched in his thick hair. I opened my eyes for a second, and I saw the building across the street, Eli's building, and I froze. With a rush, images of Eli began to fill my head, images of us, alone together, in this very room.

"Wait. Doc, wait," I cried out, my heart racing wildly.

"What?" he asked breathlessly, pulling away from me a little. His face was concerned. "Did I do something wrong?"

"No. No," I reassured him. "I just...can we take it a little bit more slowly? Have a drink first?"

He studied me. "Are you sure you are ready for this? Because...I want to do this right, Faith. I don't want you to have any regrets."

His sweetness cut through me. I put a hand on the side of his face. "I'm sure. I'm just...it's been awhile, and I'm...nervous, I guess," I lied.

"Okay," he said slowly, deliberating. He moved away and my body immediately ached for the heat of his. He still held my hands.

"Could you go to the fridge and get us some wine?" I needed a minute to pull myself together.

He looked at me doubtfully. "You're not going to run away or anything, are you?"

My smile came easily. "No. I just need a second."

"Okay." Reluctantly, he let go of my hands and went to the kitchen. When he was out of sight, I breathed a huge sigh.

I wanted this. I knew I wanted this. So why was it so hard to let go of the past? I looked around the little, barren room. This room, as empty and lifeless as it was, was enough for Eli and me. We'd laughed together here, made love for the first time, and the last time, too. I envisioned the little Christmas tree he bought me sparkling in front of the windows, sitting cross-legged on the floor eating Chinese takeout, cooking together...

I turned around and noticed Doc's cap on the floor. I walked over and picked it up, brushing it off reflectively. Eli was gone; and Doc was here. Doc loved me, and I loved him. It was time to move on. Dozens of new memories waited to be made. I only needed to open my heart up again and allow that to happen.

CHAPTER SEVENTEEN

M^{ax} I berated myself as I walked back to Faith's kitchen. Why was it I couldn't seem to keep my hands off the girl for even one evening? I knew she was fragile, yet all I could seem to think of was myself and what I wanted. I pulled a bottle of chardonnay from the refrigerator and got two wine glasses down from the cabinets, the only two there. I was suddenly struck by the thought that the last two people to drink out of them were Faith and Eli. I shook my head and poured the amber-colored wine into the glasses, picking one up and taking a long drink. I set the glass back on the counter and stared at it for a minute. Finally, I decided to take my two glasses into the other room. When I walked in, the lights were out except for a lamp behind an old recliner. Sitting in the recliner, with her legs hanging over the side, was Faith, the driver's cap perched on her head at an angle. Her shoes were off, one leg bent, allowing her dress to fall to her hips, revealing the tops of those fabulous thigh-highs. She smiled at me brightly, crooked a finger and said seductively. "You promised to help me take these off." Her fingers brushed along her legs, and I'm pretty sure my hands started shaking as I looked for a place to set the glasses and tried to roll my tongue back into my mouth. I walked over and stood beside the chair, finally finding my voice.

"Are you sure?"

Looking me straight in the eye, she raised her foot and placed it on my crotch.

"I'm sure."

I'm not entirely clear on what happened right after that because my head exploded, but the next thing I know we were clawing at each other's clothing. She had on one of those teddy things underneath, black with lace and ribbons, and what with the black stockings and black driver's cap, it about sent

150

me over the edge right there. I picked her up in my arms and took her over to the bed, setting her down awkwardly because of the height—that was one thing I would have to change, I thought.

She lay on the mattress and I squatted at her feet and pulled her stockings off slowly, laboriously as I did the last time, rubbing her and kissing her as I did. Once off I slid my hands up to her hips, where I grabbed her and pulled her strongly toward me, rising over her at the same time to kiss her, her lips full and welcoming. I shifted my weight to the side, leaning on one elbow, and turned my head to look down the length of her long, lean body. She lay still beside me, taking in deep breaths as she watched me.

I ran my hand down her torso and deftly unsnapped the teddy between her legs. I pushed it up over her smooth stomach, and brought my hands again down over her lovely, bare hips. I leaned over her again to kiss her, and I realized with sudden clarity what I wanted more than anything was to be able to show her how much I loved her, to take this burning need for her inside, and somehow translate that in a way she could understand, and not only understand, but feel. For the first time in my life, I'd found someone I was willing to be selfless for, someone whose needs were more important to me than my own.

As these thoughts were crossing through my mind, I came to the slow realization something was horribly wrong. Faith had become very stiff under me, and now began to shake. I pulled back to search her face, and to my dismay, found her concentrating her focus on some distant corner of the ceiling, trying to force the tears back that threatened to spill from her eyes. Her face was white with some unseen horror and I was almost afraid she was going into convulsions.

"What's wrong?"

As soon as I let up on her a little she rolled over on her side and tried to curl up in a ball, wracked with sobs. I was terrified. "Oh, no. No," she cried over and over again. Then she began to gasp for air. "I can't breathe. I can't breathe!"

"Please, honey. You're going to hyperventilate. Relax. It's okay." I rubbed her back trying to console her.

"No. It's not okay!" she screamed between shuddering breaths. "It's not okay. It will never be okay."

"Faith, please...tell me what's wrong."

"I can't..." she started; then she began to mumble something over and over again.

"Okay, take it easy," I said, trying to keep my voice calm. "Take deep even breaths. And when you're composed, you can explain to me why you're upset."

"I'm upset because I'm a *headcase.*"

"A headcase? Who told you that?"

"He did."

"Eli?"

"No. Brendon. And he's right."

"Brendon? You mean that kid at the hospital?"

"*He's not a kid!*"

"Okay, okay. He's not a kid," I said to placate her. "Faith, look at me." I tried to roll her on her back and she went ballistic.

"*Don't touch me. Don't touch me!*" she screamed hysterically, curling up tighter. "Okay." The hurt and shock were a gut shot. I moved away, sitting up. She immediately rolled over and reached out for me.

"Oh, Doc. I'm sorry. I'm so sorry. I didn't mean it." She laid her head in my lap sobbing, but I didn't know what to do. Should I try to hold her? Or would she freak out again?

"*He* did this to me. He did this to me!"

"Who did? Brendon?"

"No."

"Eli?" I asked, confused.

"No. Aaron."

"Aaron? What the hell are you talking about?"

She raised her head then, her arms still wrapped tightly around her body. "I came home from work." When she saw I was listening, she continued, slowly at first, then the words started tumbling from her. "He followed me into Eli's bedroom. At first, I thought he was joking around, but...he locked the door and threw me on the bed. He hit me." Her words were coming so fast I had to concentrate to keep up.

"Aaron hit you?"

She nodded.

The horror of it rocked me.

"He made me...u-unb-button—"

"Oh, my God."

She looked at me beseechingly. "I screamed, but no one heard me."

"Oh, Faith. No."

"I tried to fight him, but..." Tears ran down her beautiful, horror-stricken face.

I imagined how useless it would have been, her body against his massive brawn. "You couldn't."

"He tried to...rape me. Doc, he tried to rape me!" The way she shouted it at me, it was as if it just happened, and maybe it remained that way for her.

My mouth couldn't form any comforting words. I'd gone numb. How could this have happened? My mind reeled. "Where was Eli?" I asked suddenly, but the sobs were coming so thickly now I couldn't make sense of her garbled phrases. Heedless of her earlier warnings, I grabbed her up into my arms and rocked her like a baby.

"Why? Why did he do that?" she cried over and over again.

And I answered her. "I don't know. I don't know, baby." I held her while she rode out the storm of her grief, overwhelmed by my own shock over her pronouncement.

After about fifteen minutes, she shivered and I reached to pull her comforter over her. I sat with my arms wound tightly around her, rocking a little and kissing her hair.

"It's okay, baby. I've got you now. No one's going to hurt you." After another long while, she quieted some and became heavy. "Are you tired? Do you want to sleep?" She nodded, and I started to let her go so she could lie down, but she clung to me. Awkwardly I adjusted so I was lying on the edge of the bed, and she was lying beside me on her side, her head on my chest. I stroked her arm.

I thought she was asleep, but she startled me by saying, "I'm sorry, Doc."

"Don't be."

She sat, looking down on me. "I ruined a perfect evening."

"No, you didn't. No, you didn't," I chided. "Come back here." I pulled her into my arms.

After a moment, I said, "I'm glad you told me."

"I'm sorry I hurt you, Doc. I d-didn't mean to." Her voice was full of emotion.

"Oh, Faith. That doesn't matter."

"Yes it does. To me it does." She leaned on her side then and stroked my face with her hand. "I wanted to...I did..."

"I know. It doesn't matter now."

"Yes, it does. It does matter. *You* matter to me. More than I can tell you." She bent and kissed me, her hand still on the side of my face, and her tears hit my cheeks. I smiled through my own tears and turned my head to kiss the inside of her hand.

My throat was tight. "Thanks."

She laid down again, practically on top of me, pressing her warm body to mine. Eventually, she drifted off, but I sat awake for hours, thinking what she must have gone through. The thought of Aaron taking his hands to her... I wanted to kill him. I wanted to hunt him down like the dog he was and make him pay for every last thing that he'd done to her. How could a guy who was twice her size, three times her size, use his hands to harm her? How could a guy who I had worked beside, laughed with, drank with...force a woman to...I didn't even want to imagine it. Then, with a doubled sense of shock, I remembered I had run into Aaron before Christmas and took him out for a drink. I sat across the table from the man after he attacked Faith when she was alone and defenseless. It made me sick.

And then it dawned on me. This was the thing, the "very bad thing" she said happened causing Faith and Eli's breakup. But why? I would have thought something like that would have brought them closer together. As I sat and pondered that, she began to move in her sleep. She moaned and was quiet, then, a few seconds later, she moaned again. I was about to wake her, thinking she was having a bad dream, when she began to talk, her words distinct in the dark stillness of her room.

"Don't. Please, leave me alone. ...No, don't touch me!" She sounded frightened, and I knew she must be reliving it. Her head moved from side to side on my chest. I froze. My heart sped up, and it was as if I was there, too, like some strange voyeur, watching what Aaron was doing to her, hearing her cries. "Eli! Help me!" she called out. "Help!" She finally screamed so loudly she woke herself and she struggled away from me in a panic.

I sat and grabbed her arms. "It's okay." She shook the hair that had fallen down in front of her face out of her eyes, which were wide and disoriented, her breathing coming in great rasping gulps.

"No!" She struggled against me, but then she seemed to realize where she was, though her eyes still searched the dark recesses of the room uncertainly.

"Faith, it's okay, honey. No one's going to hurt you." She closed her eyes, and tears rolled down her face unchecked. She brought one hand to her mouth and my hand slid down to her wrist. "Your pulse is racing. Come here, lay down again. Let me take care of you."

She slumped against me. "I'm so sorry."

"Shhh." I stroked her hair and she calmed down.

"I haven't had a dream in weeks," she muttered, sounding frustrated with herself. She abruptly rose to one elbow, looking down at me and messing with the edge of the blanket as she spoke. "You can go, Doc...if you want to. I understand."

I pushed up on my elbow, too. "Why would I do that?"

"Doc, I know what I am. It's okay. You don't have to pretend." She wasn't looking me in the eye.

"What are you talking about?"

"Doc!" Her voice was edgy now. It was obvious she was getting angry at me for not understanding her, but I had no clue as to what she was suggesting. She let out an exasperated breath, sitting up all the way and clasping the covers to her chest and looking away from me. "I c-can't even make love to you. I'm...messed up...damaged...a headcase."

Damn that Brendon kid for ever saying that to her. I put one hand on her shoulder, but she wouldn't turn to look at me. "You are none of those things. And even if you were, it wouldn't matter. I love you," I blurted out. Having said it, I didn't see any reason to stop. "I've loved you since the first moment I laid eyes on you."

She turned her head now and looked at me in wonder. Instinctively I took her hand.

"But you were already Eli's, so I couldn't say anything."

She looked down at my hand as I gently rubbed my thumb over the back of hers. "I love you, too," she said quietly. "Before New Year's, I always thought of you as Eli's friend—well, Eli's and my friend, because you were always so good to me, right from the start—but when I saw you again at Amber's, after all that time, I started to feel differently. At first it was confusing, but tonight..." A pained expression crossed her face and she withdrew her hand putting both hands on the side of her forehead. "It doesn't matter. It doesn't matter because it can't work."

"Why?"

"Why? Because...you're Doc. Doc who's...well, you know..."

"N-no, I don't," I said slowly, honestly puzzled.

"Eli and the boys told me you've been with...quite a few women."

"What's that got to do—" I started angrily.

"Obviously the...physical nature—" she said, choosing her words carefully "—of a relationship, is important to you."

"Now wait one minute," I blustered; then I realized, I deserved that. I sighed, rubbing my face with my hand. "You're right. Before I met you I was...not at all select about the women I was around," I said cautiously. "And after I met you, I did sleep with Amber to try to get you out of my mind. But it didn't work. Since her, there's been no one." I grabbed her chin and turned her head so I could look her in the eyes. "*No one.* No one has even appealed to me in the least, because none of them were you, not even close."

Her eyes widened in surprise, but her brow wrinkled again. "But you saw what happened tonight, I wasn't even thinking about...wh-what happened with Aaron, and my body just...reacted. I couldn't stop it."

"So you think I'm the kind of guy who would just...leave...when I found out about what happened to you?" *Is that what Eli did? Is that why she thinks I would, because he did?*

"I didn't know what you would do. I didn't want you to find out in the first place," she admitted.

"Why? This doesn't change the way I feel about you. Listen, like you said yourself, I've had many physical relationships with women before. I'm not looking for that anymore. I want more. I want you."

Tears ran down her face and she shook her head. "I can't believe you—" She stopped, appearing totally overcome and speechless.

I think I loved her more in that minute than I ever did before. I brushed her tears away. "And as far as the...physical...part of our relationship goes, I'm willing to take whatever you can give me."

"Oh, Doc." A smile finally found its way to her face. She flung her arms around me, squeezing me tightly. "I want to give you so much," she whispered. "I only hope that I can."

I held her close, whispering in her ear. "We'll take our time. Everything will be fine. In fact, everything is going to be great." We stayed that way for several minutes, and I could feel her relax within my arms. "Now...it's two o'clock in the morning. You should get some rest. Can I stay with you?" I added softly.

She reached up and stroked my face again, and then kissed me tenderly. "Yes. Please stay."

And so I did. That night, and the next, and many more after that.

CHAPTER EIGHTEEN

F*aith*
    "I want you to go away with me for the weekend."

He had pulled me into a short, dead-end hall of the hospital that was almost always vacant. I looked at Max warily. It had been three weeks since he took me to the charity dinner and we'd spent nearly all of our free time together. He was loving and sweet, and the consummate gentleman, never pushing things beyond where I felt comfortable and seeming, somehow, to know exactly where those lines were.

"This will be strictly on the up-and-up. I promise not to coerce you into doing anything. I'll even get you your own room if you want. I just thought that it would be nice to get away together."

"Well, where do you want to go?" I asked, becoming cautiously excited.

"Oh, I don't know. I was thinking about the mountains, or the beach. When was the last time you've been to the beach?"

"I've never been to the beach."

"You've *never* been to the beach?"

"No. We never really went anywhere as a family, because of Nate's unpredictable behavior. And I've never been able to afford it on my own."

"Well that wouldn't be a problem. It would be my treat."

"Oh, no. I couldn't let you do that. I've got money now. I'll—"

"Absolutely not. It's my treat. And you will be treating me when I get to see you in a bikini." He grabbed my hips and pulled me to him. He nibbled on my neck, distracting me while I tried to respond to him.

"I don't know, Doc. You already bought me that gorgeous dress. And you never let me pay for anything when we're out. I don't want this to be a lop-sided relationship. I want to be able to give back to you as much as you give to me."

"Faith," he said, suddenly serious, "you give to me everything that matters. I make outrageous amounts of money. But it means nothing if I can't spend it the way I like. And I like spending it on you. Besides," he said, turning playful again and whispering in my ear in a way he knew drove me insane. "I know you're only after me for my body anyway."

"Well, that is true." I kissed him happily. "But still...I'm already withholding...certain pleasures...from you. Am I supposed to keep taking from you and giving you nothing in return?"

He reached up and played with my hair silently for several seconds. He looked deeply into my eyes, his own eyes darting between my eyes as he spoke. "You've given me *so much*. I've never been happier than I've been since New Year's."

"I feel the same way."

"Good," he said, as if the matter was decided. "Then you'll go with me."

So, a week later, after trading shifts around to make a long weekend, Max drove up in front of my apartment building and threw my suitcase into his car's trunk. He came back and kissed me. "This is going to be so fun." He held my hand and chit-chatted with me and I was so distracted I didn't realize we were at the airport until we practically parked the car in the parking garage.

"I thought we were driving to the beach."

"Well, I suppose we could if someone built some massive bridges." He grinned, getting out of the car.

I hurried out after him. "Where are you taking me?" I asked, trying to look stern, but feeling a smile spread across my face.

He opened the trunk which muffled his reply, but I still heard, "Hawaii."

I raced around the back of the car. "You're taking me to Hawaii?"

He whipped the bags out of the trunk and set them on the concrete to close it again. "Yep. Oh, and it's not for four days, it's for a week." He picked up the bags and started walking, his smirk a mile wide.

"What? But I have to work on Tuesday."

He paused at a crosswalk, looking straight ahead as cars whizzed past us. "Actually you don't." He turned, finally, to look at me. "I talked to that Brendon fellow. He's got your shifts covered."

"Brendon's working my shifts?"

The light turned and he picked up our bags and started walking across the street to the terminal. "Not all of them, but he got others to fill in."

When we hit the sidewalk, I grabbed his arm and made him stop and turn toward me. "We're going to Hawaii for a week?"

"Uh-huh."

"I love you, Maxwell Theobold III." I grabbed his face in delight and pulled him in for a kiss.

"I love *you*, Faith Anne Robeson," he said seriously. "Now come on. We don't want to miss our flight."

"I've never flown anywhere before."

"Well then, I guess you're in for a lot of firsts this trip."

The trip was fantastic. We stayed up drinking, or dancing, or just playing cards. During the days, we did sightseeing, or shopping, or lay on the beach. He spoiled me with dresses and jewelry...and just by being Doc. And, true to his word, we had separate rooms, although we spent every night together in one or the other. But never once did he push me to do anything beyond what we did before.

The last night of our stay I was feeling kind of sad, thinking our magical time together had come to an end. We were out on our own little patio, off the rooms in the beautiful hotel Max chose, and we were drinking the day's special, banana boat drinks. We sat in a double-wide teak lounge chair and watched the sunset. I laid my head on Max's shoulder with a sigh. "I can never thank you enough for this week. It has been absolutely heavenly." We were holding hands under a blanket Doc dragged off the bed. A storm was brewing and it had turned a little colder and we still had on our swimming suits from the beach.

"This has been great. Maybe we can open our own place here. You can do sonos and I'll perform the surgeries."

"We may need a little help," I answered wryly. "Like an anesthesiologist, and nurses, and—"

He put a finger over my lips. "Don't ruin my fantasy."

We were silent for several minutes, and then I turned my body toward him under the blanket, running my hand up his thigh. "Tell me more about your fantasy, Doc," I asked suggestively.

"Well," he said kissing me, "it stars this very hot brunette with these incredibly green eyes." And then he kissed me, taking me under, in the simple way he had, washing away everything but he and I and my desire for him. This time I listened to my body as it cried out for him.

"Make love to me," I said breathlessly.

He froze, peering into my face as the last rays of the sun warmed it. Slowly he moved forward to take my lips again, softly, seductively. My body melted with his touch. I moaned and shifted so he was over me. His kisses became more intense and his hands caressed my skin, running along my sides with a desperate skill. He reached behind to untie my top and then those wonderful surgeon's hands were on my breasts, taunting me, kneading me, making me think of a number of firsts I'd like to try with him.

Abruptly he pushed up on his arms. "I can't do it."

"What? Why?" I tried to keep the pleading note out of my voice.

"I can't. I promised you I wouldn't make you do anything."

"You're not making me," I said, reaching for him again. "I'm asking." I kissed him. "And pretty soon I'm going to be begging in a very undignified manner if you don't give in to me." I let my lips try to persuade him, my tongue hungry for his.

He moaned and seemed to give in, coming back to me and responding to my kisses until I was filled with an almost primal need for more of him.

I decided to debase myself shamelessly as his lips left mine to kiss my throat. "*Please,* Doc."

He raised his head. I opened my eyes slowly.

"Dammit, Faith. You don't fight fair." He got up and let the blanket drop back over me and went inside.

I sat stunned for a minute, not understanding what had just taken place. As I fixed my top, I couldn't help but feel slightly humiliated, and the thought of having hurt Doc's feelings made tears spring to my eyes. As I stood to go in after him, he opened the door to come out.

"I'm sorry. That wasn't right for me—" He wrapped me up in his arms and didn't speak, squeezing me tightly.

"I'm sorry. I didn't mean to...I..." We'd never fought before; another first. And being the first, it hurt more. My voice broke, giving me away.

"Oh, honey." He pulled back, putting his hands on either side of my face. "I upset you."

"No, I..." But the tears would come, no matter how hard I tried to stop them.

He searched my face. "Why are you so upset?"

"It's just...I..." I felt totally ridiculous trying to articulate my feelings of rejection. I hung my head. "You don't want me like that anymore?"

"I don't want you?" He laughed. "Honey—" he placed both hands on my shoulders, ducking his head to try to catch my eyes "—I want you so badly it aches. But I *promised* myself, no matter how hot you looked in your swimming suit—and, you did, by the way. In fact, it should be illegal for a woman to look that good in a swimming suit. But, more importantly, I promised you, *that* wouldn't happen this week. I didn't want you to feel any pressure, or to feel like this trip was some kind of bribe, or you had to reciprocate in some way."

"I don't feel that way. I want to make love to you. It's been so wonderful, and it's about to end, and I thought it would be a great place for us to...be together...for the first time."

"First of all, our time together isn't coming to an end, it's only beginning." He brought my hand to his lips and kissed it. "And, second of all, it wouldn't matter if our first time took place on the floor of a gas station, it would be magical because it would be me and you." He kissed my other hand. "Now, forgive me for being such a big jerk."

I smiled. "You're forgiven."

He raised his eyebrows. "One last walk on the beach?"

"Sure, let me grab my sweatshirt and some jeans."

And so we walked hand-in-hand on the beach together, each caught up in our own thoughts. I stopped and came to stand in front of him. The wind blew my hair, and I had to raise my voice above the crash of the waves. "I know I have no right to ask you this, but...bring me here again someday?"

He laughed, grabbing me up in his arms and lifting me off the sand. "You got it, gorgeous." And I knew he would.

It was late when we got back from New York. We trudged into his place, dragging our bags with us. As soon as we were in the door, before he even turned the lights on, Doc dropped the bags he was carrying with a loud

THUD. Before I even knew what was happening, he swept me up in his arms. I shrieked in surprise. "We're not in Hawaii anymore," he said with a low growl.

"N-no." I didn't understanding what he was getting at.

"So, all bets are off." Light criss-crossed through the apartment from outside giving us enough light to see by. He kissed me as he walked over to his bed, laying me down delicately on the comforter, his eyes no longer showing a hint of tiredness. He sat next to me. "I want you to tell me if anything I'm doing frightens you, and I'll stop. I swear."

I nodded.

He rubbed my legs and let his gaze linger as it swept over me. I brought my hands to the buttons on my shirt, wanting to prove something to myself. My hands trembled a little as I unbuttoned, but when I looked up and caught the loving way he was looking at me with his warm brown eyes, my hands steadied of their own accord. I wished I had on a prettier bra instead of the plain, smooth, black one I had on, but Max didn't seem to mind as his eyes lit up comically. He rubbed my shoulders, relaxing what little stress remained, his flesh on mine utterly intoxicating.

"Turn over," he commanded quietly. I flipped over and he removed my blouse as I did, and then started to smooth his hands over my back unhurriedly. I closed my eyes and let his strong hands soothe me, surrendering to his touch completely. He leaned down and whispered in my ear. "Do you have any idea how truly beautiful you are?" Then he began to kiss down my back at a leisurely pace that almost felt decadent. He shifted his weight and began to take his thin, black sweater off, but I rolled over quickly and came to kneel beside him and help him to take it off. He kicked off his loafers and peeled off his socks and then stood to take his pants off, but I sidled over to the side of the bed and pulled him by his belt buckle in between my legs as I sat on the edge.

I rubbed my hands appreciatively over his broad chest and then began to kiss his abdomen, which tightened in anticipation. I slowly undid his jeans and they were added to the pile we'd already started on the floor. He sat on the bed, and we kissed as my hands again explored his chest. I pushed him gently down on the pillows and straddled him, letting my hair fall around us as I kissed him, the heat within us rising to a low boil. He brought his hands to my jeans button and I sat to give him better access. He ran his hands up and down my sides and finally let them rest on my hips, half on denim, half on skin.

"You doing okay?" he murmured. I nodded with a smile and it was true; the only apprehension having been at the beginning. He brought his hands around and under the seat of my pants, rubbing gently, discovering each subtle curve of my body. He undid my jeans then sat and scooted back until his back was against the tall, wooden headboard, giving himself room to slide off my jeans and panties. I climbed onto his lap and took him into me with a suddenness that surprised him. He closed his eyes, a look of pained delight taking over his features. When he spoke, his voice was tight. "I don't know how long I can last."

I bent closer. "You'll last longer the second time." I moved my hips, watching his face and feeling a rush of power. His hands went to my bra clasp in the back, working clumsily in his haste. I helped him and threw this last article of clothing from the bed. He sucked my breasts as I grabbed hold of the headboard and gyrated my hips in a way I knew would send him over the edge. He called out my name in his ecstasy and I almost laughed with pleasure. "Oh," he moaned between his labored breathing afterward. "I'm sorry." He laughed. "You're too damned good."

"That's okay." I kissed his nose, and then slid away from him. "You rest, 'cause I'm not through with you yet."

"Oh, man, angel. Whatever I did to deserve you, I hope I do it again." He chuckled again, trying to regain a more regular breathing pattern.

I curled up next to him, and we quickly fell asleep, exhausted from our travels. Sometime later he woke me up, ready to go again, and this time he took me up until I was begging for him and then drove into me until the movement of our sweat-slicked bodies rocked the bed. We took turns throughout the night discovering the secrets of each other's bodies.

At four a.m., as we both lay on our separate pillows trying to catch our breath from the latest go round. "Good thing we gave ourselves an extra day to recover from traveling before heading back to work." I turned my head and smiled at him in the light from the window. "I love you, Faith."

Maybe it wasn't the searing passion I had with Eli, but it had a tender, lasting warmth that didn't flame up and blow out, but rather lit my life with its steady glow. "I love you, too." Maybe things could work out for us after all.

CHAPTER NINETEEN

M*ax* Months followed our trip to Hawaii, months of unrelenting happiness. I'd never understood the pure pleasure of sharing yourself entirely with someone else, mind, body, and soul, until then. Faith seemed so happy, too. I wanted to make it a permanent arrangement.

One day someone knocked on the door of her apartment. I was washing dishes, so she went to answer it. I heard the low murmur of voices arguing, so I set down my dish towel and followed her to the door.

"You *are* Faith Robeson?"

She nodded.

"Then this delivery is for you."

"But I just told you. I didn't order anything."

"I did." I said sheepishly from behind her.

"You ordered something to be delivered to my apartment?"

"Yes. It was supposed to arrive yesterday," I said through gritted teeth as I reached for the man's clipboard. "And I was going to put it together while you were at work and surprise you."

Her eyes sparkled. "I always like your surprises, Max."

"Well, I sure hope you like this one. Bring it in, boys."

She watched as they hauled in piece after piece. "A bed?"

"Lady, we've got a whole friggin' suite of furniture out here," the big, brute of a guy said with a grin.

"You bought me furniture?"

"Yes. But whatever you don't like we can send back. I made sure of that." But, as it turned out, she was thrilled with the sleigh bed, the bedside tables, the sofa, and coffee table.

When the men were all finished and left, she turned from the door with her hands on her hips, her voice stern. "Doc…"

"They had a sale," I said weakly. "Come on. It's no big deal. This is a smidgen of my salary."

"But I'll be like a…kept woman. It's not right."

"No, it's not like that. I just wanted to do something for you. No implications, no strings attached, just a gift."

"Most gifts can be wrapped up with a ribbon and held in your hand."

"I could go get some ribbon…" I suggested playfully.

She laughed. "You're incorrigible. And…I love it. I do. But—"

"Come on. Let me do this for you. Besides, I plan to make full use of the bed."

She sighed, struggling with her internal debate, then smiled. "Well…I guess in that case, it's more of a gift for you than me…"

"It is." I leaped on this. "It's just…my back can't take it on the floor anymore."

She came over and grabbed my hips. "I've never heard you complain about your back before," she said doubtfully.

"Oh, yeah, baby. It hurts."

"Does it?" she said with a smile.

"Mmm…painful," I added, clutching at my back.

"Hmm…well, doctor…what is your prescription for this back pain?"

"I think you need to make love to me, right away, in our new bed. You know, in order for me to regain a full range of motion."

She grinned. "Really?"

"Honest Abe," I said, holding up my hand like a Boy Scout.

"Well, then," she said, tugging on my shirt. "If it's doctor's orders."

We fell into bed and made love in the middle of the afternoon, with the sun shining in and the mattress tags not even torn off.

Later that night, as we lay down to sleep, Faith sat abruptly. "Ouch. There's something in my pillowcase." She reached in and brought out the jewelry box I stuck in there. She quirked an eyebrow. "What is this?"

I examined it, the picture of innocence, then, handed it back to her. "It looks like a jewelry box."

"I know that. What's *in* the jewelry box?"

I shrugged. "I guess you'll have to open it to see."

She looked at me, then, glanced down at the box. Tentatively, she lifted the lid. She gasped. I scrambled out of bed and went around to her side, getting down on one knee and taking her hand. "The past several months have been the best time in my entire life. I love you, and every day I grow to love you more. I want to love you for the rest of your life. I want to have children with you and grow old together and sit around the nursing home embarrassing visitors by talking about our love life. I want to take you places you've never been before and enjoy seeing them through your eyes. I want our children to smile and groan when I kiss you and—" I stopped, really looking at her for the first time. She wasn't smiling. In fact, she looked like she'd been struck. "I've been talking a lot about what I want," I said quietly, "but I didn't even ask you what you wanted. What do *you* want, Faith?"

Her mouth opened but no sound came out. Tears filled her eyes. "I...I don't know. Before you came back into my life, I felt so alone, and all I wanted was for the hurt to go away."

"You don't have to be alone. You'll never have to be alone again. I'm ready. I can make the hurt go away."

She brushed her hand over my face. "You already have. It's just...I haven't really thought about marriage yet. I don't want to make any mistakes—not that marrying you would be a mistake—oh!" She stood, walking away from me, unable to look me in the eye. "I'm not saying this right. You proposed to me for God's sake. The answer should be yes. I shouldn't have to think. That's like a slap in the face. See. I told you I would hurt you. I just...my feelings are so confused at times and I want to do things the right way..."

I put my hands on her shoulders. "It's okay. This is a huge decision, you should think about it. In fact, I would worry if you didn't think about it."

But I can't deny it hurt, initially. The path was *so* clear to me. There weren't any deviations, there weren't any choices—it was her. It was always her. But I knew she went through a lot, with Eli, and then again what she went through with Aaron. Who could blame her for being scared? I knew she loved me. I knew she was happy with me. I was sure she would eventually say yes.

And I was right.

ELI

The phone rang and I dove on my bed, snatching it from my desk at the same time. I answered it with a smile. "What's up, old lady?"

"Oh, Eli." Mom laughed. "How are you?"

"Good. Good. How are you doing?"

"Oh, we're fine. Weather's been a bear lately. Unseasonably warm for this time of year."

"Yeah, in Chicago, too. And you don't want to open your window because of the smog."

"Maybe you should move back to New York...there's no smog here."

"Yeah, right, Mom." I sensed something in her voice and sat straighter. "Hey, what's up? You usually save that whole 'move back to New York' thing for the end of the conversation. What's going on?"

She didn't speak for a moment. "I saw Faith today."

Despite the years away, my heart skipped a beat. "And..."

"She was...with somebody."

I was shocked by how badly it hurt. I wanted her to have somebody, to be happy. Or so I'd always told myself. But to actually hear it... I cleared my throat. "Well...that's good. Good. She needed somebody."

My mom read right through me. "Eli? You're not going to go out and drink, are you?"

I sighed. "No, Mom. I know now that doesn't solve anything, no matter what it is." But I wanted one so badly I was salivating. "Listen, I have a class in about a half hour. I need to go. But I'm fine. Really. Faith needed somebody."

"Okay, son," she said sadly. "Will you call me later?"

"Sure, Mom," I answered tiredly. I hung up the phone. I didn't have a class, but I needed to think.

FAITH

The day was like any other day. Max and I went for a jog and came back to my place for a late breakfast. It was one of those glorious mornings where everyone was that much more pleasant to each other just because of the sunshine. We sat at our little kitchen table by the window, where my bed used to be, and enjoyed eggs and bacon, the reason why we ran in the first place. The phone rang and I hurriedly swallowed my orange juice to pick it up.

"Faith...so good to hear your voice."

The blood drained out of my face and my hair felt prickly. My hands started shaking so badly I had to put my glass down. Doc was reading the paper, not paying any attention.

"How did you...where did you...?" I sputtered.

"Find your number? Well, funny story...I was going through some things of mine and I found this piece of notebook paper with your name and number on it in Eli's handwriting. It was sure nice of him to provide that for me, don't you think?"

"Wh-what do you w-want?"

Hearing the note of panic in my voice, Doc pulled the paper down to look at me from over the top. He straightened. "Faith, who is that?" His voice sounded nearly as frightened as mine.

The voice continued. "Oh, Faith...I think you know what I want. I want you. We never got to finish—"

Doc ripped the phone out of my shaking hands and listened for a second. Then his face went from white to red in a heartbeat.

"Listen, Aaron, you sick son-of-a-bitch—"

I could hear Aaron's overloud voice pouring out of the receiver. "Doc? Is that you? Great. Stupid bitch screws everybody on the crew except for me."

"She is not—" His face became even redder and it was like he'd lost his capacity to speak. I'd never seen him this way.

"You tell Faith I'm coming down there to fucking screw her, too. I'm not finished with her."

"You do that, Aaron. You come down here, because I know what you did to her and I'll make you pay. I'll make you pay for every second you tortured her. I'm gonna—" Doc threw the receiver against the wall and it broke. "Son-of-a-bitch! Son-of-a-bitch!" He pulled his hair back and left his hand on the top of his head. "I can't believe—"

My knees suddenly turned to mush. I reached back for, and fell into a chair. Doc looked up and immediately rushed over to crouch in front of me. "Are you all right, honey?"

I nodded, not able to trust my voice yet.

He stroked the side of my face. "Oh, God. I'm so sorry this happened. But don't worry about a thing. I'm gonna pound that goddamn son-of-a-bitch's face in."

"No," I managed to breathe. "We have to get out of here. We have to go to your place."

"Faith, if you think I'm running away from a fight—"

"Please, Doc. I don't want to see anybody get hurt."

"Thanks for the vote of confidence. I know Aaron's big and all, but—"

"Dammit. This isn't some kind of ego contest. You don't understand. Violence makes me sick, physically sick. I don't want to see *anybody* get hurt, not even *him*." I spat out the word.

"Okay, I'll take you back to my place and then I'll come back and you won't have to see me beat his face in."

"No." I brought my trembling hands to his face, completely distraught now. "That would make it worse. I'd worry about you. *Please, please* do it for me." I could see by his face he was going to argue with me. I had to do something, *something* to stop him. I said the first thing that came into my mind. "Besides, you'll be too happy to pound anyone's face in."

"Really?" he chortled sarcastically. "And why's that?"

"Because...I'm saying yes."

"Yes to what?" he asked irritably.

I smiled. "Yes to you."

"Yes to—" A glimmer of comprehension showed on his face. "You mean..."

I nodded happily. "I thought about it, and I love you. I'll marry you, if you still want me."

He sat on his heels, dumbfounded, unable to go from mad to gleeful in 0.2 seconds. He took my hands and peered into my face. "You mean it?"

"I do."

He picked me up and swung me around, whooping loudly.

I heard somebody nearby yell, "Hey. Keep it down."

When he stopped, I smiled down at him. "Now, please, can I get my fiancé out of here?"

His smile faded slightly. "Geez, Faith. You sure make it hard on a guy's ego. I could take him, you know."

"I know, babe," I responded, kissing his forehead. He let me slide down to my feet. "But I don't want anybody messing up my husband-to-be's beautiful surgeon's hands." I held them in mine.

After a second he grabbed his coat, and walked with me to the door, still holding my hand. "But I could take him," he mumbled as we shut the door behind us.

"I know."

A month or two passed. I'd managed to put off any wedding arrangements. Though I hadn't told Doc, I still felt apprehensive about my decision. Not that Doc wouldn't make the most wonderful husband, the most perfect husband...but I couldn't shake this feeling that somehow it was wrong.

And then I saw him.

We had gone out to dinner to celebrate our engagement, and out of nowhere, I saw him across the street. My heart lurched in a way only Eli could make it. Some say your first love is the strongest. It makes sense. After all, I'd given him my heart. It would only be right for him to still have a part of it.

Had Max been anything but ecstatic about our engagement, he would have noticed something was wrong. I sat next to him in the car, fidgeting with my ring, staring at it as I twirled it around and around on my hand. Max was talking, but I wasn't listening anymore. I sought him out again, although I knew he turned and walked away. Eli.

"Faith?"

"Huh?"

"You certainly are distracted. Rethinking your decision?"

"What?"

"Your decision to have the ring sized."

"Oh. Yeah, yeah. I think I should have it sized down."

"They said that wouldn't be a problem. We'll take it on Friday when we're off."

I gazed out the window. "Okay."

"Are you sure you're okay?"

"I'm fine." I forced a smile and squeezed his hand.

But I wasn't fine. I was as far from fine as I could be. I was engaged to a man whom I loved, while I was in love with another.

CHAPTER TWENTY

E *li* When I saw her with Max it was like the bicyclist who just whizzed past punched me in the stomach. Max. It just had to be Max, didn't it? I turned and walked blindly away, not even knowing where I was going or what I was doing here in the first place. I didn't want to go back to my hotel alone, so I decided to wave down a cab and go to my mother's.

I hadn't told her I was coming, so she nearly broke my eardrums with her squeal. "Eli! Oh, Eli!" I had to smile when she wrapped me up in her arms. I was so glad I made things up with her years ago. It was one of the few things I had done right in my life. Falling in love with Faith was another.

"Come in, come in. Al. Look who's here." She folded her apron up to dab at her eyes as she pulled me into the house. Al came from the back of the house with a dish towel slung over his shoulder.

"You guys weren't eating dinner were you?"

"No, no. We've been finished for a while. Just doing the dishes." He wiped his hands on the dish towel before shaking mine. "You look good, Eli. You've filled out some."

"Yes, sir. I actually eat now, rather than drink my meals."

They chuckled, but I could tell they were a little uncomfortable with me talking about my drinking.

"Well, you do look marvelous, honey." My mom patted my cheek. She eyed me keenly. "So...why are you here in New York?"

I stuck my hands in my pockets, and watched my toes as I rubbed my foot in the carpet, making a rainbow-shaped swipe in the nap. Then I looked up into her eyes. "I came back to see Faith." It wasn't the only reason, but I wasn't ready to tell her the other one yet.

She didn't look surprised. "And did you see her?"

I paused, looking at my foot as it continued its arc across the carpet. "In a sense. I saw her across the street, with Max."

"You know him?" she said, surprised now. She walked over to the couch and sat. Al followed.

"Yeah. I know him. At one time I would have considered him my best friend." I sat in the chair across from them.

"Oh, honey. Are you sure it was him? That doesn't sound like Faith."

"I'm sure, Mom. Max has been in love with Faith almost as long as I have."

My mom looked at Al tearfully and he spoke up. "Well, what are you going to do, son?"

"I don't know," I returned honestly. I sat back in the chair with a sigh, folding my arms behind my head. "And the weird thing is...I hadn't even tried to find her yet. She showed up across the street from my friggin' hotel. Sorry, Mom," I added, knowing she didn't like me using strong language.

My mom and Al exchanged a look. They were smiling now. Al's hands rested on his knees when he pushed up to stand. "You've got to go talk to her, son." My mom nodded beside him, standing, too, and taking his arm. "Sooner the better."

I stood also, protesting. "I just got here."

Al clapped me on the back. "You'll be back when you straighten things out."

"I'm not sure that I can," I sputtered. "I'm not even sure that I should."

"Eli," my mom said, shocked. "Why not?"

"Maybe she's better off without me."

"Better off with her heart torn in two? I don't think so." My mom grabbed me roughly by the arms and gave me a little shake. I was surprised by how strong she was. "And, Eli Batronis, you are a good man. You made some mistakes, but you're sorry for them and you fixed things and that takes a lot of courage in my book."

"Mine, too." Al punched me in the shoulder.

I rubbed my shoulder, starting to feel ganged up on. "I'll go. But I don't know if she'll talk to me."

"Give her a chance, son."

I left their house, feeling somewhat better, but I was nervous about facing Faith. I let her down in so many ways. If I could have done it all over again... But, I couldn't, that was a fact. All I could do was move forward, and I'd have to see in what direction she was moving.

I caught a cab, and as it pulled up in front of her apartment building I was filled with the strangest and most wonderful feeling of homecoming. I got out and paid the cabbie—I think I gave him a twenty dollar tip in my euphoria. I rushed up the steps and into her building. I pushed the button for the elevator, *our* elevator, but it didn't come fast enough. I took the stairs two at a time and arrived at her front door, sweaty and breathless. I banged on it loudly three times and tried to catch my breath.

When she opened it, we stared at one another. She was as beautiful as the day I left, more beautiful even. Doc's voice carried from behind her.

"Who is it, honey?" He came from somewhere behind the door and grabbed a hold of it with one hand, and the frame with his other hand, leaning against them slightly. "Eli." He exhaled my name with what sounded like both surprise and resignation; it felt like a curse. He stared at me for a second, his mouth hanging open and ran his tongue in front of his bottom teeth, his eyes hard. He smiled, or sneered, I wasn't sure which. "Won't you come in?" He backed away from the door with a flourish of his arm, gesturing toward the room. Faith stepped back hesitantly, and I brushed past her, feeling my own jaw tighten.

Max sat on the couch, stretching his arms over the back of it with a proprietary air, playing up his lord of the manor role, but every muscle was tensed. Faith went and sat stiffly beside him. "So good of you to come," he said snidely. "Although I wish you would have called first. Then we could have made sure we had a drink waiting for you," he added with an edge.

I took my eyes from Faith for a moment to glare at him. "I don't drink anymore."

"Really?" He raised his eyebrows in disbelief.

I wanted to punch him.

I sat in a chair closest to Faith, leaning with my arms on my legs, my hands folded, on the edge of my seat. An awkward silence followed in which I stared at Faith with longing, and she stared back at me with a look of shock. Like I'd walked out of her dreams, but whether it was a pleasant dream or a nightmare, I couldn't quite tell. For Max, I was definitely a nightmare. He glowered at me with his show of desperate overconfidence as if he could power me away with his eyes alone.

But, at that moment, it was as if Faith and I were in the room all alone. "How are you?" I asked her, my voice soft.

"She's fine." Max spat, sitting up so quickly Faith jumped. He mirrored my stance, leaning forward aggressively and rubbing his hands together loudly. "So, Eli...where've you been?"

"Chicago," I said to Faith.

"Mmm..."

I finally looked at him and sat back, relaxing my position, but still talking to Faith. "You got furniture."

"That's right," Max answered. "I bought it for her."

Faith shot him a look of displeasure.

"It looks good, but it kind of ruined the whole minimalist thing she had going," I responded with a grin. Faith smiled, remembering, too, the conversation we had the first time I'd seen her place.

Max was not nearly as amused. "Wrecked any cars lately?"

I winced. *Low blow, Max.* Apparently we both knew the scars on her body. "No, I don't drive."

"Lost your license, huh?"

"No. That's been reinstated."

"Three years is a long time to not get behind the wheel." I didn't comment. He looked at me, contemplating. "So, what have you been up to in Chicago?"

"I'm working on my degree in architecture."

He was clearly surprised by this. He nodded his head exaggeratedly, then stood. "It's been good catching up, but Faith and I have a full night ahead of us, don't we, honey?" He put his arm around her, but she glared at him.

I stood slowly, but as I did, I caught a glimpse of the ring on her finger and froze for a second. Noticing, she quickly hid her hand behind her back, like a kid caught stealing a cookie. A hole opened up in my gut, like I'd been kicked by a donkey. I walked to the door stiffly and they followed. When I got through the door I turned back. Max was holding it with one hand, the other on Faith's shoulder. She looked sad. "Good luck in Chicago, Eli," Max said dismissively.

"Yeah," I answered, numb.

He closed the door quietly in my face. Reflexively, my hand shot out to touch the wood. I curled it into a fist, and laid my head on it, closing my eyes. After a minute or two, I left.

FAITH

Three loud bangs on the door sounded. I should have been afraid it was Aaron, but I was still thinking about seeing Eli on the street and my guard was down. When I swung the door open and he was there, I froze in disbelief. After dreaming about this moment for so many nights, to have him just appear seemed so surreal, like I would reach my hand out and it would pass right through him.

He came in. He and Max sniped at each other. And all I could do was force myself to breathe and soak him in. His voice. His voice was so painfully, familiarly, wonderful, like returning to your room after you've been away at college and finding that nothing has changed. Only it was better than that. I wanted to touch him so badly, but I couldn't hurt Doc...wouldn't do that. My heart was so full of love for both of them that its walls strained against the contents and the blood surging through my veins numbed me instead of energizing me.

He talked to me, his green eyes soft and compelling, but Max answered him. Before I even knew what was happening, he got up to leave. It was like my heart was being ripped out a second time. For the rest of the night, I couldn't even function properly. I'd pour myself a cup of water, and set it down somewhere, and then pour myself another cup of water. By the end of the night, I probably had four glasses of water in my little apartment. I didn't sleep well that night. Every time Max touched me I felt myself involuntarily draw back.

In the morning, I slipped out of bed early and got myself a cup of coffee. The first rays of light flickered in the window and set my ring ablaze where my hand hugged the steaming mug of coffee. I set the mug down, to lose it for the morning, and looked at the ring on my hand. I'd dreamed about wearing Eli's ring. I loved Max, truly I did...I could even say I was in love with Max. He definitely had the ability to make my heart soar when he walked into the room, or told me he loved me, or made love to me, and he made me happy. But with Eli...it was like two souls touching, melding...in heartache, and in joy. We'd both been through the ringer, together, and separately, earlier in our lives, before we met, and that kind of connection left its mark. You could not sacrifice and forgive without leaving a piece of your heart with the other. And he needed me. I could feel that.

But at the same time, I knew Max's need for me was real, too. Although he was lighthearted, he wasn't playing at loving me, his commitment was there. And he'd never once hurt me...gave and gave, as a friend, and as a lover. I took the man's ring. I made him a promise.

But I never realized what I was giving up.

I was torn.

MAX

Man, just when you think you have it all, it falls down like a sand castle at high tide. I couldn't believe it when we opened the door and he was standing there. It was my worst nightmare come true. Why now? Why not in a year from now when I had her married?

Faith was moody after Eli left our apartment that night. She didn't say more than a dozen words, and she didn't melt into me like usual when we went to bed. She didn't respond to my touch either, and I needed her so badly. She said it was because she had an early shift in the morning, but that never stopped her before.

She crawled out of the bed at dawn. Without moving, I watched her get dressed. I saw her looking at the ring on her finger, twirling it around, and then watched in horror as she took it off and set it on the dresser. *She doesn't want to wear it to work. It's too big. She's afraid she might lose it.* But deep down, I knew it was a lie.

After moping around the apartment all day, I headed up to the hospital when her shift was supposed to be over.

"Hey ya, gorgeous," I said to Becky, the girl at the front desk at the sono lab. "Is my fiancée available?"

"Fiancée? You mean Faith? You guys are engaged? That's great. Congratulations, Dr. Theobold. Wow. I can't believe Faith didn't tell me."

"She didn't tell you?"

"Well...it has been awfully busy today. We were slammed. Faith has been running around like crazy."

"Hmm." So Faith didn't want to spread the good news. But my concerns were erased when she came out, showering me with her bright smile. "Hey, babe."

"Hey," she said, giving me a kiss on the cheek and looping her hand through mine. "You came in on your day off?"

"Well," I said, stealing a kiss on the lips. "I came in to see my girl, and I thought I'd take you to the jewelry store so we can get this sized." I pulled the engagement ring out of my pocket.

"O-oh, okay." I thought I perceived a slight dimming of her smile, and she glanced away.

The jewelers took her measurement and told me they'd have to send it out to be sized down and that it would be back in a week. I wanted to take it to another jeweler, to see if we could get it sooner, but Faith quickly told them a week would be fine.

I pouted on the way home, but Faith told me she would go to the store and get ingredients to make her cannelloni, which was my favorite, so I perked up. She dropped me at the door and leaned over for a quick kiss, which I tried to lengthen, but she claimed someone needed her spot and zipped away.

I trudged up the stairs a little despondent and waited impatiently for her return. Keys jangled outside my door about an hour later, so I opened it. To my surprise, Eli was messing around with the door across the hall.

He looked over and said casually, "Oh, hey, Doc."

I was dumbfounded. "What are you doing?"

"Hmm?" he responded, feigning innocence. "Oh. Just locking up. This is New York City, you know...Crime Capital of the World."

"No...I mean, why are you messing around at that apartment?"

"Oh, now I see what you mean." He chuckled. "I moved in last night."

"You moved—" All of a sudden his plan became clear. "Geez." I paced in front of Faith's door, running a hand through my hair, then, stopped abruptly. "Man, you're a piece of work, aren't you? You couldn't leave her well enough alone. You had to come back here, just when she's found a little bit of happiness with me. Just when she's gotten past the nightmares of Aaron's hands all over her while you were passed out drunk in the next room."

His jaw tightened and his eyes flashed. "Shut up!"

"Yeah," I stated with conviction. "She never told me, you know. She would never be that disloyal to you. But I figured it out. I figured it out when she was screaming out your freaking name in my bed. Dammit, Eli. Why'd you have to come back here?"

"I love her," he stated simply.

"Do you? Do you really? Well I love her too, man. And I won't go down without a fight. So you can go on and play your little games next door, but it's me she's lying next to in bed every night—"

"Yeah, screaming out *my* name—"

I'd had enough. I went from zero to really pissed off in a heartbeat. I reached back and coldcocked him in the face and immediately blood squirted out of his nose. Before I had time to react, he clocked me one right in the jaw and then we started grappling with each other. The war waged back and forth across the hall, both of us bouncing each other off the walls and not one person came to check on the ruckus. We beat on each other until we stumbled back against opposite walls, producing a short truce inspired by sheer exhaustion. Eli leaned against the wall, and I put my hand down and sat, awkwardly, with my back against the other wall. Both of us were huffing and puffing and staring at each other. Eli wiped the back of his hand under his nose, smearing the blood there while I sat holding my sore ribs.

"Geez, man," Eli finally said between breaths, rubbing his knuckles. "You have a hard-assed jaw."

"Yeah, well you've got a bony chest. You need to put some meat on that."

He grinned. "Nah, what you're feeling there are muscles of steel."

I laughed, grimacing at the pain it caused. "Yeah right."

We both started laughing so hard we didn't hear Faith's footsteps on the stairs. "Uh-oh," I said, catching sight of her.

She rushed up the last couple of steps, dropping her paper sack of groceries on the floor and rushing to my side. "Oh, my gosh! Doc! What happen—" She turned and saw Eli looking back at her sheepishly, blood on his shirt, his face, and his hands. She stood and I scrambled to my feet next to her. "What are you doing here?"

He gestured at his door. "I live here. Moved in last night."

"You what?" She shook her head. "Did you two get into a fight?" She didn't wait for an answer. "You morons!" She looked back and forth between the two of us. "Doc. How could you risk hurting your hands?" She took my hands and looked at them.

"Ooh, Doc. You're in trouble," Eli joked.

She spun around. "Shut up, Eli. What were you thinking?"

"He started it," Eli retorted childishly, pointing at me, but looking suddenly frightened of her. And he should have been. She looked like a hellcat. Faith turned on me.

"Doc?" I shrugged and then I caught Eli's eye. We both started laughing. Without even looking, and quick as a flash, Faith planted her tennis shoe squarely in Eli's crotch, sending him to his knees.

"Ohh!" he cried out. "Shit! Why'd you do that?" he moaned, obviously in considerable pain. I gave him credit for not throwing up there on the spot. "What about him?" he managed to ask, gesturing to me sloppily, and lifting his head a little, though still staying doubled over. "Isn't he gonna get it?"

"Oh, don't you worry about him," she spat. "He's going to be wishing I kicked him in the balls when he sees the cold shoulder I'm going to give him." She stormed into her apartment, and slammed the door shut, leaving the two of us in the hall.

Eli laughed through his pain. "Ooh. I feel sorry for you, man."

"Yeah, sure." I started to pick up the groceries spilled out on the floor. Eli handed me a can of stewed tomatoes that had rolled over by him. I took it. "Thanks."

"I've got an open couch if you need it," he called as I opened the door to Faith's place. He was still too weak to rise.

"In your dreams, pal," I retorted, but I couldn't help but give him one last grin before I closed the door.

CHAPTER TWENTY-ONE

Faith

F I was so upset with Doc I didn't talk to him for the rest of the evening. I refused to cook my cannelloni, but I almost felt sorry for him while he sat glumly eating a salad, his right hand in a bag of ice. He left around nine-thirty for a late shift at the hospital, giving me a kiss on the cheek and a humble, "Sorry," which I duly ignored.

After he left, I was restless and got up and paced the floor of my apartment. After about fifteen minutes, I rashly left my place and crossed the hall, knocking on Eli's door. He opened it and I pushed past him as he jumped to a defensive position. I couldn't blame him seeing as the last time we saw each other I racked him. I walked across the empty floor to the opposite side of the room, barely seeing his mattress, and the little lamp beside it with an open textbook under its glow. But I did see the worn picture of me propped up under the lamp by his bed, and it sent a sharp pain through my chest. His apartment was the mirror-image of mine, and looked almost exactly like mine did when we lived together there, even down to the placement of the mattress on the floor. I stood with my arms crossed, staring blindly out the window, his facing a courtyard, rather than the street.

In the glass I caught his reflection as he looked back out into the hall, as if expecting to see Doc follow me in, and then he slowly closed the door and walked over to my side. He stood gazing at me wordlessly while a minute ticked by.

"Why did you come back?" I asked him without turning my head.

He looked at me as if deciding whether to tell the truth or not. "My mom told me she saw you with another man."

I turned and looked at him then, suddenly tremulous. "You didn't know it was Doc?"

He shook his head. "Not until I saw you on the street."

I nodded, fighting back the tears angrily. I looked at the window again, swallowing. His reflection still was turned toward mine, searching me. My arms remained stubbornly crossed. I closed my eyes. "Why did you leave me?" I whispered, barely able to get it out at all.

He looked at his fingernails for a second. "You told me to," he said quietly, "and I thought that was what you wanted."

My head snapped around. "What about what you wanted?"

He shrugged. "I figured I forfeited that when I let Aaron trick me into drinking that night. He told me it was just a Coke. But after I tasted it, I knew he put rum in it, and I could have stopped." His voice became choked. "Oh, how I wish I would have stopped. I'm *so, so* sorry." Tears rolled down his face and I couldn't do it anymore. I ran into his arms. We shook with sobs, holding each other and sinking slowly onto the bed.

"I shouldn't have blamed you." I pulled back, but still kept my arms around him. "I know you wouldn't have let him hurt me if you could have stopped it."

"But it's my fault. I drank until I made myself useless to protect you."

"You didn't realize there was anything to protect me from."

"Don't defend me, Faith. Don't you do that." He took a breath. "I wasn't there for you, and he..." He broke down, laying his head on my chest and I ran my fingers through his hair. His familiar scent wafted up to me like some healing balm.

"Eli. Eli." I whispered his name. "You didn't hurt me. Aaron did. I don't blame you for what happened. Sure, I was angry at first...but my thoughts were so unclear at the time."

He pulled his head back. "How can you forgive me when I can't even forgive myself?"

I thought about this. "That's harder to do." He was so close to me, so close now. "I'm sorry I told you to leave. I still loved you," I choked out.

"What about now?" he asked quietly.

My voice cracked. "Now I belong to someone else."

"Not yet," he said, lifting my left hand and rubbing my empty ring finger.

"If you only told me..." I said stomping my foot. "I would have waited. I would have waited. ...Dammit! I told him 'yes'." I cried and then it all came pouring out. "I was scared. Aaron called and Doc threatened him and I had to do something to get him out of the house."

"Aaron called you?"

I nodded.

He jumped up. "That son-of-a-bitch called you?" His voice pitched high. And he paced. "Unfuckingbelievable! Where is he? Where is he?" He acted, irrationally, like Aaron was hiding in the closet or something. He strode across the room purposefully. I jumped up, too, following him. "Is he still at that place? At that filthy place where he..." Eli couldn't bring himself to say it.

I grabbed his arm. "No. No, Eli. He moved away. We don't know where he is."

He clutched me in a viselike hug. "I won't let him hurt you, Faith." His voice was strained. "I won't let him touch you again."

The desperateness of his actions alarmed me. "It's okay." I looked up at him and he looked down, his brow wrinkled with worry, but his face began to change. His green eyes turned smoky and he leaned in. The combination of the familiar feel of his arms around me, the scent of skin, and the intensity of his gaze made me feel nervous, but at the same time alive, like I was breathing in the fresh air after being trapped in that trunk of my childhood. His lips came down on mine and it wasn't even remotely within my capabilities to resist him. He held me so closely it was impossible to see where he began and I ended, melded into one, the heat of our bodies searing the edges closed, his mouth stealing my breath away with each passing second. I wish I could say I ended things quickly, but I didn't. We stood locked together for some time, my lips responding with his and seeking their own pleasures.

I pulled away finally, and he spoke my name imploringly as we parted, verbalizing the pain of our separation, now and in the past. I gazed into those fathomless green eyes for a second, speechless. Then, shaken, I broke free from him and ran out the door, saying only, "I can't do this." He called out to me again but I streaked into my apartment and bolted the door, as if he would try to break in. I slid down the door, clutching my knees and crying bitterly for what could never be. I could not, I would not, break Doc's heart, though mine was splintering in two.

FAITH

When Doc crawled silently into bed at six-thirty, he seemed surprised when I snuggled closer. He was lying on his side, and I wrapped my arms around him, lifting my head to whisper in his ear. "I'm sorry." He thought I meant only about being mad at him, but I was guilty of more than that. I made a promise to him while being in love with another man...that was unforgivable. I tried to push it from my mind as he rolled over to face me. The morning light showed the bruises on his face and I cringed. I gently reached up and stroked his face.

"I look like hell don't I," he whispered gruffly, smiling.

"I'm sorry, Doc."

He reached out and pushed a section of hair back from my face. "Don't say that," he returned, his voice cracking, shaking his head a little. His eyes moved back and forth as he gazed into mine. "You know, I love you, Faith."

I could hardly find my voice. "I know."

He stroked my arm. "Let me show you now."

I nodded. He made love to me slowly, deliberately. At first I had to fight myself to keep from drawing back from him. I thought of Eli across the hall and the guilt tasted metallic on my tongue. I think Doc sensed my inner turmoil, but he brought me to him patiently, caressing me gently until I was able to relax. I'd been with Max for as long as Eli and I were together, or maybe even a little longer, and he knew how to move me just as well. We lay together afterward, the morning sun warming our bare skin. He drifted off with his head on my chest, and I played with his hair idly. I thought of the electric feel of Eli's lips on mine, and fought back the tears.

Later, I slid out from underneath Doc and got ready for work. I made it through my morning at the hospital without major catastrophe, though I misplaced a couple of charts, and called a few co-workers by the wrong name. By eleven-thirty I was ready for a break.

I was headed to the cafeteria, when I saw Eli. What was he doing at the hospital?

He was making a beeline for the chapel. I'd never known him to attend church. Maybe AA meetings were held there. I made up my mind to walk on past, but at the last minute veered and entered the chapel quietly. The room was empty, though candles were lit and lights were on. Eli knelt in the first pew, seeming to look up at the cross behind the altar. To my shock, he spoke out loud.

"Lord, why now? Why, after I've straightened out my life—" His voice cracked and I felt my heart squeeze in my chest. I involuntarily took a step toward him and his head whipped around. I could see the tears in his eyes even from the back of the room. He sat back on the pew.

"Eli, what's wrong?"

"Faith," he cried, hurriedly blinking away his tears and sniffing. "Wh-what are you doing here?"

"I work here. What are *you* doing here?"

"I..." He seemed at a loss for a plausible answer. He rose and came toward me.

"Eli, are you sick? Or...it's not your mom, is it?" I asked, alarmed.

"No. No. My mom's fine."

"Then what?"

"Oh, just some routine tests. No big deal." He tried to shrug, but it came off awkward.

I stepped closer. "Eli," I answered, my voice accusatory, "tell me."

He closed the gap between us and ran the back of his hand down my face. I froze at his touch, and closed my eyes. "Eli..." I murmured, a weak sort of warning.

"I've missed you." His voice was thick.

We turned when we caught a movement. Max was heading out the door.

"Oh, no." I ran after him.

MAX

I showed up so I could join her for lunch, but her co-worker told me she had already headed down to the cafeteria. I went to find her, but as I turned down the long hall leading to the cafeteria, I saw her slip into the chapel. I smiled, feeling better just seeing her, and picked up my pace. But when I opened the door, I was floored. I caught them as he stroked her face. So, she had come to the chapel to meet Eli. Sickened, I turned around and left.

Faith barreled out after me. "Wait, Max." I stopped dead in my tracks. She came around to face me.

"Well, I guess I know why you're not wearing my ring." My voice dripped with sarcasm.

"Max," she said reproachfully. "He was upset. He's sick."

"What?" I didn't expect this.

"He won't tell me what's wrong, but I think it's something bad. When I came in—" She dropped her voice. "—I heard him praying out loud and asking God 'why?' Tears were in his eyes. It's something bad. I know it is."

She was clearly upset, and I had to say, I was a little panicked myself. Sure, I hadn't been glad to see Eli on my doorstep the other day, but he was my friend, and I didn't like seeing Faith this worried. I held her shoulders. "I'll find out, babe. Don't worry. You go get some lunch, and I'll meet you down in the cafeteria after I check things out." I kissed her cheek and then hurried off.

"Hey, Carmelita. How are you, gorgeous?"

"Good, Dr. Theobold," the receptionist said with a smile.

"I like that top. Red is definitely your color. Say...could you do me a favor? I was supposed to meet my friend, Eli, after his doctor's appointment, but I can't remember who he was seeing. Could you look it up for me?"

"Sure. What's the last name?"

"Batronis. B-a-t-r-o-n-i-s, I think."

"One second. Yes, he was seeing Dr. Leonard Thompson. But his appointment was at ten. You may have missed him."

"Well, shoot. I guess it pays to be an active listener. Hmm...well, where is Dr. Thompson's office, maybe Eli's waiting for me up there."

"Third floor. Near Internal Medicine."

"Thanks, doll. See ya around."

My heart beat faster as I took the elevator up to the third floor. Dr. Leonard Thompson. He was a liver specialist. Could Eli's excessive drinking have taken its toll? As I approached Internal Medicine, I saw the good doctor walking toward me down the hall with a colleague. I'd met him a while back at a benefit and found him arrogant and dull.

"Dr. Thompson?"

The doctor eyed me. "I'll see you downstairs, Jim," he said to his co-worker. "Yes. Can I help you?" he asked brusquely. Thompson was about six-feet tall with gray hair and wire-rimmed glasses. He gave the impression of a man who knew that his time was more valuable than yours.

I held out my hand. "Dr. Max Theobold. I'm a surgical intern. We met at the Cancer Research Center Benefit."

"Yes. How can I help you, Dr. Theobold?"

"I won't keep you long," I assured him, sensing his impatience. "You saw a friend of mine this morning, Eli Batronis. I ran into him downstairs and he seemed pretty upset. He was trying to explain to me your prognosis, but, to be frank, he wasn't making much sense. I was wondering if you could fill me in a little so I don't misspeak when I try to explain things to him."

"Well, it's pretty simple, doctor," he said condescendingly. "His liver is shot. He needs a transplant."

"Ahh..." I replied, taken off guard. Then I exclaimed, more to myself than him, "But Eli hasn't had a drink in at least two years."

"Oh, yes, but doctor, as you know, the sins of the past often come back to haunt us. Mr. Batronis's have caught up to him." He seemed to take some sick satisfaction in this. "Now if you'll excuse me."

"Yes, sure," I murmured absentmindedly. Eli had liver disease, and it was pretty serious if he needed a transplant. Faith would be devastated. I took the elevator back downstairs feeling bad for my old friend, and dreading having to tell Faith. When I got to the cafeteria, she was sitting by herself, staring forlornly off into space. She had a ham sandwich on her plate with one bite out of it. I sat across from her. "Hey."

She scrutinized my face. "It's bad," she said hollowly.

I took her hand, nodding my head. "He needs a new liver."

She inhaled sharply, her hand going to her mouth. "Oh, Doc." Her eyes filled with tears.

"Now, it might not be that bad. Plenty of people get liver transplants and survive to a ripe old age."

"Do you think Eli has a chance?" she asked, cautiously hopeful.

"Well...he's young," I hedged, but seeing her eyes brighten, I realized I needed to tell her the whole truth. I couldn't give her false hope; it would be too cruel if things were to go the other way. "But...his history of alcohol abuse will go against him."

"But he's quit drinking now."

"I know. It's just...sometimes they frown upon someone who has purposefully destroyed their own liver—"

"But that's not fair. He's worked so hard to be sober."

"I know, honey. I feel bad for him, too. And you're right. It's not fair." I sighed, rubbing her hand and thinking. "I'm going to see about getting Eli another doctor. I get the feeling this Dr. Thompson isn't fully in his court."

"You'd do that?"

"Of course. You know, Eli was my friend long before you met him."

She smiled finally and stood to give me an enthusiastic kiss on the cheek. "That's why I love you, Max Theobold."

"And I love you, too," I said seriously.

CHAPTER TWENTY-TWO

E*li* I'll admit, when I heard the knock on my door later that afternoon, I was hoping it was Faith. When I opened it and Max was there, I was prepared for the worst.

"Can I come in?" he asked tensely.

I moved aside and waved my hand toward the center of the room.

He glanced around at the interior. "Copying Faith's style, I see." He grinned, and I relaxed a little. He cleared his throat and became more serious. "Eli, I want to talk to you about something I did this afternoon after Faith saw you in the chapel. Something, that was, perhaps, not totally ethical."

My mind whirled with the possibilities, but I simply nodded.

"After Faith left you, she was upset. She knew you were sick, but not why. To ease her mind, I, sort of...tricked people into giving me your medical information. I'm sorry I snuck around behind your back to find out, but..." He lifted his hands as if indicating he felt he had no other choice. He looked at me evenly. "I know how sick you are. I know you need a liver transplant."

I sighed and turned away from him, quiet for a moment. "Faith knows?"

"Yes," he answered contritely.

I closed my eyes. I didn't want her to know. I didn't want her to feel sorry for me or for it to change the way she felt about me in any way. It's just how it was. "Well, I guess it's no more than I deserve, huh?"

"No, man. That's not true," he said adamantly. "You deserve much better. You've worked hard to overcome your addiction. It's a bad break this has happened to you, that's all."

I turned around, surprised. "Thank you, Doc." My throat was tight with emotion. "I appreciate that."

"I mean it, Eli. And that's one of the reasons I'm over here in the first place." He took a folded up piece of paper from his pocket. "This is Dr. Steven Triberg's phone number. He's a liver specialist I researched, and, frankly, I think he'd be a better doctor for you than Dr. Thompson. Thompson's good at what he does, be he's an egotistical S.O.B. and, in my opinion, he doesn't really have your best interests in mind. Dr. Triberg is a recovering alcoholic himself. I've already talked to him, and he will go to bat for you one hundred percent. He's not going to stand in judgment of you and will work as hard for you as he would for someone who was born with liver disease."

"In other words, he doesn't think I deserve this because of my past."

He sighed. "Exactly."

I hesitated, looking at the number on the paper but not really seeing it. "Can I ask you a question?"

He shrugged. "Sure."

"Why are you doing this for me?"

"Because...no matter what feelings I have about...you and Faith...you are still my friend. And I hope you still consider me one of yours."

I offered my hand. "Of course." We shook vigorously, and then clapped each other on the back.

"Well, I need to be getting back to help with dinner."

"Wouldn't it be a bigger help to stay over here and have a cold one with me and stay out of Faith's hair?"

"Why does everyone assume I can't cook? I'm an excellent cook," he commented. "Then again, I could use a beer."

"You'll have to go back to your place to get one. All I have is Coke, re-member? But we could watch the Mets game, if you want."

"Sure," he responded enthusiastically. "But I'll have a Coke."

"No, really. Have a beer if you want. It won't bother me." *Too much.*

"Okay. I'll be right back."

He left, and I looked at the paper in my hand and thought about what he'd done. He'd gone out of his way to help me. "Well, I'll be damned," I mumbled to myself.

MAX

I read the results again. HIV positive. Talk about the sins of your past. Why I'd never thought seriously about the possibility was beyond me. I'd always been a big condom user, but as a doctor I knew that wasn't always effective, so it shouldn't have come as such a big shock when I was given a random blood test at work and the results showed I was HIV positive. After all, before Faith I had been with many, many women, most of them of loose morals, but I guess I was the classical example of thinking such a thing would never happen to me.

I wasn't exactly sure how to mention this to Faith. "Guess what, honey? I'm HIV positive," just didn't seem like a great conversation starter. And what if I gave it to her? I didn't even want to think about that. One thing was for certain, she needed to be tested. I was sitting down eating dinner, trying to figure out a way to broach the subject, when someone knocked at the door.

"I'll get it," I said, grateful for any kind of distraction. I couldn't have been more surprised to see someone. "Well, you've got some balls."

"Listen, Doc. You've had your turn. Now I want a go at a little fun with Faith."

I exploded and, without thinking, ran and threw myself at Aaron, driving him across the hallway and into Eli's door with a *crash* and a splintering of wood. With a noise that was a cross between a growl and a shout, Aaron grabbed me and threw me off him, and then pushed off the door to come after me. I grabbed his arms, planting my feet to try to stop his momentum, but skidding across the hardwood anyway, until my heels hit the wood baseboard of the wall. Faith was screaming, but I wasn't even aware of where she was.

Aaron took a swing and I ducked, coming up under his arm to plant my fist in his ribcage. It was like hitting a brick house. No give at all. He shoved me into the wall to gain some room between us and followed up with a hook to my midsection, which, I knew for certain, is nothing like a brick house. The pain was so intense, it blinded me for a second and Aaron connected on the opposite side, actually lifting me off my feet with that one. While my head was down, he aimed an uppercut to my face, snapping my head back with the power. Faith screamed again and grabbed at his arm to try to pull him away from me, but he slapped at her viciously, without looking, hitting her in the shoulder, I think, and forcing her back. Rage sliced through the pain that was nearly cutting me in two.

I surged forward again, landing some blows which seemed to be of little effect, and Aaron pushed me again, lifting me in the air and tossing me until I crashed against the wall and slid down. My arm snapped making a sick sound as I landed at a weird angle. Howling in pain, I tried to straighten up, my vision starting to blur. When I looked up, I could see Aaron towering over me, lifting a fire-extinguisher over his head and I had a comical flash of a caveman hefting a rock. I put my good hand up to block, and prepared at the same time to dodge whatever attack he launched.

All of a sudden, from out of nowhere, Eli was on Aaron's back, screaming like a madman. Furious, Aaron tried to shake him off, but Eli clung like a bar patron to a mechanical bull. Incensed, Aaron spun in circles, absurdly, like a dog chasing his tail, and then, finally, dislodged him by throwing himself backward, wedging Eli between his enormous body and the wall. Eli lost his grip and slid to his feet. Aaron turned on him, but, quick as lightening, Eli landed two uppercuts to his rock-hard jaw, knocking him back a few feet. With a roar, Aaron brought the extinguisher down and changed his grip on it, swinging it with all of his might into Eli's side. His body flew against the stair rail and he crumpled to the floor without a sound. Loud footsteps preceded someone racing up the steps. Aaron turned toward Faith. His anger seemed to drain out of him and he raised his eyebrows at her suggestively.

"It's just you and me, baby," he said roughly, his voice thick with lust. I cringed and tried to pull myself to a standing position. Faith backed up, her eyes wide, her hands out in front of her defensively.

"No, Aaron," she said forcefully, but fear was evident in her eyes. Two linebackers wearing police uniforms sprang from the stairwell and grabbed Aaron from behind, slamming him face first into the wall and wrestling his hands behind his back.

Aaron was shouting. "Dammit! I saw you first, Faith, you stupid, bitch!"

While the cops fought handcuffs onto him, I crawled over to Eli, my ribs aching. "Eli, are you okay, man?"

"Doc," he said weakly, grimacing and breathing heavily, "something's wrong. Don't tell Faith, but I need an ambulance." He grabbed his side, his coloring a pallid gray.

As if in response, one of the police officers offered. "Hold on, guys. An ambulance is on the way."

The other one spoke to Faith. "Can you tell me what happened here, ma'am?"

"That man tried to rape me three years ago," Faith said loudly, her voice shaking, "and he came back tonight to—" A sob escaped from her and she brought a shaking hand to her mouth, backing up another few feet.

"Help her!" Eli said, his face tortured by her pain. I nodded and struggled to my feet, using the bars supporting the railing behind Eli. I stumbled over to Faith, throwing my good arm around her. Two EMTs popped off the elevator and made their way over to Eli.

"Oh, Doc. You're bleeding." She reached up to touch my face but I pulled back in horror.

"Don't! I'm HIV positive!"

"Wh-what?" Suddenly everyone turned to me. Eli, the EMTs, the cops, everybody.

I took Faith's hands, making sure mine were clean. "I found out today."

Her mouth hung open, her damp eyes flitting back and forth between mine. "Are you sick?"

"No," I reassured her.

"Okay. We'll deal with it."

One of the EMTs approached. "Sir, are you injured?"

"Yes. I'm a doctor, and I'm pretty sure I broke my right radius bone and I may have some cracked ribs."

"You'll need to come with us, then."

"I'll meet you at the hospital," Faith said, going back in to grab her purse.

The police were leading Aaron away. "What hospital? We'll come and take your statements there."

"Bellevue."

Before they could leave I called out. "Officer?" One turned back. "How did you guys get here so quickly?"

"We were here already, answering a disturbing the peace call on the floor below." He grinned. "But we couldn't hear anything above you guys, so we came up to see what was going on."

"I'm sure glad you did." I shook his hand. "Thank you." Then looking over at the other policeman, who was waiting a few steps below, I addressed him. "Thanks."

"No problem," the first guy answered. "See you later at the hospital."

In the ambulance, Eli became confused and disoriented. "It's acute liver damage," I told the EMTs. "He's already on the transplant list. I think he injured what's left of his liver."

"Okay, Doc," the EMT said warily, not used to getting diagnoses from his patients.

"You need to call ahead and get him bumped up the transplant list."

The driver glanced back over his shoulder at his partner. "You heard the man, Sam. Call it in."

By the time I was casted, they were already pulling together a transplant team. By an odd stroke of luck, a suitable match had been found for Eli. I talked to Dr. Triberg. "I want to be in on the transplant."

"And, why again, would it be good for a surgeon with a broken arm to assist?"

"Listen, I found out today that I'm HIV positive and I don't know if I'll be able to perform surgery again myself—"

"And, why again, would it be good for a surgeon who's HIV positive to assist?"

"My fiancé is in love with the patient."

"Which would make you more prone to kill him, not save his life."

"He's my friend."

He glanced over at Eli's bed where Faith was holding his hand.

"The hot chick holding his hand is your fiancé?"

I nodded.

"And you're sure you don't want to kill him?"

"Look, I've had a piss-poor day. I found out I have HIV, the guy who tried to rape my fiancé showed up on my doorstep and then proceeded to snap my arm like a twig, and it would make things go a whole lot better if I could watch you save my friend's life. So what do you say?"

He sized me up. "You're in."

"Thanks."

"Get someone to suit you up."

"You got it."

Watching the surgery was mind-bogglingly awesome. They got rid of Eli's old, damaged liver and put in a new one like switching a light bulb. Okay, it was a little more complicated than that, but, still and all, awesome. Eli came through like a trooper. I was in his room when he came around. He took in my scrubs, the cast, and the way I looked over his chart and said weakly, "I must be in some alternate universe where they let handicapped guys perform surgery on stiffs like me."

I smiled. "You should be so lucky." I walked over and sat on the bed next to him, observing his color. "So, how are you doing?"

"You tell me. You're the doc."

"Damn fine, I think." I was unable to hide my glee. "Man, Faith's going to be pissed she missed you waking up. She's been sitting here by your side since they wheeled you in and you pick the sixty seconds she has to go pee to wake up."

He chuckled, and then groaned a little.

"You in pain?" I asked quickly.

"Nothing as bad as your jokes." He felt along the line of stitches on his abdomen. "What happened to me?"

"Well, Aaron did you the huge favor of sending you into acute liver failure."

"I'll be sure to send him a thank you card."

"No, man, seriously. Your condition upped you on the transplant list. You've got yourself a brand-spanking-new liver."

His eyes opened wider and he pulled back the sheets to look at his incision, as if he could see his new liver through it. "No shit?"

"No shit." I grinned. "Have I ever lied to you?"

"On several occasions."

I waved my hand. "Bah. When it counted?"

We both laughed. "Doc...I want to thank you...for everything you did."

"You were the one who saved me from becoming an Aaron-sized pancake."

He grinned. "Oh, yeah. I guess I did."

Faith came in and ran over to the bed. Eli scrambled to pull the sheets up so as not to reveal anything, which had me stifling a laugh. She sat on the opposite side of the bed and touched his face, tears coming to her eyes. "Oh, Eli," was all she could manage.

"Hey," he said gently. "Don't cry. I'm doing fine." I studied the two of them for a second, and I was struck by the way they looked at each other—Eli's eyes soft and concerned, and...I could almost feel Faith's heart clutching as she looked at him, pale and weak in that bed. I realized this is how love looked. They were in love with each other. Although I didn't want to, I visualized them as I had seen them, so many times before, laughing together as he walked her home from the diner, watching each other on the dance floor at Harry's, Faith's horror when Eli had his fall, that warm look they would get when relating some story of their adventures into the city... And, perhaps for the first time in my life, I had an unselfish thought. These two belonged together. It was as plain as the hospital-white walls surrounding us. I knew she would stay with me because of the promise she made me, and because she loved me. But I knew it was wrong; I knew it in my very soul. Faith didn't love me like she loved Eli, or even like I loved her, with that same soul-scathing, all consuming fire. But maybe love didn't have to be that way, I told myself, maybe it could be a quiet, but steady fire, one that would never go out. Somehow, though, I couldn't convince myself.

Eli spoke again, telling her brightly, "Doc here tells me I have a new liver."

She looked up, as if just remembering me. She smiled at me proudly through her tears and reached over with her free hand to cover mine. "How's your patient, doctor?"

I cleared my throat, unable to speak for a second, but recovered quickly. "He's doing great." I turned to Eli. "Your biggest risk now is that your body will reject the new liver. But it was the right blood type, and the right body size. You're young and healthy, so everything looks good. I think you're going to be okay, man."

"I can't thank you enough."

"You owe me a beer."

"No, a Coke, remember?"

"You're no fun anymore, Batronis." Seeing Faith's frown, I added, "No, I'm kidding. Seriously, I really admire what you've done, Eli. You've stopped drinking, built a career as a budding architect...that takes a lot of strength and guts, man. You've put yourself on the straight and narrow, and that's not easy."

Eli and Faith stared at me, both of them speechless. Eli's voice was choked when he finally said, "That means an awful lot coming from you, Doc. I've always admired how you seem to have it all together, and I couldn't have asked for a better friend."

I wondered about that. "Well, you should probably get some sleep. Give that new liver a rest." I stood, and Faith did, too, although I could see it was tearing her up inside to leave him.

"We'll be back soon," she reassured him.

"Okay," he said, and I could tell he was still emotional. As much as she hated to leave, he hated for her to leave.

We walked down the hall, my good hand flung over Faith's shoulder. Her head was bent, and she was quiet, though she brought her hand up to cover my fingers on her shoulder. I was reflective as well.

"Faith," I said, after such a long time that it startled her. "After Eli gets out of here, can I take you out somewhere nice, where you could wear that dress I bought you when we first started seeing each other?"

She nodded, but didn't say anything at first. "That would be nice," she commented, although I could see her struggling with something.

Three weeks later, after we got Eli settled back into his apartment, we set out to have dinner as we'd planned. We hadn't spent a lot of time together, what with visiting the hospital and all, and our schedules not jibing, so we were both looking forward to the evening. When Faith was nearly ready, I snuck out to the hall and retrieved a rose I stashed in the fire extinguisher compartment Aaron took his weapon from. When Faith took a nap in the afternoon, I slid out to get the flower for her, and run another errand. I knocked on her door. It took her a couple of minutes to realize I was not there to answer it.

When she opened the door, she took my breath away as always. I produced the rose from behind my back and she laughed. She took it from me and brought it to her nose, breathing in its fragrance.

"You're crazy." Her eyes sparkled with laughter. Then she turned suddenly serious. "Do you know how much I love you?"

I took her hand and kissed her fingers, trying to disguise how moved I was. "I think so. Are you ready?"

"Yes."

I escorted her out, and wined and dined her. We laughed, and she seemed to relax for the first time in a long time. I took her out on the dance floor.

"You look absolutely beautiful tonight." She blushed. God, that was the thing I would miss the most, I think.

"Thank you." She tugged playfully on my tie. "You look quite dashing yourself."

"Can we go home now? I just want to go home."

"Sure," she replied, looking at me curiously.

When we got home, I sat with her on the couch, and took her hands in mine. She seemed to sense I needed to speak to her about something and sat quite still.

"Faith, I'm leaving tomorrow."

She looked at me, confused. "Leaving where?"

I cleared my throat. "Africa. I'm going to Africa to work there."

Her brow furrowed. "What are you talking about?"

"I love you. I love you more than anything." Suddenly it was too hard, tears poured down my cheeks.

"Doc, what are you saying?" She sat, searching my face.

I reached into my jacket pocket. "I went and picked this up today." I pulled the ring box out and laid it on the table. "I want you to keep it, although I'm sure you'll be wearing another ring before long."

She shook her head. "Doc...I don't understand."

"This is the right thing to do. I've known it all along. I've been kind of a placeholder until Eli got back."

"Doc, no." She put her hand on the side of my face. "I love you."

"I know you do, Faith. I do. And I don't regret for one moment any of the time I've spent with you."

She sobbed, shaking her head in disbelief. "What are you doing?"

My voice cracked. "I'm letting you go."

Her voice was a whisper. "But I never asked for you to let me go."

I nodded my head, barely able to get the words out. "I know. I know you didn't. You wouldn't do that."

She laid her head down on our hands, bawling. "I'm so sorry. I'm so sorry."

I laid my head on top of hers. "You shouldn't be. You've done nothing wrong. You've given me the best three years of my life."

We cried and held each other on the couch for a long time. Hours later, I stretched out, my feet on the coffee table, my tux shirt opened, my tie hanging loosely. Faith lay in my arms, spent and sad. A large pile of Kleenex lay in front of us on the table; our eyes were swollen and I had a headache from trying to hold it all in. We hadn't said a word in minutes, but when Faith spoke up, it was like a natural part of the conversation.

"Where will you go?"

"Kenya. There's a hospital there." My fingers glided over her bare arm without thinking.

"This is killing me." She started to cry again.

"Oh, baby." I pushed her to a sitting position so I could see her. "Don't say that." I wiped away the tears, but they came faster than I could keep up with.

"I mean it. I don't know if I can make it without you."

"Eli will make it better."

"But...part of me belongs to you now."

"But the greater part belongs to him. It always has, and it always will."

Her eyes moved back and forth between mine. "How can you be so selfless?"

"Damned if I know. This is all new to me."

She laughed through her tears. "Are you sure about this? Is there nothing I can say?"

I shook my head. "Nothing at all. My mind's made up. But I do have a favor to ask of you."

"Anything."

"Make love to me one last time."

She cried but she nodded through her tears.

I don't know how we found the strength, but when I looked back years later, it was those few hours together I remembered most. It was the most fantastic lovemaking. I felt her love like never before, and, strangely enough,

I felt happier afterward than I had in a long time. She cried, and begged me to stay, but my mind was made up.

CHAPTER TWENTY-THREE

E*li*   I packed my bags and locked my apartment, but when I turned around, she was standing in her doorway.

"What are you doing?"

I hung my head. "I'm leaving."

"You're leaving," she repeated, a strange expression on her face.

"Faith," I said quietly. "I love you, and I want you and Doc to be happy."

She gave this weird, little laugh and shook her head. "Well, Doc beat you to the punch." Holding the doorframe as if unsteady, she carefully sat cross-legged on the floor in the middle of her open doorway, putting one hand to her forehead.

"What are you talking about?" I set down my suitcase and came and crouched in front of her. She had me scared; she looked a little crazy.

When she lifted her head, tears pooled in her eyes, and that's when I realized how swollen her eyes already were. "He left me."

"He *what?*"

"He went to Africa. He said he was setting me free."

I reached out for the doorframe and slid down, my back against the wall, my feet out in front of me. I sat still for several seconds, absorbing this new information. Faith remained seated beside me, not elaborating.

"He left?" I said dully.

"Yes! He left, Eli. He left. How many times do I have to say it?" She started to cry. I woke up from my stupor and put my arm around her. "Man, I'm a *real* loser," she added bitterly. "I had *two* men leave me in one day."

"You know he only left because he loved you."

"I know. I know. That's what makes it so hard." Her crying became more uncontrolled.

"Let me take you inside," I said, getting to my feet and helping her up. As we passed through the doorway, my arm around her, she turned back.

"Your suitcase."

"Leave it. It just has stuff in it," I said, absentmindedly.

"But it's New York City."

"Leave it," I repeated. I closed the door and led her to the couch.

She sniffed, and grabbed a Kleenex from a box. From the pile around it, I guessed she'd been shedding a lot of tears lately.

"So..." I was at a loss for words. "He left..." She made a low growling noise in her throat at my repeating that again, but I couldn't get over it. What now? "How do you feel about that?"

"How do I feel about that? How do I feel about that?" She jumped to her feet and I began to think I'd asked the wrong question. "I feel like crap. I feel like worse than crap." She turned on me. "Go, why don't ya? Just go. You've got your suitcase packed. You don't have to sit around here and feel sorry for me."

"I'm not here because I feel sorry for you."

"Why are you here then?" she screamed, her eyes wild with grief. "Why are you here?"

"I don't know. I guess I—"

"You guess?"

"I know!" I yelled. "I know I love you."

"You know you...?" She threw up her hands and stormed away from me, then turned back with an exasperated sound. "Well you sure have a weird way of showing it. Both of you. You both love me, but you both are going to leave me. That's great." She was shouting now, nearly hysterical. "Well, get out then. If you're going to leave, then go. *Go!*"

I looked at her, confused. I'd made my decision to cut my soul out and leave her so she could have a shot at happiness, and here she was, sick and miserable. I couldn't understand it. As she continued to shout at me, I stumbled toward the door, my mind like a punch-drunk prize fighter, and opened it. Then, with sudden clarity, I saw an image of her standing in the street, her uniform top pulled open, Aaron's grotesque teeth marks blaring through her skin...she was shouting, 'It's over, Eli. This is over,' and I realized her words and her anger now were bubbling out of the hurt she felt inside, just as they had before. I slammed the door shut.

"No. Not this time, Faith." I turned around to face her. "I love you and I'm here to stay, for as long as you want me. I know you're upset, and angry, and you have every right to be. I messed all this up. I threw what we had away for a drink, and I couldn't be sorrier for that." My voice became fierce with emotion. "But I'm here now, dammit. Ready to do what's right. If it's just to be your friend and hold your hand, or if you want me to chase him down and bring him back to you, I will. I owe you that much, and I owe him, too. But I'm not walking away now because it's difficult. That's what the old Eli would have done, but I'm not that man anymore, and I refuse to ever be him ever again. When you figure out what it is you want, I'll be across the hall. You just let me know."

I turned to leave and she shouted to me again, her words reverberating off the walls. "I want you, Eli." I turned around and studied her face. She stepped closer, speaking more softly, "I want you. I always have. And as much as I've tried to stop loving you, I just can't." She stepped forward into my arms and I held her, held her while our two hearts quivered and then started beating again as one. I closed my eyes, concentrating on the way it felt to have her in my arms again. "I never wanted to hurt him," she cried desolately, her head on my chest. "I love him, too."

"I know, babe." I held her head to me, my hands in her hair. "Shh, now. It's going to be okay. I'll help you through this." She cried quietly, worn out from all the emotional turmoil. "I'm here now, Faith. I'm not going anywhere again." We continued to stand together in silence for a while. Finally, I asked, "Do you want to sit?"

She glanced over at the couch, the couch Doc bought her, I supposed, and shook her head, "Not here."

"Okay, we can go over to my place."

We crossed the hall to my apartment, where we didn't have any furniture to complicate things and I walked with her to the bed. We sat on the edge. Nerves made my stomach tight. "Do you want to be alone for a while? I can leave..."

She shook her head.

"Okay." I couldn't shake the feeling of apprehension. Where we once shared everything together, a black hole of three years without each other stood between us. I hadn't been with a woman, hardly touched another soul, in all that time, and part of me worried about opening up again. It should have been easy with Faith, but it wasn't; I was afraid to hurt her again, afraid to trust myself with her. She leaned into me heavily, and I could tell she was bone-weary. Should I lie so that she could rest? Or would that make her feel uncomfortable? How do you start over with someone you've already shared everything with? I contemplated my options, feeling awkward, like a teenager. I cleared my throat. "Do you want to lie down?"

She nodded, and I scooted back onto the pillows, holding my arm up for her. She slipped into place and I couldn't help but sigh; she felt so right beside me. "I didn't sleep much last night," she said, her voice tentative.

"Relax, then."

She seemed to heed my advice and within minutes became like a wet noodle beside me, molded to me, the heat of our bodies lulling us. Her head was on my shoulder and her hand stretched across me on my other shoulder, one leg hooked over mine.

"Are you comfortable?"

"Mmm," was her only reply. She breathed steadily, and I thought she fell asleep, but she murmured in my ear softly. "I've missed you so much." I turned my head, and was surprised to see her eyes were wide open. Her face was inches from mine. I swear my heart stopped beating for a second.

"I've missed you, too," I choked out. And then she leaned forward, a fraction, but a fraction was all it took. Her warm lips were on mine and I closed my eyes, focusing on the sensation they created. The soft sound of our lips meeting and parting, changing angles, and intensity, swirled inside of me, making me tingle everywhere, bringing me to life, as if I been some frozen Neanderthal. I reached up and touched the side of her face, her skin creamy smooth. I slid out from under her, rising on my elbow so I could kiss her better, my leg coming to swing over hers now, a little. A need rushed inside, a need so strong it was terrifying. My lips traveled to her chin, and then down to her neck.

"Eli, Eli," she moaned, as if she had been holding my name inside of her a thousand years and it was now liberated from her. I wanted her with a savage intensity I never felt before—wanted to be inside of her, wanted to have her scream my name in desire, and then in ecstasy, wanted it *now*, with no preliminaries. My hand went to the inside of her thigh, nearest to me...and then I pushed away, pushed off her and sat, my heart pounding. I was breathing heavily and I couldn't seem to slow it down at first.

"What's wrong? I didn't hurt you, did I?"

I actually considered telling her she had. "No," I muttered, absentmindedly passing a hand over my scar. I jumped out of the bed.

"Wh-what?"

"I've got a class." I grabbed my backpack and shoved my books in it. "Sorry. But if I'm going to stay here, I need to attend my classes." I rushed out the door, slamming it behind me without even looking back.

Once out of the building, I took my time; I had over an hour to kill.

FAITH

When Doc left, it hurt more than I could imagine, more even than when Eli left, because things were so screwy between Eli and me when he went to Chicago. I was still in shock over what happened with Aaron, so the pain, with Eli, came later. But to watch Doc walk away from me... It was gut-wrenching. I loved him so much, and to know he was tearing himself up inside in an effort to make me happy, and to watch him trying to be so brave, and to sit there while he faded out of my life, and love him all the more, it was like a slow, agonizing death. The fact he made the effort to make our last night together special—that was so Doc. He believed that he was a selfish person, when in truth he was the most generous person I had ever known, far better than I.

And when you have spent so much time together, and been so intimate with someone, you missed them with each breath. I missed the way his hair would be all ruffled in the morning. I missed the way he looked when he jogged beside me, stocking cap on, air frosted in front of him as he breathed, eyes twinkling and teeth shining. He would reach out at some random moment as we jogged and squeeze my hand, and it was as if he squeezed my heart. I missed his off-key singing in the shower, the way he would make up strange band names when we didn't recognize a song, "Oh, this is Fred Win-kleman and His Band of Renowned" or "Teddy and the Tar-Heaters". One time he came up with some off-beat name, and swore it was a real band, and when we got home and Googled it, I found out he was right and we laughed and laughed until I nearly fell out of my chair. I felt lost and bereft when Eli was gone, but in many ways it was worse without Doc, as he had always been beside me, always supported me, and I leaned on him. My support post had been ripped out from under me.

At the same time, I was excited by the chance to fix things with Eli, to start again, to have a chance to love him as I once had. Where Max's love had been like the sun, lighting my world and warming me to the core, Eli's had once been like a supernova, bursting with brilliance and power, but, at times, scorching me and searing my flesh. I hoped the changes he made in his life would bring that love more under control, that we could learn to not hurt each other anymore, that the fire would burn strong and constant and would never cease.

That is, if we could get over the awkwardness that settled over us. After Eli left for class, I was at loose ends, left alone in his apartment. I eventually made it back to my place to change for work. When I got home from that, a light shone from under his door into the hallway, looking so inviting. I went to knock on the door, rather than return to my empty apartment, but I felt unsure. Maybe he had second thoughts. The way he ran out of his place af-ter we kissed made me feel uncertain about his feelings. I turned around and headed back into my apartment.

After a few minutes, there was a knock on the door. My heart rose and I hurried to answer it. He leaned on the doorframe, his arm bent, staring down at me while a slow, sexy smile spread across his face.

"Hey."

I loved the way he breathed that word, full of warmth and intimacy.

"Hey."

He glanced at his feet a second, then looked up, his eyes squinting. "I'm sorry I ran out on you earlier. Not much of a gentleman."

"That's okay." I looked away, trying not to remember the hurt.

He reached down and curled a finger under my chin to lift my face. "It's not okay. I won't do that again." He sounded sincere, but changed the subject. "Wanna grab some pizza?"

"Sure. But let me change out of these scrubs. Come on in."

He came in, closing the door behind him. "You look cute in those scrubs."

I turned back and stuck my tongue out at him, and rummaged through my closet and drawers until I found the right thing. "Umm...I'll be back." I went into the bathroom to change, thinking again how strange it was to feel modest in front of him, after having left no stones unturned in the bedroom in our day. But it would have felt equally wrong to just strip down in front of him. I left the door open a crack so I could talk to him, peeking out now and again to see what he was doing.

He wandered around the apartment, looking at things, running his hands along the smooth wood of the sofa table. His eyes fell on my closet, and he drew out the black dress Doc gave me. I wondered what he was thinking as he gazed at it. I yanked on the bottom of the red sweater I put on to straighten it and stepped out. He turned with the dress still in his hand.

"This is pretty."

I rubbed at an invisible stain on the top of the couch, my cheeks getting hot. "Uhh...yeah."

He studied me and I tried to look him in the eye, but ended up glancing out the window, before walking over to take the dress from him, trying to appear casual, and hanging it back up.

"Doc bought it for you." It was more of a statement than a question, but I nodded. His jaw tightened. "I guess he could buy you about anything you wanted on a surgeon's salary." I pushed the University of Hawaii sweatshirt back farther in the closet.

"Eli," I said softly, a little reproachful. "You know that doesn't mean anything to me."

"I know. But it means something to me." His brow creased. "I want to be able to give you all the things that he could."

I reached up and stroked his face. "I have all I've ever wanted right here."

Slowly the worried lines disappeared from his forehead, and he pulled me in by my hips to kiss me. He hugged me, sighing in my ear, "I'm such a screw up. Why do you love me?" Before I could answer, he spoke again, pulling back so he could look me in the face earnestly. "Someday I will be able to do things for you. I swear. The internship could turn into something steady. And—"

I put a finger to his lips and cocked my head with a frown.

He laughed. "Okay, no more insecurities. Just pizza. I'm not going to even think about how Doc wined and dined you while I'm only taking you down to Little Tony's."

"But you know how much I love Little Tony's."

He chuckled, relieved. "So that much hasn't changed, huh?"

I grinned. "No way."

"Then this way, m'lady." He crooked his arm for me and led me out.

We had a nice meal. This part of our relationship seemed to be back on track, at least. We talked about anything and laughed. I enjoyed watching his face in the crummy restaurant light. He seemed more relaxed and genuine. But when he walked me to my door, he seemed suddenly uncomfortable. He dropped my hand.

"Well...good night. I had a nice evening."

I looked at him in surprise. "You're not coming in?"

"Umm...I have to be up early to get into the office."

"Oh, okay." I tried to hide my disappointment. He backed off toward his door. So no kiss, then, either. "Well...good night then."

I entered my place with a sigh of frustration. I wanted him so badly my body quivered sitting across the table from him at dinner. I stared around my apartment apprehensively. It felt so empty; and I felt so empty.

I wondered where Doc was and what he was doing. Was he on a plane? Or was he in some hotel room, feeling as lonely as I was? I drove myself crazy envisioning him, staring out some black plane window, or sitting on the edge of a bed in the light of a hotel lamp, unbuttoning his cuffs. In my imagination he was wearing a white shirt and tan pants. I'm not sure why, but that's what he had on when I saw him on the plane, and in the hotel room. I imagined him flopping back in the bed, laying his head on his arms, crossed on top of the pillows, staring at the ceiling, alone. Or worse yet, I envisioned him with some nameless girl, whose features shifted—sometimes she was a blonde, sometimes, a brunette—and he touched her, needing comfort.

"Oh, Doc," I said out loud. I missed him so much. Dully I changed out of my clothes and pulled on an old Bronx Zoo tank top and some skimpy cotton shorts. I sat cross-legged on the couch, staring at nothing, wondering over how things changed. I forced myself to get up, finally, and cross to the bed. I stared at it for a while, and then made myself crawl under the covers. I turned the light out and closed my eyes, curling on my side. But when I breathed in, I could still smell him there. The feeling was so strong, I rolled over and felt his side of the bed. But, of course, he wasn't there. I started to cry, longing to be held by him again.

The phone ringing exploded through the apartment. My head spun around and I stared at it, afraid I imagined it. It rang again. It could only be one person. I lunged for it.

"Doc?"

Several seconds passed. "Faith."

I squeezed my eyes closed. The warm familiarity of his voice pierced me. We didn't speak for a while. I gripped the phone so tightly my knuckles and the insides of my fingers ached.

"How are you?" he asked finally, his voice sounding strange.

I couldn't answer.

"Faith? Faith? Are you there?"

"I'm here. I'm here." My voice was so weak, I was surprised he could even hear me from half-a-world away.

"How are you?" he asked again. "How's...Eli?" He forced the name out.

"I don't know."

"What do you mean you don't know? He lives across the hall from you," he snapped, then sighed. "You didn't tell him I left?"

"No." I nodded my head, although I knew he couldn't see me. "I told him."

There was another long pause, and when he spoke again, his voice was tight. "And?"

"We went out to eat."

It was as if he could read my non-answer.

"Give it time. It's going to be strange at first."

Tears rolled down my face. "You're comforting me from across the globe?"

"I just want you to be happy."

But I'm miserable. I wanted to say. "Come home," I pleaded.

He was silent. "I can't do that."

My throat hurt, and I tasted the salt of my tears. "I know."

"This is the best thing for us. For all of us. I know it may not seem like it now, but you have to trust me."

"I love you."

"I know."

I could tell he was crying.

"I shouldn't have called. I just needed to hear your voice."

I cried quietly, unable to respond.

"I'll call you in a couple of weeks."

"Okay." But we both knew he wouldn't.

Silence. "Faith?"

"Yes."

"I will love you forever."

I swallowed. "Me, too. I'll never forget you. Not one minute with you."

The phone went dead. I fell apart.

And then I got up. I was sick of crying, sick of being a victim. My nose was sore from blowing it, my eyes stung, and I was exhausted. I crossed to the couch, dragging a blanket with me, but I could still smell him. I lay awake for hours.

CHAPTER TWENTY-FOUR

E*li* I tossed and turned for hours, staring up at the ceiling and watching the shadows the fan threw above my head. Finally I got up and pulled on my jeans, going to stare out my window at absolutely nothing. A few lights shone in the building across the courtyard from mine. I wondered if the poor slobs in those apartments were as confused about their love lives as I was. How was it possible to feel so at home with someone and yet feel so...odd, around her?

I roamed the streets earlier in the day considering the same question. Despite having to kill an hour, I ended up late to my class. I was so absorbed in my thoughts I lost track of time. Did I love Faith? No question. Did I want Faith? *No question.* So what was it making me draw back? I considered our long, convoluted history, and I knew the answer. I hurt her time and again, and the possibility I could do it again, if we became involved again, was terrifying me.

But I was a different man than the one she knew before, I reasoned with myself. I no longer drank, and that was the root of all of our problems before. So what was keeping me from loving her? What was keeping me from being happy? By morning, I came to the conclusion it was the fear of that other man returning, the one who clung to the past, the one who surrendered to the bottle to take it all away, the one who hurt Faith.

I snuck out early, and avoided seeing her. I heard her come home, as I had the night before, while I sat and studied and had the same urge to see her. I followed my instincts and knocked on her door. When she opened it, I was struck by the dark circles under her eyes, and the way her shoulders slumped. So I was hurting her already.

"Hi."

She eyed me warily. "Come in." When I stepped through the doorway, I was surprised to see her mattress on the floor in its old spot, and all of the furniture stacked on the near side of the room, on the opposite side of the door.

"You've done some rearranging," I commented with surprise.

"Uh-huh," she replied, yawning loudly. She stood in the middle of the barren room, her arms crossed.

"Did you move all that yourself?"

"Yep."

"Today?"

"Last night."

"Last night?"

"I couldn't sleep," she said with a shrug. "Can I get you something to drink?"

"Sure. I'll take a water if you don't mind."

She shuffled away without commenting and returned with two glasses of water. She still had her scrubs on. I took a drink and watched her. Her eyes looked flat and emotionless, and she was trying not to look at me.

I shifted my weight. "Are you mad at me?"

Instead of answering, she blurted out, "Why won't you touch me?" I could tell she was hurt and angry.

I walked away from her and set my drink down on the window sill, looking out at the street blankly as I tried to formulate an answer. She came to stand beside me, gazing up into my face to gauge my response. "I don't know." I sighed. I shook my head, and said, more to myself than to her. "Maybe I shouldn't have come back."

She set her glass down next to mine with a sharp knock. "Maybe you shouldn't have," she agreed. She turned away, but not before I saw the hurt in her eyes. She stood with her back toward me, rigid, her arms crossed in front of her, then she sagged, and turned around. "I'm sorry, Eli. I'm just so drained today. You didn't deserve that." She still wouldn't look me in the eye. I imagined it was too painful. "Maybe you should go so I can try to get some sleep." She hurried to the door and held it open for me, her gaze on the wall across from her.

I stood for a second or two, stunned, then, followed numbly. "I'm sorry," I said at the door.

She sighed. "It's all right. I'm just tired. Tired and numb. I'm not sure I ever fell asleep last night."

I took her hand, rubbing my thumb over the back of it. "Well, you get some sleep then. I'll see you tomorrow?"

She was looking at our hands. "Yeah," she breathed tremulously, and I left.

I went back to my place feeling like a heel. What was wrong with me? I was with the woman I loved, but somehow found myself incapable of showing her that love. I tried to study, but it was useless. I read the same page over and over again and finally tossed the book aside in frustration and snapped off the light. I was getting ready for bed, taking off my shirt in the light from a streetlight outside, when I heard a soft knock. I rushed to the door.

Faith stood on my doorstep in a tank top and shorts, wide-eyed. "I can't sleep."

"Come here." I pulled her in and closed the door behind her. She looked so small and unhappy. I wanted to soothe her. For some reason, I swept her off her feet. She laid her head down on me, her body limp. I took her to my bed, climbing in after her. She lifted her head and laid it on my chest, her hand running over the skin of my chest and arms.

"I love you, Faith. I really do. I just don't want to hurt you again," I whispered. Somehow it made it easier, saying it into the darkness.

She rose on her elbow. Her eyes peered into mine, the outside light coming in from over her shoulders; like Faith, I hadn't been able to afford curtains yet. "You won't," she said, her voice clear. "I know you better than *anybody*," she stated with utmost confidence, "and you *won't*."

She kissed my lips lightly, then laid her head down and prepared to snuggle in. But her words washed over me, caressed me, soothed the area in me where I had not yet been able to forgive myself. I turned on my side, scooting down so we were face to face. We sat like that for some time, staring into each other's faces, and then I kissed her, long and tender.

She was mine. We did belong together, and we could make it work, I knew it now.

We made love that night, long and slow, each movement a statement, a promise, a vow. Our love was expressed more unmistakably in those hours than it was at any other time in our lives; more so than even during the day of our wedding, or anytime after. My past was to remain in my past, and, along with the houses I was going to make, I would build a life with Faith, a good life, the life I had waited for.

PROLOGUE

F*aith*
  I could hear Eli reading to Grace in the next room. He was an awesome father, loved Gracie beyond measure, but didn't let her get away with much. I couldn't hear the words, but I could tell from the rhythm he was reading *Listen, Buddy!* I should have known; that was one of our little girl's favorite books. His voice got gruff as he did the voice of the "Scruffy Varmint" that the bunny in the story runs into. I laughed, then a sharp pain made me cry out. I grabbed the bedpost to steady myself, catching my reflection in the dresser mirror. My eyes were drawn to the necklace that never left my neck, made from the diamonds in the engagement ring Max gave me. It rested near my heart, a reminder of the man who was never far from it. I wished he was here now, his doctor's hand a comfort in my time of need.

I glanced at the clock as another pain seized me. One minute apart. Had I waited too long? I hobbled over to the door and peeked out. Their heads were so close together on the couch, Eli's, with the gorgeous, thick brown curls, and Grace's, soft and fine, the color of melted milk chocolate with streaks of caramel.

"Eli?"

"Yeah, babe," he said lightly, turning the page and nuzzling Gracie, making her giggle.

"It's time."

"Time? Time for what?" He lifted his head, reading the clock on the mantle then turned to see me smiling with my hand on my bulging stomach. He slammed the book down. "Really?" he asked excitedly.

Another wave hit me and I grimaced. "Oh, yes. Really." He jumped up and helped me over to the couch, talking to Grace as he did.

"It looks like you are about to have a little brother or sister, hon."

"Really?" she squealed in delight. "Mommy? The baby's ready?"

She made it sound like it was a cookie or something. "Yes, I think so."

"Oh, goody. Goody. Goody." She danced around clapping her hands. "I want a boy."

Eli and I exchanged a glance over her head and I smiled. "I'll see what I can do."

He phoned his mother and passed the word on quickly. "She'll be here in five minutes. I already have the bag in the back... Ooh!" He had his hand on my rigid stomach. "That's a hard one. Do you want me to get you anything?" His leg shook.

I squeezed his hand as Grace squirmed up on the couch beside me. "Nope. I've got everything right here." I pulled her to my side, and looked down into her beaming face. "Are you excited?"

Her head bobbed up and down, the ribbon in it flying comically. I sucked in my breath. "Ooh. Your baby brother or sister is strong and they want to come out *now*." I looked into Eli's eyes and hoped he would understand my meaning. As if on cue, the doorbell rang and he flew to answer it.

"Grandma. Grandpa." Grace left me. I may as well have been invisible when Grandma and Grandpa appeared; she was especially fond of big-heart-ed Al.

Betty gave her a squeeze and cooed over her, and then let Al have his turn as she walked over to me, her smile radiant. "How are you doing?"

"Good. Now that you're here—mmm."

"Another one? You and Eli better get going." She helped the Goodyear Faith off of the couch, Eli scrambling to the other side to get me upright. As I looked back from the door, Betty picked up Grace's books and put them into the basket we had for them, and Al happily sported a tiara and what looked to be pink streamers of some sort in his thinning hair.

This was the wonderful gift Max had given me, another chance to make things right with Eli, another shot at happiness. And I had hit the jackpot. A husband I adored, a wild, happy-go-lucky little princess, and...who knew who was on the way here in, probably, only a couple of hours. And add to that the bonus of great in-laws, and my world was a virtual Paradise. I only wished, somehow, it could have contained Max, too, but I knew that was not possible. I counted my blessings and hoped and prayed he was happy, because he deserved that.

SUSAN

Dr. Max Theobald was not a happy person. He appeared so on the surface. Most people believed him to be so. But, perhaps because I was attracted to him, I noticed what others did not. I saw that even when he was joking, and flirting with the nurses, he had some hidden wound. I would catch him from time to time, when he didn't know anyone watched, staring out some window, as if searching for someone out there. But I got the feeling the someone he was looking for was back in The States, where he'd left her.

When we started seeing each other, I dreamed of eclipsing this other woman in his thoughts. But, after a time, I became resigned to the thought he would always love her; it didn't make him love me any less. And I knew he needed me, needed someone to love him, to worship him just as he worshipped her, and that was easy for me. Max was patient and kind, you could see that when he was working with patients, or flirting with even the most homely girl in the hospital; he would treat her with the same respect and attention he would give any knockout that walked into the place, perhaps with a little more, even. His good humor was infectious, and his sex appeal, unequalled. But it really wasn't any of these that appealed to me the most.

It was the sad, lost little boy I saw within him, the one who needed someone to care for him, who had me twisted around his finger. Maybe it was the nurse in me who wanted to heal the pain. But one thing was for certain, I wanted him, and I would take whatever he could give me.

MAX

I came back to New York with my wife, Susan, a nurse from Australia whom I had met in Ghana. Ironically, we had come to know each other during a blackout when I was trying to perform surgery by the feeble light of an auxiliary lantern. My HIV status made me uniquely qualified to serve in Africa, where AIDS was out of control. Susan was also HIV positive, the re-

sult of a careless needle prick when she first began nursing. Despite being in-
fected, we both had the great fortune to not develop AIDS for many years
and we were able to help thousands of sick people in our time overseas.

We were on a short visit to the States and celebrating our one-year anniversary in The Big Apple. I opened the door for her to get into a cab, and
then, above the noise of the rumbling taxi, and a random honk up the street,
and a vendor kibitzing with a customer, I heard her laughter

I turned and saw the family of four. The little girl stood at the foot of a
navy stroller, leaning over it with an ice cream cone. She looked to be about
four, with a white-eyelet sundress and soft brown hair that curled gracefully
at the ends. She had a bright red bow in her hair with long streamers hanging
down.

"Gracie, honey, Baby isn't old enough for ice cream yet."

Faith stood behind the stroller in her own white, floral sundress, looking
as incredible as ever. Eli bent and scooped the girl up, while Faith came
around to the side of the stroller and straightened the robin's egg blue blanket
over the squirming little bundle inside.

"Ice cream would give Max a nasty tummy ache, sis," Eli explained. "Sorry."

"What about you, Daddy?"

He rubbed noses with her. "That's nice of you to want to share, Gracie-
bear, but Daddy already had an ice cream cone, remember?"

"Oh, yeah." He swung her down and set her on her feet, taking one of
her—no doubt—sticky hands in his. He wore a white, linen shirt and tan
pants, and a smile the size of Texas. My eyes returned to Faith, who watched
the pair with a look of utter contentment. Eli glanced over and slid his free
arm around her waist as they walked.

"Hey, Mack," the cabbie hollered at me. I looked at him confused; how
did he know my name? Then I realized he was simply speaking to me generi-
cally. "You gonna get in or what?"

"Oh, yeah. Sure." I walked around to the other side of the cab but continued to watch them as they walked off together, Faith reaching up now to
wipe something from Eli's face, both of them smiling.

"Honey?" Susan called to me from the depths of the back seat.

She was a good woman, and I loved her. She made me happy, and I was lucky to have her. She was sweet, like Faith, always looking out for others; that's what made her a great nurse. She had a good sense of humor, was classically beautiful and intelligent; she was one in a million.

Did I think about Faith? Every day of my life. Did it make me unhappy? No. I'd been blessed with three wonderful years with Faith. Some people go a whole lifetime without love like that. And she did love me, of that I am sure.

I climbed into the back of the cab and slid over to give Susan's hand a squeeze. She looked out the window. "Is that Faith?" she asked quietly.

I blinked. "How did you know?"

"The only woman who could get you to react that way is the woman whose name you call out in your sleep all the time."

I felt the blood drain from my face. I was too stunned to speak.

"She's pretty," she commented serenely.

"Susan. I'm so sorry. I—"

She patted my hand. "You needn't be. I knew part of your heart belonged to someone else from the start."

I grimaced. "Am I that transparent?"

"To me you are. But that's because when I'm looking at you all the time, I can't help but notice certain things about you." She laid her head on my shoulder tranquilly, but I shifted so she raised her head.

"Hey—" I put my hand on her cheek "—you know I love you and I would never hurt you—"

"It's okay, Max. I made my peace with it a long time ago. I know you love me, and that's enough."

I gulped. I did not deserve her. I considered, briefly, whether I should let her go. She deserved to be loved with the same intensity as I loved Faith; she was a wonderful woman. But, in the end, I was selfish. As it turned out, our marriage was happier than most of our friends' marriages were. I was forever grateful to Susan for rescuing me and loving me more than I deserved. Eventually, after many, many years, my past with Faith was able to be blacked out from my mind, and Susan did become my world so I came to love her with a passion almost equal to the one I had for Faith. Faith's name no longer created the depth of pain it once had, and that pain faded quickly, especially in

Susan's presence. All in all, I consider myself to be a very lucky man to have been able to love and be loved by two such fabulous women.

I also felt blessed to have seen Faith on the street that day. It gave me a sense of closure, knowing the hardest decision I had ever been forced to make in my lifetime had turned out to be the right one for all concerned in the end. How could I want anything more?

DEDICATION

This book is dedicated to award-winning author Laurie Larsen. Several years ago a friend told me about a writing contest Laurie was hosting and I entered and won. When she sent me the prize, she also invited me to a Romance Writers of America meeting. At that time I knew virtually nothing about the publishing industry. Through fellow authors' critiques at the meetings I grew as a writer and learned the ins and outs of the business. Laurie's criticism was always dead on, but gentle. That's not easy to do. She later became my editor and has always gone out of her way to help me and her other author friends. Here's to you, Laurie! Thank you for all the advice and encouragement over the years. You've made me a better writer and brightened my world at the same time.

Note from author

Thank you for reading BLACKOUT, part of my REAL ROMANCE COLLECTION. I hope you enjoyed it. Now that you've read the book, won't you please consider writing a review? Reviews are one of the best ways readers discover great new books. They don't need to be fancy or long, just a sentence or two honestly describing your opinion of/experience with the book. I would sincerely appreciate it.

Want more from M.J. Schiller?

Page forward for

an excerpt from

A KNIGHT TO REMEMBER

Book Three in the ROMANTIC KNIGHTS SERIES

BOOK THREE
A KNIGHT TO REMEMBER
CHAPTER ONE

Her name was Lt. Danica Jonas. Tall and slender, she had a muscular build, and long, flowing dark hair. With piercing green-grey eyes, she was, by all accounts, stunning. Despite her lower rank, she possessed a sense of command Orion knew would have her gunning for his job in a few years. *Hell, she'd probably be better at it than I am right now.* She had volunteered to help him with a small repair job, and now they were stuck together in a maintenance shaft. *How in the galaxy did I let this happen?*

He always believed in order to maintain the respect of his crew members, it was important for a Commander to be able to reach them on their level. That's why he was often seen taking a turn at watch, or cleaning landing pods, or tackling some other low-glamour job. He had even taken a shot at cooking the evening meal—once. That was an arena the crew decided it was best for their well-meaning Commander to stay out of. So when a small repair job came up, and his engineering crew had been riddled with bouts of the Meridian flu, he decided to handle the problem himself. *After all, I used to do a lot of tinkering before I became Darius's novice. How much could things have changed since then?*

"Apparently enough to have gotten me locked inside a maintenance shaft for a couple of hours," he admitted ruefully to Danica. A huge grin lit her face. "You seem highly amused by my predicament."

She nodded her head. "Um-hum."

He frowned. "I find that a tad annoying."

After realizing their com-links didn't work well in the titanium shafts, and banging on the door for quite awhile, hoping to catch the attention of the odd passerby, they decided to make the best of the situation and sit and wait.

"Luckily I did leave the job location on the bridge. Eventually, someone will come looking for us. So you can wipe that smirk off of your face, Lieutenant. You could have remembered the access code too, you know." He smiled to offset his stern tone.

"Yes, Sir." She executed a mock salute, and they both broke into laughter.

"You are *so* not telling anyone about this," he said when the laughter had ceased.

"Well, let's see now... How can I work this to my advantage?" She rubbed her chin. "I'm thinking my next performance review is going to be pretty stellar."

"I wouldn't count on that," he joked back. Her mouth hung open, and he laughed. "I'm just kidding. You're doing an excellent job. There's no one I would rather turn to with a problem right now than you."

"Thank you, Sir."

"Since we're stuck in what amounts to little more than a crawl space, I think you can drop the 'sir' for now."

"Yes, Commander."

"Orion would be fine."

"Orion, then." She smiled. A mouthful of white.

"So—" He patted the ground next to him. "—I read in your file that you're from Randon. I've never been there. What's it like?"

"Oh, it's an old dust bowl of a planet. But we call it home." She stretched out her long legs. "My parents are still there, and my brothers and sister. They're farmers, actually. At least that's what it says on their profiles. They really do a little bit of everything. My mom sews for people and does some artwork. My dad repairs small engines—"

"Ah, so that's where you got your flair for repair work," he said drolly, raising his eyebrows.

"Hey!" She swatted him good-naturedly. "I did get that coupling fixed, and that's—"

"More than you can say for me. I get it." He laughed at himself. "Man. I really thought I could handle this. I'd say it's pretty much been a disaster from the start."

"Oh, I don't know about that."

She was studying him intently. Her manner changed abruptly, and she bit her bottom lip. Gazing into his eyes she leaned forward. He became acutely aware of her proximity.

As if reading his mind she said, "It's getting hot in here all of a sudden, don't you think?" Her long fingernails glided down her uniform blouse deliberately, undoing a button. Orion's palms began to sweat, and he felt like he was trying to breath in zero atmosphere. At the same time, he was riveted to her actions. She reached up unhurriedly and undid his top button. And then another. And another, sliding her hand underneath his shirt. Her touch excited him.

His body went on autopilot, remembering what it was like to be with a woman. He reached his hand under her glossy hair covering her neck and drew her in little by little. Her lips were warm and inviting. A groan escaped his throat. *What was that?* He sounded like someone who had been carrying a burden too long and was just allowed to set it down. It had been a long time since he was seduced by a woman's touch. The kissing became more intense. They shifted so that their bodies were pressed against each other.

And why not this woman? She's decidedly HOT—absolutely knockout gorgeous—intelligent, funny...and HOT!

She was, in fact, everything he wanted in a woman. She was not, however, the woman he wanted. He pushed away from her.

"What is it?" she said breathlessly, searching his eyes. She straightened up. "Is it because of my rank?"

The blood was still pounding in his head. And other parts. "Well, yeah. There is that," he snarled. He worked the buttons on his shirt.

She studied him coolly. "But it's not that."

He shifted. *Damn it's hot in here!*

"There's some woman."

"No. There's no one."

She hastily fixed her blouse. "An old girlfriend? Someone who doesn't love you back?"

He wished in vain that someone would come and open the door and let him out. Were they running out of air?

"No. It can't be that. She would have to be a fool... Or married!" Her eyes glowed with her discovery. "That's it, isn't it? She's married."

"Was married," he found himself saying.

"And..."

"Her husband died in an explosion."

"Ahh." She was quiet for a second. "How long ago?"

"Two years."

She let out an exasperated laugh. "So when are you planning to make your move, Space Stud?"

"It's complicated," he growled.

"Really?" She pulled her legs up, drumming long nails on her knee. "She has kids?"

"One daughter, actually. But she died in the same explosion that took her father."

"Oh!" For once she seemed stymied.

After several seconds of awkward silence, he turned to her, grabbing her hands. "I'm sorry, Danny. You're a great girl. You really are. It's just that..."

She disengaged her hands from his and scrambled to her feet. "You're in love with her, and you always will be." She crossed to the keypad, jabbing at the buttons. To his amazement, the door slid open, and from his position on the floor he saw her stride down the corridor without looking back.

As he watched her voluptuous figure disappear out of sight he silently berated himself. *Orion. You're an idiot. A complete, and utter, idiot!*

Twenty minutes later the door opened. A young officer looked down at him.

"Thank you, Jakes." He accepted his hand up. "I forgot the door locks automatically." He brushed off his pants. "Has Lt. Jonas reported to the bridge?"

"No, Sir."

Of course she wouldn't.

"I'll take her shift then."

It's going to be a long night. A very long, and lonely, night.

Jakes frowned. "Is she ill, Sir?"

"Yeah. Something like that," he muttered.

Maggie sat at the edge of the pond, knees pulled up to her chest. She wore a pair of denim pants with a long-sleeved shirt and a poncho, her hair pulled up in a pony tail. She gazed out at the water as she had done every day for...she didn't know how long. Time was irrelevant. The happy little life she created here with Darius and her little Bella was gone. She didn't want to care about anything anymore. Because in her book, caring was synonymous with pain. She was like a fish that had been gutted, her insides lying out on the table, torn and bloody; the hole they created vast and unending. She had quit singing, quit everything, retreating to the pond and waiting.

Only she didn't know what it was she was waiting for. All she knew is that here she felt Darius's presence like nowhere else. It was not like before, a live presence. But still, she consoled herself, it was a presence. Or had been.

Today was overcast, and chilly. The previous days had held a promise of spring, but, she decided, like so many other promises in life, it amounted to nothing. The wind blew her hair back against her face, the strands stinging her, but she made no move to subdue them. Despair crept over her. Why could she no longer feel Darius? Had she forgotten him already? In desperation she cried out his name. As the tears flooded her eyes the wind carried the sound of her voice back to her, a desolate moan. She bent her head into her knees, crying freely, whispering his name over and over again, needing to feel him beside her.

Darius watched Maggie from The Other Side. He watched her as she became an emotional roly-poly, curling up to protect herself. He lingered, watching, waiting, wanting her to come out of the black hole that was now holding her captive. He wanted to tell her he and Bella were fine, and the one who needed her now was Orion.

He observed Orion, too. Watched him going through the motions, as emotionally unattached as Darius himself had been before he met Maggie. He witnessed him hiding his heart away from Danica, like a squirrel with a nut. He watched...and his heart ached for them both.

Maggie roamed the edges of the pond. *Why? If Darius isn't on one side, will he be on the other?* She shook her head savagely at her own stupidity...or was it insanity? It was so hard to tell these days. She sat after a while in the place where she'd started. She had worn away a patch of the grass, she noticed idly.

There were no tears today. She had spent all her tears. Part of her was mad at herself for this stagnation she had fallen into...but sometimes holding on to the pain was the only thing keeping her together. More and more she found herself thinking of Orion. *Why did he leave me when I needed him most?* She had to bury a child and a husband all alone. Her heart shattered, a mirror of their ship. Of course Polonius had been there. He contacted her every day, and she tried to do her "I'm-okay-dance" for him.

But he too had passed away. There was no one. Why did Orion leave without even saying goodbye? And why hadn't he contacted her since? Maybe he, too, was haunted by guilt because of what they had done together.

But the thoughts of Orion that really disturbed her were the thoughts that came in the night. Vivid memories she tried to push away. But they always returned, leaving her even more riddled with guilt. She ran a finger over her lips and recalled the way his felt when they tasted her, how his hands felt as they explored her body, how it made her feel to look into his eyes and know that he loved her.

All that was in the past, she reminded herself. *Orion has moved on with his life, and I... I'm stuck here.*

"Maggie."

She scanned the grasses surrounding the pond. There was no one. *Must be the wind*, she reasoned.

"Maggie."

This time she recognized the voice. Her heart clutched. She turned. A shimmering image strode toward her, a blinding white light pouring over his shoulders. She squeezed her eyes shut. "My God," she said aloud. "I've finally lost my mind."

"No, Maggie. I'm here from The Other Side. I needed to talk to you one more time."

She squeezed her eyes tighter. "No. Please no." She fought her heart. Barely separating her lashes, she slit open her eyes. He was still there, standing beside her. She remained frozen. *This isn't right.* She gulped, closing her eyes to block it out.

"Ah, yes."

His voice! My God! His voice!

"Your eyes have been wrong before. But what does your heart tell you?"

She took a breath through her nose, opening up and allowing herself to test her feelings. She let go and went deep inside. She felt...calm. The kind of calm she felt when she was with Darius. She opened her eyes. He was sitting on the grass, his knees drawn up, his head turned toward her. His smile. She never thought she would see it again. She studied his face, every familiar crease. "You've come back to me," she breathed.

"Only for a moment. Only this once."

It was a stab wound to her chest. Her joy receded. She continued to stare at him, then took another breath. If they were only to have this time, then she would sip up every second they shared. She was surprised when her voice worked. "Why did you come back?"

He gazed out over the pond for a minute, as if the words were painful to him. "I've come to say goodbye." He paused, then, turned to her again. "Maggie. My heart. I'm dead, but you're not. I don't want you to waste the rest of your time here, alone. Bella and I are fine."

At the mention of her daughter's name the tears rolled past Maggie's eyelashes in quick succession. He was silent for a while, then murmured, "The Knights' Gala is tomorrow night. You should go. Orion will be there."

She started at the mention of his name.

"He needs you, and you need him. Go. Please, go."

She dropped her head. "You're wrong about that, Darius. He hasn't talked to me..." She lifted her head, but he was gone. She swung around but she was again alone.

Find out what happens next by purchasing A KNIGHT TO REMEMBER!

ALSO FROM M.J. SCHILLER

ROMANTIC REALMS COLLECTION:
TAKEN BY STORM
AN UNCOMMON LOVE
LEAP INTO THE KNIGHT
LADY OF THE KNIGHT
A KNIGHT TO REMEMBER

ROCKING ROMANCE COLLECTION:
TRAPPED UNDER ICE
ABANDON ALL HOPE
BETWEEN ROCK AND A HARD PLACE
ROCK ME, GENTLY
MIDNIGHT MELODY

LOVE AND CHAOS SERIES:
ROCKED BY GRACE
ROCKED BY LOVE
ROCK IT TO THE MOON
ROCK OF SALVATION (Coming soon!)

REAL ROMANCE COLLECTION:
UPON A MIDNIGHT CLEAR
THE HEART TEACHES BEST

DAMAGE DONE
BLACKOUT
HOMETOWN HEARTACHE
TAKE A CHANCE ON ME

DEVILISH DIVAS SERIES:

TO HELL IN A COACH BAG
DAMNED IF I DO
THE DEVIL YOU KNOW
SATAN, LINE ONE
PITCHFORK IN THE ROAD
SIN WORTH THE PENANCE
HELL HATH NO FURY

ABOUT THE AUTHOR

M.J. Schiller is a lunch lady/romance-romantic suspense writer. She enjoys writing novels whose characters include rock stars, desert princes, teachers, futuristic Knights, construction workers, cops, and a wide variety of others. In her mind everybody has a romance. She is the mother of a twenty-year-old and three eighteen-year-olds. That's right, triplets! So having recently taught four children to drive, she likes to escape from life on occasion by pretending to be a rock star at karaoke. However...you won't be seeing her name on any record labels soon.

www.ingramcontent.com/pod-product-compliance
Lightning Source LLC
Chambersburg PA
CBHW071150170626
46809CB00002B/846